DEADLINE AT DAWN

CORNELL WOOLRICH (1903–1968) was one of America's best and most influential crime and noir writers, who also published under the names George Hopley and William Irish (the moniker under which *Deadline at Dawn* was originally published). His novels were among the first to employ the atmosphere, outlook, and impending sense of doom that came to be characterized as noir, and inspired some of the most famous films of the period, including *Rear Window*, *The Bride Wore Black*, *The Phantom Lady*, *The Leopard Man*, and *Deadline at Dawn,* among many, many others.

DAVID GORDON was born in New York City. His first novel, *The Serialist*, won the VCU/Cabell First Novel Award and was a finalist for an Edgar Award. It was also made into a major motion picture in Japan. His work has also appeared in *The Paris Review*, *The New York Times*, *Purple*, and *Fence*, among other publications. His "Joe the Bouncer" series of capers, which features an ex-Special Forces Agent who works as a strip-club bouncer and moonlights as a fixer for the New York mob, is now in its fourth installment.

DEADLINE
AT DAWN

CORNELL
WOOLRICH

Introduction by
DAVID
GORDON

AMERICAN
MYSTERY
CLASSICS

Penzler Publishers
New York

Published in 2022 by Penzler Publishers
58 Warren Street, New York, NY 10007
penzlerpublishers.com

Distributed by W. W. Norton

Cover image: Andy Ross
Cover design: Mauricio Diaz

Paperback ISBN 978-1-61316-326-9
Hardcover ISBN 978-1-61316-327-6

Library of Congress Control Number: 2022900822

Printed in the United States of America

9 8 7 6 5 4 3 2 1

INTRODUCTION

FIVE HOURS and twenty-five minutes.

That's how much time the novel you are holding in your hands will take. Not how long it takes to read—that will vary, depending on the reader, and whether you have opened this book while browsing in a bookshop, on a short ride home after buying it, or tucked up in bed with a cup of tea. Rather, it is the story itself that unfolds over exactly five hours and twenty-five minutes. And we know this because the author not only alerts us to the time, he makes each chapter heading another click of the hands, (1:39 . . . 2:52 . . .) so that we are precisely, at times excruciatingly, aware of those precious minutes running out.

"A ticking clock" indeed. But this author goes further. Here the metaphorical clock is an actual clock: The Paramount clock, set on a building that looms over the characters' lives as it towers above the city in which they live and die, shining like the moon over their destinies. It becomes a presence, an omen of good or ill, even a kind of character as our heroine, Bricky, addresses it, first as a comforting pal over her shoulder, and then as a lurking threat.

This combination of extreme precision (5:25) and almost surreal or dream-like imagery, of expertly-wrought suspense and mytho-poetic symbolism, is characteristic of this novel, this author, and of the genre and place in which he lived and worked.

The place is New York, Gotham at its most hard-boiled. The author is Cornell Woolrich, who rose from the pulps to become the dark prince of noir. And the time-haunted novel of danger and suspense, of course, is *Deadline at Dawn.*

Cornell Woolrich. If he didn't exist, it would take a writer of just his unique bent to create such a character. Born in 1903 in New York, into what seems to have been an unhappy marriage, he was a pale, sickly, underweight child who lived with his father in Mexico for ten years before his mother retrieved him at thirteen and returned him to his hometown. He never saw his father again. He attended Columbia University just three blocks from where he had been living on 113th street but dropped out when his first novel, *Cover Charge*, was published in 1926.

His goal at the time was to become a Jazz Age novelist like his hero F. Scott Fitzgerald. This aspiration was not meant to be, but the influence remains in his work—in the lyricism, the choice of characters, the romantic fatalism . . . The debutantes become dance-hall dime-a-dance dames, the daring chancers like Gatsby become small-time thieves and shady operators, and that famous green light at the end of a dock becomes, well, a big clock on a tower, among other things.

Like Fitzgerald and so many others, Woolrich went to Hollywood after his novel *Children of the Ritz* won a contest held by First National Pictures. It didn't work out; the most memorable event of his Hollywood sojourn was a short, disastrous, and by all accounts deeply miserable marriage. Again, he returned to New York where he remained, living in residential hotels with his mother until her death in 1957 and, after that, reclusive and alone.

He was never able to establish himself as a mainstream novelist, whether it was because of the Great Depression, which ended the Jazz Age, or because of his own more personal, but still pretty great, depression. Instead, in the thirties he turned to the pulps, becoming so prolific that he spun off multiple pseudonyms (William Irish was first credited with this book) and so successful that the movies came calling after all, with directors from Hitchcock to Truffaut adapting his work.

But success did not seem to brighten his inner gloom. He remained a haunted figure. The reasons for this remain mysterious, subject to wild speculation: He was a closeted gay man, tormented by repression and self-loathing. He was an extremely-uncloseted gay man, wildly promiscuous and cruising the streets in a sailor suit. He cynically married merely as a cover. He was a deeply lonely soul who longed for a human connection but was unable to ever make one, except perhaps with Mother. His cadaverous, ghostly appearance was due to illness, or congenital reasons, or alcoholism. The truth is that we may never know. A solitary who confided in no one, he died with his secrets intact.

What we do have is the world he created. It is a night world, a world set not only in the crime genre but more specifically the hardboiled crime fiction that emerged from the pulps, most notably with such masters as Dashiell Hammett, Raymond Chandler and David Goodis. Even more precisely, it is a noir world—a sub-genre noted for its fatalism, its dark glamour, its expressionistic style, its cynical and critical view of the human heart. Woolrich is as noir as it gets, perhaps *the* noir writer par excellence.

This book, *Deadline at Dawn*, is a perfect example. It is the story of Bricky, a small town girl gone wrong, a taxi dancer clinging to the shreds of her dignity, counting the seconds until her shift ends, and just one night away, it seems, from surrendering to the darkness that New York has left in her soul after leaching away all her dreams. By sheer chance, or fate (and the distinction will matter), she bumps into Quinn, minor thief and desperate character who wandered into the dancehall for a brief respite from his own torment, and who, as it happens, hails from the same small town. His family even lives right next door. Each one sees the other as their last chance at redemption, their one hope of escape from this dirty town on a dawn bus back home. But to do that they will need to undo the jam that Quinn has gotten himself into and, to do that, they will have to solve a murder—without getting killed or arrested themselves.

What unfolds next is a night of tension and suspense: a minute-by-minute thriller full of sudden twists and hair-pin turns, driven by our frantic but brave and resourceful lovers and played out in indelibly rendered settings—streets, bars, alleys, taxis, and hotel rooms—where a cast of thieves, hustlers, cheats, rapists, killers, and a few decent souls struggle to survive. All characters, however minor, have their defining traits, their story. Every detail of mid-century Manhattan rings true.

But there is also a kind of hyper-real, mythic feeling to the novel. Objects and places take on a symbolic, almost magical, power. I mentioned the clock above. There are keys, cigars, matchbooks, scraps of paper. The flour dusting from a loaf of pumpernickel bread. All of these items have a specific role in the plot but they also seem to glow and hiss, to take on good or evil power. Even a hall of doors in a cheap hotel becomes a "row of stopped-up orifices in this giant honeycomb that was the city." And the city itself is the most malevolent creature of all, a living, breathing monster that hunts Bricky, licking its claws, waiting to suck the last life out of her and Quinn. It is the beast from whose belly they are trying to fight their way out. At one point, she even whispers, afraid that it will hear her.

Another noticeable trait is a high degree of coincidence, spins of fortune that propel and ricochet these characters through the tale. At first, as a skeptical contemporary reader, I took this in stride the way I do, for example, with Dickens. But once thoroughly seduced into Woolrich's world, I realized this was not wild luck (for the characters) and convenient coincidence (for the author). This was fate.

The world of noir is ruled by fate, whether that means the inner drives and demons of the characters, who cannot change their nature even if it kills them, or the unbeatable workings of a rigged system in a corrupt society, or the narrative necessity of dream logic, forged by fear and desire. Of course the key that you should never use just happens to fall into your satchel. Of course the dark room contains a corpse, the stranger at the bar a secret, the scrap of paper a vital if inscrutable significance. As in a fairytale, everything has the inevitability, the interconnectedness, the meaning and potency of dreams. But for Woolrich, that dream is a nightmare from which the characters cannot awake.

Without giving away the ending, I will say that, this time, Woolrich does hold out a ray of hope. Morning does inevitably come, after all. Light chases away the darkness. The bus leaves the city for the open country. But even so, a shadow always remains, like the daytime remnants of a nightmare. We, like Bricky and Quinn, will never be quite the same.

Woolrich's own fate was as noir as it gets. He ended up alone, in his hotel room, in a wheelchair, after losing a foot to gangrene, in an uncanny replay of one his own most famous tales, "Rear Window." His life, like his work, is full of twists and shadows, and beneath it all, the mysterious unraveling of fate. Luckily, we can enter this strange and thrilling world as we wish and leave when we close the book. I suggest you start with a visit of exactly five hours and twenty-five minutes.

—DAVID GORDON

HE WAS just a pink dance-ticket to her. A used-up one at that, torn in half. Two-and-a-half cents' worth of commission on the dime. A pair of feet that kept crowding hers before them all over the map, all over the floor, all over the night. A blank, a cipher, that could steer her any which way he wanted until his five minutes were up. Five minutes of hailing, pelting two-quarter-time notes, like a stiff sandstorm hitting an accumulation of empty tin buckets, up there on the bandsmen's box. And then suddenly silence, as at the cut of a switch, and a sort of tonal deafness for a moment or two after. A couple of free breaths without your ribs being corseted by some stranger's arm. And then the whole thing over again; another blast of sand, another pink ticket, another pair of feet chasing yours around, another cipher steering you any which way he liked.

That was all any of them were to her. She loved her job so. She loved dancing so. Especially for hire. Sometimes she wished she'd been born with a limp, so she couldn't manage her two feet alike. Or deaf, so that she'd never have to hear another slide-trombone fingering its nose at the ceiling. That would have kept her out of this. Then she would have probably been bathing somebody's soiled shirts in a basement-laundry, or scouring somebody's soiled dishes in a lunchroom scullery. What was the good of wishing, anyway? You didn't get anything. Well, what was the harm? You didn't lose anything.

She had only one friend in all this town. It stayed still, it didn't dance, that was one thing in its favor. And it was always on hand, night after night, seeming to say: "Buck up, kid, you've only got another hour to go. You can do it, you've done it before." And then in a little while: "Hang on tight, kid; another thirty minutes now, that's all. I'm working for you." And then finally: "Just once more around the floor, kid. Time's up now. Just one more complete turn, and your sentence has been commuted for tonight. Just once more around, you can last *that* long, don't cave in *now;* look, my minute-hand's muscling in on my hour-hand. I've done it again for you, I've gotten you off. By the time you get back this way it'll be one o'clock."

It seemed to say those things to her every night. It never let her down. It was the only thing in the whole town that gave her a break. It was the only thing in all New York that was on *her* side, even if only passively. It was the only thing in all the endless world of her nights that had a heart.

She could only see it from the two end windows on the left, the ones overlooking the side-street, every time she made the circuit down around that way. The ones in front, overlooking the main drag, didn't show it to her. There was a long row of them on the left, but the last two were the only ones that were any good, the rest were blocked off by buildings in the way. They were always left slanting open, to get in ventilation and to publicize the din up here to the sidewalks below; it might pull strays off the pavement. It was through the end two that she got it. Peering benignly in at her from way up high there, with sometimes a handful of stars scattered around it further back. The stars didn't help her any, but it did. What good were stars? What good was anything? What good was being born a girl? At least men didn't have to peddle their *feet*. They could be low in their own particular ways, but they didn't have to be low in this way.

It was pretty far-off, but her eyes were good. Glowing softly against the taffeta backdrop of the night. A luminous circle, like a hoop. With twelve luminous notches around the inside of it. And a pair of luminous hands to tell them off, that never jammed, never stopped dead and played a dirty trick on her, always kept plugging for her, kept inching ahead, to get her off and out of here. It was the clock on the tower of the Paramount, all the way across the town from here at Seventh Avenue and Forty-third. Diagonally across, and still visible in here where she was, through some curious canalization of building-tops and angle of perspective. It was like a face—all clocks are. It was like the face of a friend. A funny friend for a slim, red-haired girl of twenty-two to have, but it spelled the difference between endurance and despair.

And another funny thing about it was, she could still see it further over where she roomed, from the windows of her rooming house if she got up on tiptoe and stretched her neck, although it was at an even greater distance there and all the way around in a different direction. But over there, on sleepless nights, it was just a detached onlooker, neither for her nor against her. It was here in the mill, from eight to one, that it really helped her out.

She looked at it longingly over this anonymous shoulder

now, and it said to her: "Ten-to. The worst is about over, kid. Just grit your teeth, and before you know it—"

"Plenty crowded here tonight."

For a minute she couldn't even tell where it had come from, she was in such a vacuum of non-awareness. Then she centered it in the disembodied cipher steering her about with him at the moment.

Oh, so he was going to talk, was he? Well, she could take care of that. He was slower in reaching that point than most of them, at that. This was the third or fourth consecutive number he'd claimed her for. And before the last intermission, she seemed to recall a similar suit-coloring before her blurred eyes a great many times, although she couldn't be sure, for she didn't bother trying to differentiate one from another—ever. The tongue-tied or the bashful type, perhaps, that was the reason for the delay.

"Yuh." She couldn't have made the monosyllable any shorter without swallowing it altogether.

He tried again. "Is it always as crowded as it is tonight?"

"No, after it closes it's empty."

All right, let him look at her like that. She didn't have to be agreeable to him, all she had to do was dance with him. His ten cents just covered footwork, not vocal exercise.

They'd darkened the place for this last number. They usually did, toward the end of the session like this. Direct lights out, and the figures on the floor moving about like rustling ghosts. That was supposed to make the customers mellow, that was supposed to send them out into the street feeling as though they'd had a private tête-à-tête with someone up here. All for ten cents and a paper-cupful of vegetable-coloring orangeade.

She could feel him poising his head back a little, looking at her closely, as if trying to figure out what made her that way. She centered her own eyes blankly on the flashing, silvery spirochete that went swirling endlessly across the walls and ceiling, cast off by the spinning mirrored top overhead.

Why look into her face to find out what had made her this way? He wouldn't find the answer there. Why not look into the casting-offices all over town, where her ghost still lingered, poised on the chair nearest the door? Or should have, she'd haunted them so. Why not look into the dressing-room of that tawdry Jamaica roadhouse, the one job she'd actually gotten, that she'd had to flee from before rehearsals for its floor-show even got under way, because she'd been foolish enough to loiter behind the others at the proprietor's suggestion? Why not look into the slot at the Automat on 47th?— the one that had swallowed up the last nickel she had in the world one never-to-be-forgotten day, and given her back two puffy, swollen rolls; and from then on wouldn't open again for her, no matter how often she stood longingly before it, for she had no further nickels to put in. Above all, why not look inside the battered dog-eared valise under her bed back at the room at this moment? It didn't weigh much, but it was full. Full of stale dreams, that were no good now any more.

The answer was in all those places, but not in her face. *So* what was the sense of his looking for it in her face? Faces are masks, anyway.

He tried his luck again. "This is the first time I was ever up here."

She didn't bring her eyes back from the pelting silver gleams streaking down the walls. "We've missed you."

"I guess you get tired of dancing. I guess by the end of the evening, like this, it starts in to get you." He was trying to find an excuse for her surliness, so that his self-esteem could tell itself it wasn't on account of him, was for some other reason. She knew; she knew how they were.

This time she brought her eyes back to him, witheringly. "Oh no. I never get tired of it. I don't get half enough. Why when I go back to my room after I leave here at nights I practise splits and high kicks."

He dropped his own eyes momentarily, as the barb made itself felt, then raised them to hers again. "You're kind of sore about something, aren't you." He didn't ask it as a question but stated it as a discovery.

"Yeah. Me."

He wouldn't give up. Couldn't he take a hint, even when it was driven home with a sledge-hammer? "Don't like it here?"

That was the crowning irritant of the whole series of inept remarks he'd been awkwardly tendering her as conversational fodder. She could feel her chest beginning to constrict with infuriation. An explosive denunciation would have surely followed. Fortunately, the necessity of answering was removed. The spattering and jangling of tin buckets that had been going on ended on a badly-fractured note, the mirror-gleams faded off the walls, and the center lights went up. A trumpet executed a Bronx cheer of dismissal.

Their enforced intimacy was at an end. His ten cents had spent its course She dropped her hand from the turn of his arm, inertly, as though it were something that had died long ago; and in doing so managed unobtrusively but definitely to push his own arm off her waist.

A sigh of unutterable relief escaped from her, that she made no effort to quell. "Good night," she murmured tonelessly, "we're closing up now." She turned to leave him and walk away.

Before she had quite time to complete the act, the look of surprise she saw on his face held her there a moment longer, her back half to him. More than that even, it was the way he was fumbling in his various pockets, bringing out coils and spirals of linked tickets from each, until he had a massed, overflowing double-handful.

He looked down at them. "Gee, I guess I didn't need to buy all these," he murmured ruefully, but more to himself than to her.

"What did you expect to do, camp in here all week? How many did you get, anyway?"

"I don't remember. I think about ten dollars' worth." He looked up at her. "I just wanted to get in here, and I didn't stop to—" he began. Then he stopped again.

She'd caught that, however. "You just wanted to get in here?" she said on a rising inflection. "That's a hundred dances! We never play that many in a night." She glanced over toward the foyer. "And I don't know what you can do about it, either. The cashier's gone home for the night and you won't be able to get a refund now any more."

He was still holding them, but helplessly rather than with any air of acute loss. "I don't want a refund."

"Then you'll have to come back again tomorrow night and keep coming till you've used them all up. They'll be just as good then."

"I don't think I'll—be able to," he said quietly. Suddenly he'd edged them slightly toward her. "Here. Want them? You can have them. You get a cut on the ones you turn back, don't you?"

For a moment her hands strayed uncontrollably toward the mass; then she quickly checked them, drew them in again, looked up at him. "No," she said defiantly. "I don't get it, but no thanks."

"But they're not any good to me. I'll never be back here again. You may as well take them."

It was a lot of commission. A lot of easy commission, too. But she'd made a rule for herself long ago, out of bitter experience. Never give in *any*where, about *any*thing, even if you couldn't see what they were driving at. If you gave in about one thing, no matter what it was, you'd find yourself giving in about the next, somewhere else along the line, that much easier.

"No," she said firmly. "Maybe I'm a chump, but I don't want any commissions I haven't danced for. Not from you or anybody else." And this time she completed the act of leaving him, turned on her heel and walked across the barren floor, upon which they were almost the last two to have remained standing.

She glanced back toward where she'd left him just once, from the dressing-room door on the other side of the ballroom. It was more of a posture-reflex that went with the act of widening the door to enter, than an intentional deliberate look back to him.

She could see his hands going in a sort of compressing motion, kneading the mass of tickets more compactly together. Then right while she looked, he flung the lumpy ball indifferently away from him, offside toward the edge of the parquet, and turned and went strolling forward toward the foyer entryway.

He'd danced about six times with her, all told. He'd just

thrown away well over nine dollars' worth of tickets. And it was no pose or act to impress her; she could tell he hadn't been aware of her scrutiny at the moment it occurred.

Pretty easy with his money, as though he didn't know what to do with it, couldn't get rid of it fast enough. Meaning—if anything—that he wasn't used to having it. Because, she was shrewd enough to have learned by now, those who have had money for any length of time are never at a loss as to what to do with it.

She gave a shrug with one shoulder, went in and closed the door behind her. She called this next step, the departure from the premises, running the gauntlet, but it no longer held any real terrors for her. It was like stepping over a puddle of dirty water that lies in your path; inconvenient, but in a moment you're on the other side of it and it's done with.

The lights had gone down again, this time for good, when she came out. Just one in back, so the scrubwomen could see to work by. She said to someone, invisible behind her as she reclosed the dressing-room door, "Well, then don't ask me to go out on double dates with you any more, and you won't *get* turned down!" She made her way down one side of the gloomy, barren, cavernous place, her footfalls muffled by the strip of carpeting that ran along it, except in one place where she cut a corner and they echoed out in hollow woodenness for a moment.

The pattern of the darkness had reversed itself. It was lighter now outside the open windows than in here in the interior of the dance-hall. She passed the two at the end, and her friend, her ally and accomplice, was up there limned against the sky. Her head turned slightly toward it as she moved rapidly by, until the casement cut them off from one another again with her passage. If any message or look of gratitude passed fleetingly between them at the moment, that was between her and it.

She parted the swing doors and stepped out into the still-lighted foyer running to the head of the stairs, with its alcoves for the ticket-seller and cloakroom-attendant and its two decrepit rattan settees.

There were two of them out there. There was always somebody. They always hung around. If you waited until daybreak to emerge, there would still have been one or two of them hanging around. One, a leg draped from the edge of the settee, must have been waiting for someone who was still in there; he gave her only nominal attention. The other, standing out at the very head of the steps themselves, was, she saw as she passed him, the very one who had just been with her for the past half-dozen dances or so.

He was, however, looking intently down the stairs toward the street rather than expectantly inward toward the doors she had just come through. As though delayed more by inability to decide where to go than by intent to meet anyone. In fact, she could tell by the surprised look of recognition he turned on her as she passed, that he hadn't seen her approach at all until then.

She would have gone by without a word, but his hand went to his hat—he had one on now—and he said: "Going home now?"

If she'd been astringent inside, she was vitriolic out here in the vestibule. This was strictly enemy territory. There was no bouncer out here to protect you, you were on your own. "No, I'm just checking in. I come up the stairs backward like this so they won't see my face, know who I am."

She went down the rubber-matted, steel-tipped steps and out into the open. He stayed behind up there, as though still at a loss what to do. And he wasn't waiting for anyone, because there was just one girl left behind in there and she was already preëmpted. Again she gave that slight shrug of one shoulder, but this time mentally and not in actuality. What was it to her? What was any of it to her, anyone to her?

The open air felt good. Anything would have, after that place up there. She always gave a deep exhalation on first emerging, that was part relief, part exhaustion. She gave it now.

This was the real danger zone, down on the street. There were a couple of indistinct figures loitering about, well-off-side to the doorway, cigarettes dangling from mouths, whom she refrained from glancing at too closely as she came out, turned, and went up the street. There always were; she had never seen it to fail yet. Like tomcats watching a mousehole. The ones who loitered about up above, they were waiting for some one particular girl as a rule; the ones down here, they were waiting for just anyone at all.

She knew this hazard by heart. She could have written a book. She wouldn't have smirched the good white paper to do it, that was all. There was always a time-lag, when there was to be the challenge direct. It never came at point of closest propinquity, at the doorway itself; it was always withheld until she was some distance away. Sometimes she thought this had to do with courage. Rather than tackle the mouse face-to-face, the valiant toms waited until its back was turned. Sometimes she thought it was merely that their stunted developments needed that much longer to come to a decision about their choice of prey. Sometimes she just thought, "Oh, the hell." And often, very often, she didn't think about it at all; it was just a puddle of dirty water to be overstepped along her homeward way.

The challenge came in the form of a whistle tonight. It often took that form. It wasn't an honest, open shrill whistle, at that. It was bated, surreptitious. She knew it was for her. And then a verbal postscript. "What's your hurry?" She didn't bother quickening her pace; that would have been giving it more respect than was due it. When they thought you were afraid, that emboldened them all the—

A hand hooked detainingly around the curve of her arm. She didn't try to pull away from it. She stopped short, looked down at it rather than up into his face.

"Take that off me," she said with lethal coldness.

"What's the matter, don't you know me? Memory's kind of short, ain't it?"

Her eyes were taut slits of white against the street-darkness. "Look, I'm on my own time now. It's bad enough I've got to talk to guys like you—"

"I was good enough for you when I was upstairs two nights ago, though, wasn't I?" He'd followed his own hand around forward, was blocking her way now.

She wouldn't give ground, nor even pay him the homage of trying to step around him at the side. "Heavy spender," she said evenly. "Shot sixty cents to pieces in one night, and now you're trying to collect a bonus on it down here on the sidewalk."

A cab had sidled up on the outside, drawn by some unobtrusive signal on his part that she had missed, its door dangling encouragingly open.

"All right, you're hard to get; you've played your act. I believe you. Come on, I've got a taxi waiting."

"I wouldn't even get in a five-cent trolley-car with you, let alone a taxi."

He tried to turn her aside toward it, partly by indirection, partly by main force.

She managed to slam the door closed behind her, and then it acted as a bulwark as he crowded her back against it.

A man had stopped opposite the two of them. That other one, who'd been in the upstairs foyer when she came out. She caught sight of him over this one's shoulder. She didn't appeal to him, ask him for help in any way. She'd never asked anyone for help yet in one of these passages. That way you were sure of never being disappointed. This wasn't anything, anyway; it would be over in a minute.

He came in closer, said to her uncertainly: "Do you want me to do anything, miss?"

"Well, don't just stand there. What do you think this is, an audition for the Good Will Hour? If you're musclebound yourself, call a cop."

"Oh, I don't have to do that, miss," he answered with a curious disclaiming sort of modesty, totally unsuitable to the circumstances.

He pulled the other man around toward him, and she heard the blow instead of seeing it. It made a taut impact against thinly-cushioned bone, so it must have been the side of his jaw. The recipient went floundering back against the rear fender of the cab, and overbalanced down the curve of that to the ground, half-prostrate and half-upright on one elbow.

None of the three moved for a minute.

Then the recumbent member of the small group scrambled to his feet with a curious recessive movement, pushing backward with his legs along the ground until he could be sure of rising at a safe distance from further blows. When he had risen, he turned, with neither threat nor sign of animosity, as one who is too practical to waste time on such heroics, and scuttled from their ken, dusting himself down the leg as he went.

The cab withdrew second, its driver deciding there was nothing further for him in this after a briefly questioning look to see whether she intended making use of it with her new partner.

Her thanks were scarcely overwhelming. "Do you always wait that long?"

"I didn't know but what he was some special friend of yours," he murmured deprecatingly.

"According to you, special friends have a right to hijack you on your way home. Is that what you do yourself?"

He smiled a little. "I don't have any special friends."

"You can double that," she said crisply. "And you can stick in for me I don't want any." And she shot him a look that added personal point to the remark.

He saw that she was about to turn and continue on her way without further parley. "My name's Quinn Williams," he blurted out, as if seeking by that means automatically to detain her a moment longer.

"Pleased to meet you." It didn't sound as pleasant as the word-arrangement presupposed it to. It sounded like a lead quarter bouncing against a zinc counter.

She resumed her withdrawal, or rather continued it without having interrupted it at all.

He turned and looked behind him, in the direction in which

her recent annoyer had disappeared. "Think maybe I should walk with you a block or two?" he suggested.

She neither acceded nor openly forbade him to. "He won't come back again," was all she said. He translated her indecisive answer into full consent, fell into step beside her, though at a formal distance of several feet.

They walked an entire block-length from the dance-hall entrance in mutual silence; she because she was determined not to make the effort to say anything, he—judging by several false starts he made that died stillborn—because he was unequal to it, was self-conscious, didn't know what to say now that he had gained his point of accompanying her. They crossed an intersection, and she saw him look back. She made no comment.

The second block passed in the same stony silence. She looked straight ahead, as though she were alone. She owed him nothing, she hadn't asked him to come with her.

They reached the second and last intersection. "I go west here," she said briefly, and turned aside, as if taking leave of him without further ado.

He didn't take the hint. He belatedly turned after her and came abreast again, murmuring something indistinct about: "May as well go the rest of the way, now that I came this far."

She'd seen him glance back again, though, a moment before he did so. "Don't let him worry you," she said caustically. "He's gone for good."

"Who?" he asked blankly. And then, as if remembering whom she meant, "Oh, I wasn't thinking about him."

She stopped short, to deliver an ultimatum. "Look," she said. "I didn't ask you to walk all the way over with me. If you want to, that's up to you. Just one thing. Keep your own thinking clear. Don't get any ideas in your head."

He accepted it in silence. He didn't protest that she'd misjudged him. That was almost the first thing she'd liked about him, the first favorable comment she'd permitted herself to make upon him, since he'd first come within her orbit an hour or two ago. But she had a prejudiced mind against all who came her way as he had, a mind that had long ago learned: the less obnoxious you found them in the beginning, the greater care you had better take, for the more obnoxious they were likely to prove in the end, having partially disarmed you.

They went on again, still at their spaced width of several feet, still uncommunicative, being together only in the act of going forward simultaneously. It was the strangest escorting she had ever had, and if she must have any, she preferred them all to be like this.

Up a tunnel-dim side-street, that had once carried a lateral branch of the Elevated over to Ninth Avenue. It was now shorn of it but permanently stunted in its development by the sixty-year strait jacket it had endured. The slab-like sides of windowless warehouses, the curved back of a well-known skating-rink that looked like a cement tank, gaps torn in the building-ranks here and there by the Depression, particularly on corner-sites, and never rebuilt upon, used now for parking lots.

The street lampposts, few and far apart, would talcum them thinly white for a moment or two like something sifting downward from the punctures of a reversed container, then their figures would darken again, blend into the gloom.

He said something finally. She couldn't remember precisely, but she thought it was the first remark he'd made since the fracas at the taxi. "You mean you come through here alone other nights?"

"Why not? It's no worse than back there. Along here, if they'd make a grab at you, it would only be your purse they'd be after." And then she felt like adding, "Why, are *you* afraid?" but forbore. Mainly because he hadn't said or done anything deserving the slash, at least up to this point, and she was tired of having her claws out and ready all the time; it felt good to leave them in where they were for a change.

He looked back again. That was the second or third time he'd done that now. Even if there'd been something to see back there, in the gloom through which they'd just now passed, he wouldn't have been able to see it.

This time she didn't let it pass unnoticed. "What are you afraid of, he'll come after you with a knife? He won't, don't let it worry you."

"Oh, *him*," he said, "you mean that guy," and gave her a surprised look, as though again she had recalled him from a separate train of thought wide of her own. He smiled a little, sheepishly, and rubbed his hand across the back of his neck, as though the fault of the act lay therein and not in his volition. A moment later he'd put it into words, half to himself. "I didn't know I was doing it, myself. Must be a sort of habit I've fallen into."

There's something on his mind, she told herself. People didn't look behind them like that, every few steps of the way. And strangely enough she believed him, that it had nothing to do with the recent incident of the blow. The way he reacted each time she caught him at it bore that out. His wariness wasn't of the immediate stretch of sidewalk behind them, of someone skulking up in back of him, it was more general, more widespread, it was of the entire night behind him. On two dimensions: both the hours of it, and the island-wide depths of it.

And now that she recalled it, that monstrous purchase of tickets he'd made, back at the mill, and then flung extravagantly away, as though they'd lost their value with tonight, there were never going to be any later time in which to use them, that was of a piece with it.

She remembered something else, and asked him a question.

"When I came out, and you were standing there in the foyer, up at the top of the stairs, you know—were you waiting for someone?"

"No," he said. "No, I wasn't."

"Then why were you standing there after the place was already closed?" She'd known he hadn't been, because he'd been looking *down* the steps and not over toward the inner doors.

"I don't know," he said. "I guess I—didn't know where to go, or what to do, after the place was once closed. I guess I—I guess I was trying to make up my mind where to go from there."

Then why didn't he stand outside, at the street entrance; that would have been the natural place for him to stand and do his thinking. She didn't ask him that. The answer had come with it. Because you couldn't be seen from upstairs in the stair-foyer, you were safe while you stayed there; you could be seen downstairs at the street entrance. If anyone were looking for you. Or you thought they were.

But chiefly she didn't ask him because of another reason,

and not the self-evident explanation that had occurred to her. She didn't ask him because her own mind had just dropped shut at this point, like a portcullis catching itself open; rolling down with a harsh grating injunction, that had no mercy, no admission in it for anyone: What do *you* care? What is it to you? What do you want to know about it for? Let him keep it to himself. What are you, a settlement nurse? Did anyone else ever worry about you?

And in bitter silence she upbraided herself, "You *still* haven't learned, have you? They beat you black and blue, and you still hold out your open hand to the next one that comes along. What does it take to get it into your head, a pounding with a lead pipe?"

He looked back again, and she let him.

They'd come to Ninth, wide and dismal in its grubby shadowiness, and not all the red and white beads whisking along it could make it anything but that.

They stood for a moment, toes overlapping the curb. The streaming beads slackened, dammed into sleazy diadems, reared facing one another, two to each intersection, all down the long billowy vista, that would crumble again and be strewn along as before in another moment.

She had already stepped down. There was an instant's recoil on his part. A false start, nothing more. A small thing. "Come on, the light's all right," she said. He went over after her immediately, but that unaccountable hitch had been self-revelatory. Effect had been shown, so cause had to be somewhere around, it only remained to identify it. Then she saw that it wasn't the light that had checked him, it was that lone figure all the way over on the other side, and going steadily away from them, that patrolman pacing his beat.

She saw that by the way his eyes came back from following him along, and then and *only* then went upward to the light, attracted to it by her remark.

The portcullis remained stubbornly closed.

They climbed the opposite curb, and went on into the maw of the ensuing westward block. Three anemic light-pools widely spaced down its seemingly endless length did nothing to dilute the gloom; they only pointed it up by giving it contrast. As if saying: See, this is what light is like— when there is any.

There was a clamminess to the air now, a sense of nearby water, that had been lacking further over. A tug-siren groaned dismally somewhere in the night ahead of them. And then another one answered it, way over near the Jersey side.

"Pretty soon now," she said.

"I've never been this far over before," he admitted.

"You can't get very much further in off the river than this for five dollars a week." And then, though she realized full well he hadn't offered any objection, she couldn't resist adding: "You can drop off anytime it gets you down."

"It hasn't got me down," he murmured diplomatically.

She opened her bag and felt for her key ahead of time; a preparatory reflex, to make sure it was there.

She halted as they reached the midway pool of light, and its downward-fuming motes powdered them back into visibility to one another. "Well, this is it here," she said.

He just looked at her. She thought it was almost stupid, the way he looked at her. Sort of bovine. As though he were trying to grasp the fact that they were separating and he would be by himself once more. Something like that. At least there wasn't any of that other stuff in it; no amorous ambitions.

There was a doorway opposite them, or very near-ly so. Left open to the street, but with the perils of in-gress ameliorated to some slight extent by a faltering lem-on-pale backwash that came from deep within it and failed to reach all the way to its mouth, leaving an intervening twilight zone. Still it was better than nothing. They'd for-merly left it dark, and she'd dreaded having to enter it late at nights. Until someone had been knifed on the stairs one night, and since then they'd left a light there at their foot. Now, she reflected wryly, you could see who knifed you, if you were to have it happen.

She cut their parting short; carrying it into effect while holding him where he was under a delaying barrage of a few last words. That was simply to gain distance, get beyond arm's reach. She'd learned by experience to do it that way, and not to stand still listening to remonstrances and purring objections. She'd had to.

"Take it easy," she said. And suddenly she was already over in the door way and he was standing alone on the side-walk. "I'll see you around," she said from there. Meaning just the reverse: she never would see him again, he never would see her, this ended it.

But even before she'd quite gone inside, she'd already seen him turn his head away again and look back into the ob-scurity through which they'd just come. Fear was uppermost over dalliance in his mind.

What was he to her? He was just a pink dance-check, torn in half. Two-and-a-half cents' worth of commission on the dime. A pair of feet, a blank, a cipher.

SHE WENT down the constructed hallway inside. She was alone now. She was alone for the first time since eight to-night. She was without a man. She was without a man's arms around her. She was without somebody's breath in her face. She was by herself. She didn't know much about what heaven was like; but she imagined when you died and went to heaven, heaven must be like this—to be alone, without a man. She passed under a solitary light at the back, looking white, looking tired, and began to climb the slatternly stairs. At first fairly erect, fairly firmly if not jauntily; at the last, after two full flights of them, sagging forward over her own knees, wavering from side to side, supporting herself by contact now against the wall, now against the wooden guard-rail.

She went all the way to the top, and then, breathing expiringly, leaned against a door there at the front, face downward as though she were looking intently at something on the floor. She wasn't. She was just being tired.

Presently she moved again. One more little thing to do, one slight little thing, and then it was all over. It was all over until tomorrow night this same time, and then it would have started once more. She got out her key and put it into the door blindly, head still down. She pushed the door in, took the key out, and closed the door after her. Not with her hands, or the knob. With her shoulders, falling back against it so that it flattened shut behind her.

She stayed that way, supine, and reaching from where she was, found the lever, put on the light. Her eyes dropped as she did so, as though they didn't want to see it right away, didn't want to look at it any sooner than they had to.

This was it. This was home. This. This *place*. This was what you'd packed your valise and come here for. This was what you'd looked forward to when you were seventeen. This was what you'd grown pretty for, grown graceful for, grown up for. All over the place, you could hardly move, it was littered with shards. Ankle-deep, knee-deep. You couldn't see them. Shattered dreams, smashed hopes, busted arches.

Here you cried sometimes, cried low and quiet to yourself, deep in the night. But on other nights, that were even worse, you just lay dry-eyed, not feeling much, not caring any more. Wondering if it would take very long grow old, if it would take very long to— Hoping it wouldn't.

. She came away from the door at last, and as she dragged off her hat, off her coat, drew nearer to the light—tired as she was, pallid as she was, question was answered. Yes, it would. And it would be a darned shame.

She toppled into a chair, and fumbled with the straps of her shoes, wrenched them off. That was the first thing she did, always, as soon came in. Feet weren't meant to do what hers did. If they must dance, should be of their own volition, joyously, for just a little while, a measure two. They shouldn't be driven to it, for endless hours beyond all endurance.

Presently she thrust them into a pair of felt slippers whose cuffs yawned shapelessly about her ankles. Then she still stayed where she was longer, somnolent, head thrown back upon the top of the chair, arms hanging limply down toward the floor, before doing anything else of the little remained to be done.

There was a cot of sorts over against the wall, depressed in its middle section even when untenanted, as though worn away by years of being in. Sometimes she wondered if they'd cried like she had, those who had in it before her turn came. Sometimes she wondered where they were. Selling sachets of lavender on a street-corner in the rain, scrubbing vestibules at dawn; or perhaps by now lying on another sort of cot, for—a firmer one, topped with sod— their perplexities eased.

There was a table with a straightbacked chair drawn to it out in the middle, under the light. An envelope lay on it, stamped and addressed, ready to but for the insertion of its contents and the sealing of its flap. Inscribed "Anna Coleman, Glen Falls, Iowa." And beside it the sheet of notepaper was to go in, blank but for three words. "Tuesday. Dear Mom—" Then nothing more.

She could have finished composing it with her eyes closed, she'd written so many others like it. "I'm doing fine. The show I'm in now is a big hit, turning them away at the door. It's called—" And then she'd pick a from the theatrical columns and fill that in. "I don't do so much in it, just little dancing, but they're already talking of giving me a speaking part next this season. So you see, Mom, there is nothing to worry about—" Things like that. And then: "Please don't ask me if I need money, that's ridiculous, I never heard of such a thing. Instead, I'm sending you a little something. By rights it should be a great deal more, they pay me a big enough salary, but afraid I've been a little extravagant, you have to keep up appearances in the profession, and this flat, lovely as it is, comes quite high, what with colored maid and all. But I'll try to do better next week—" And then two single dollar-bills would find their way in, with her blood invisible all over them.

Things like that. She could have finished it with her eyes closed. She'd finish it tomorrow, maybe, when she got up. She'd have to finish it soon: it had been lying there like that for three days now. But not tonight. There are times when you are too tired and vanquished even to lie. And something might have crept through between the lines.

She got up and she went over to a sort of cupboard arrangement, a niche without any closure, gaping against the back wall. It held, on a shelf, a gas-ring, with a rubber tube leading up and cupping onto a jet that protruded from the wall overhead. She struck a match, uncocked the jet, and a little circle of sluggish blue fire jumped into being. She placed a battered tin coffee-pot over this, readied for brewing from earlier in the day, when it had not been so much agony to move about.

Then her hands went to the shoulder of her dress, to open and discard it. She remembered, and looked toward the window, fronting the street. Its shade had been left up. There were rooftops across on the other side, if nothing else, and vermin sometimes crawled upon them. Once, during the summertime before, a jeering whistle had come in to apprise her of this. She'd never forgotten that since.

She let her dress be for a moment, went over to it to pull the shade down.

Then with her hand to the cord, she stopped and forgot to go ahead.

He was still down there. He was lingering down there in the street, directly before this house. The very same one who had walked over with her just now. The street-light falling on him identified him to her beyond the possibility of a mistake.

He was standing out there at the margin of the sidewalk, as if at a loss, as if, having now come this far, he didn't know where next to go from here, where to go on to. As if her defection had stranded him. He was motionless, yet not quite still. He kept fluctuating a little in the one place where he stood, shifting about like a jittering compass.

It was not herself that held him there, that was implicit in his very stance. His back was to her, or at least partially so; he was standing semi-profileward, parallel to the direction of the street. He wasn't looking up, seeking her at any of the windows. He wasn't looking in, questioning the doorway through which he had last seen her go. He was doing again as he had done while she was still with him, staring intently and with only momentary interruptions off into the distance, down the street and beyond, scanning the night in the direction from which they had last come, he and she. Anxiously, worriedly, fearfully. Yes, there was no mistaking the emotion the whole cast of his body conveyed, even from a height of three floors above; fearfully, as well.

Though she had every evidence that this was no trespass upon herself, that it had nothing to do with her, yet it did something to irritate her. What did he want down there? Why didn't he go elsewhere and do his shadow-boxing? What did he hang around *her* door for? She wanted to be away from all of them, she wanted to forget them, all those who had to do with the mill. And he was one of them. Why didn't he go on back where he belonged?

Her mouth tightened into a scowling pucker, and her hands sought the finger-grooves of the lower window-frame. She was going to fling it up high, and lean out, and rail down at him: "Go on now, beat it! Go on about your business! What're you waiting down there for? Move on, take a walk, or call a cop!" And other things at fishwife-pitch she knew well how to say, would have effectively dislodged him no matter how reluctant he was, or forced him to brave the opening of every window all around him to see what the cause of the tirade was.

But before she could do it, something happened.

He turned his head and looked up the other way. Still along the street-level, but westward now, toward Tenth and beyond. It was just an intermission, a respite, in the steadiness with which he'd maintained his gaze the first direction. And then suddenly she saw him give a half-crouched abortive start, though she could still see nothing from where she was, within the window-pane.

An instant longer, no more, he waited to confirm the first glimpse whatever it was, and then he darted aside, bolted from view somewhere directly underneath her vantage-point. Obviously, judging by his direction, he'd sought refuge in the doorway of this same building she was in.

For a moment there was no sign of what had caused his hasty retreat. The street stretched lifeless under her, gunmetal-dark save where the forlorn halo of the lamppost down there whitened it a little.

She stayed there, face pressed to the window, waiting,

watching. Then suddenly, without any warning sound, something white, shaped like an inverted boat, came drifting past on the dark tide of the night. It took her moment to understand what it was, it was coursing along so insidiously. It was a small patrol car, making its routine rounds late at night. Approaching without lights or clamor, to catch malefactors off-guard.

It had no objective, it was not stalking anyone, least of all him; she could tell that by its lackadaisical gait. It was just cruising, it had turned in through here at random.

It had already gone on past now. For a moment she toyed with the idea of throwing open the window after all, as she had first intended, and hailing it to stop; of telling them: "There's a man lurking in the doorway underneath here. Ask him what he's up to." She didn't. Why should she, she asked herself? He hadn't done anything overt against her, or anything wrong to her knowledge. She held no brief for him, but neither did she for them. He wasn't her brother, but neither was she his keeper.

It had gone too far by now, anyway. Its occupants hadn't even glanced over this way, at the door of this house. It coasted on down to the next corner, more boat-like than ever on the invisible current of its own motion, shrinking to the size of a pod, and then it turned to the right and was gone.

She waited a moment or two to see if he would come out again. He didn't. The street before the house remained as barren as though he'd never been there. He stayed out of sight inside somewhere, wherever it was he'd gone, his courage all spent.

She drew the shade down at last, as she'd originally intended to before it all happened. She turned away, but she didn't begin her delayed undressing. She crossed the room to the door and stood there by it listening. Then she opened it slowly, quieting it with a hand to its edge as she did so. She advanced out into the barren hall beyond, tread muted in her soft-soled foot-gear.

There was no sound to show that anyone was astir but herself, that anyone was in the building, up or down, who did not belong there. She moved back to where the railed gap surrounding the stairs began, leaned cautiously over it and looked down their dimly-lighted well, all three rungs of it, to the very bottom.

She couldn't see anything from her first stance, they intercrossed too much. She shifted on a little further, and there got a diagonal insight at their bottom reaches.

She saw him down there. He was sitting huddled on the first flight, disconsolately up against the rail, about halfway between the last landing going down and the bottom. His legs were tucked up to within a step below his body. He'd taken his hat off; it must be resting on the step beside him, but she couldn't see over that far. The only thing that moved about him were his hands, otherwise he was sitting quite still. She could see the one on the outside ploughing endlessly through his hair, over and over, as though some deep-seated predicament were gnawing at him.

He couldn't stay there like that. He couldn't stay there in the hall all night. Yet, when she made her unguessed presence known to him, as she did a moment later, it wasn't as she had originally intended to, through the window before, by means of a strident tirade. Something had happened to change her mind. Perhaps it was the hopeless, helpless way he was sitting bunched there. Who knew; she didn't know herself. She revealed herself to him without at the same time betraying his presence to others. She gave him that much of a break, at least. And it was a long time since she'd given anyone a break. Almost as long as since she'd last had one herself.

She hissed down, forcefully but surreptitiously, to attract his attention, gave him a sort of sibilant signal.

He turned and looked up, startled, ready to jump until he'd located the segment of her face far up the canal of opening between them.

She hitched her head sharply away from him a couple of times, in pantomimic order to him to come up and join her where she was. He rose in instant acquiescence, and she lost him for a moment or two, but she could hear him climbing hastily, two and three steps at a time. Then he showed up on the last flight, made the final turn of the railing, and stopped short beside her, breathing heavily. He looked at her questioningly, and at the same time in a half-hopeful sort of way, as if any summons to him, at this pass, was bound to be a good one.

He looked younger to her than he had before, somehow. Younger than she'd taken him for over at the mill. The lights over there, more than that even, the setting itself, made everyone look more sinister and seasoned than they actually were. She knew he hadn't changed, it was her impression of him that must have. Perhaps the sight of him she'd had just now sitting the stairs, rudderless, had retouched her mental image of him. And after all, everyone came to you through the filter of your own individual lens, not as they were in actuality.

"What's your trouble, Joe? Whatiya got on your mind?" She asked it with intentionally-emphasized, grating harshness, to cancel out the interest implicit in her asking it at all in the first place, and not just letting him down there on the stairs. Because she was breaking one of her own self-imposed rules, so she did it as grudgingly as possible.

He said, "Nothing—I—I don't get you," and faltered badly over it. Then got his second wind, and said, "I was just resting up down there a minute."

"Yeah," she observed stonily. "People rest on the stairs of strange houses at two in the morning, when they've got nothing on their minds. I know. Listen, it all adds up. I don't need my fingers to count off on. The way you kept hinging behind you, all the way over here; don't you think I got that? The way you were roosting there in the corner, when I first came out of the barn—"

He was looking down at the rail beside him as though he hadn't seen until just now, as though it had suddenly appeared there where it hadn't been before. He kept swivelling his palm around on it, as if he were polishing it off in one particular place, a place that wouldn't come clean.

Yes, he kept getting younger to her by the minute. He was down to about twenty-three now, which was probably a little below par. And when he'd first come in the dance-hall he'd been—well, rats have no age. At least, you don't inquire into it.

"What'd you say your name was again? I know you gave it to me outside before, but it slipped my mind."

"Quinn Williams."

"Quinn? I never heard that name before."

"It used to be my mother's before she married."

She shrugged with her eyebrows. Not about the name, about their preceding discussion. "Well, have it your way," she dismissed it. "It's your own spot. Hang onto it, if you feel that way about it."

Something from within her own room attracted her attention. A slight clattering commotion, that she could identify instantly, from long experience. She turned hastily and went in, left him out there without a word. She went over to the gas-ring and turned it off; the twinkling blue diadem fluffed out and the commotion subsided.

She picked up the tin coffee-pot and transferred it to the table. She'd left the door open. She stepped over to close it between the two of them.

He was still standing out there, back a little ways, by the stairs, where she'd last left him just now. There was a sort of passive, fatalistic air about him. He was still kneading his hand on the rail and looking down and watching himself do it.

She held her hand arrested to the door. What a dope you are, she wrangled with herself. Don't you ever learn? Don't you know any better than to do what you're thinking of doing? Then she went ahead and did it anyway. Offering this to herself in extenuation: I've got one last friendly impulse left in me. Exactly one, that this town has overlooked and left me. May as well get it out of my system and get it over with, then I'll be in the clear.

Again she gave him that curt, peremptory hitch of the head. "I've got some coffee in here. Come in a minute, and I'll split a cup with you."

He came forward again as eagerly as he'd come up the stairs. He needed bucking up, she could see; partly, that was what was the matter with him, someone to talk to.

But her arm stayed up, crossbarring the door-gap and blocking him when he'd come up to it. "Only get one thing," she warned him lethally. "This is an invite to share a cup of coffee with me, and nothing more. No sugar goes with it. You give me one blink too many and—"

"I'm not thinking of that sort of stuff," he said with an odd sort of demureness that she hadn't known males could show until now. "A fellow can tell just by looking at someone whether they mean one thing or mean the other."

"You'd be surprised how many of them ought to see an optician," she commented sourly.

Her arm dropped and he came through.

She closed the door. "Keep your voice down," she said. "There's an old bat in the next room to me—"

"You can take that chair that's there already," she said. "I'll move over this other one—if it don't fall apart on the way there."

He sat down with polite rigidity.

"You can throw your hat on the cot over there," she condescended hospitably. "If you can reach it."

He tried uncertainly from where he was, over table and coffee-pot both, but he made it.

They both turned from watching it land, smiled tentatively at one another. Then she remembered herself, quickly checked her own. His died of loneliness after it.

"I never can make enough for one in this thing, anyway," she remarked, as if apologizing for her own softness in asking him in. "It won't hit the roof if I do."

She brought over an extra cup and saucer. "The reason I have a second one," she said, "is because they were two for five in Woolworth's. You had to take both or lose your change." She turned it upside-down and shook it, and some flecks of straw fell out. "First time I've used it," she said. "I'd better run some water in it." She took it over to a greenish, mildewed tap lurking under the shelf in the cupboard-arrangement. "Go ahead," she invited while her back was turned, "don't wait for me."

She heard the loosely-contrived pot rattle as he picked it up to pour from it. Then it fell back rather heavily. So bumpily, in fact, that the cup that was already on the table sang out. At the same time his chair gave a slight jar.

She stopped what she was doing, which was drying the cup by sailing it up and down so that the drops of water were flung out, and turned quickly to ask him: "What'd you do, burn yourself? Did you get some of it on you?"

His face had whitened a little, she thought. He shook his head, but he was too engrossed to look at her. He still had his hand to the pot, where he'd let it down. He was holding that envelope she'd addressed to her mother in the other, staring at it as though he were stunned. She saw at a glance what must have happened. The pot must have been squatting on it the first time and the heat had made it adhere when he'd lifted it. He'd pried it off, and that was how he'd noticed whatever it was seemed to amaze him so.

She came back to the table, stood by it, and said: "What's the matter?"

He looked up at her, still holding the envelope. His mouth was open; both before and after he'd spoken it stayed that way. He said, "Do you *know* someone there? Glen Falls, *Iowa?* Is that where you're sending this?"

"Yes, why?" she said crisply. "That's what it says on it, doesn't it? That's my mother I'm writing that to." A little defiance crept into her attitude. "Why, what about it?"

He started to shake his head. He started to slowly rise to his feet as he did so, then changed his mind midway and sank down again. He kept looking at her for all he was worth. "I can't get over it," he gasped, and felt himself for a minute across the forehead. "That's where I'm *from*! That's my home town! I only came away a little over a year ago—" His voice went up a pitch in incredulity. "You mean you're from there too? You mean the two of us—out of all the hundreds of little towns there are all over the country—?"

"I'm from there originally," she assented warily. She left off the "too." She sat down opposite him, with watchful deliberation. Suspicion was crackling like an electric current alive in her, generated at the first word he'd let out of his mouth. She was conditioned that way. She'd learned not to believe anybody, anytime, anywhere. That was the only way to keep from being taken in. What was this anyway? What was the angle? He'd got the name of the town from the envelope, it was there for anyone to see; so far, so good. Now what was he trying to build from that? What was the come-on? What was the frame leading to? A touch? A half-nelson on her affections, before she woke up and snapped out of it? One thing she gave it; it was a new gag, and she'd thought she knew them all.

Wait a minute, he was wide open. She'd get him. "So you're from back in Glen Falls." She stared at him searchingly. "What street did you live on back there?"

She timed him with her fingernails tapping the edge of the table. His answer beat them to the first tap. It spilled out before the starting-gun even. "Anderson Avenue, up near Pine Street. The second house down between Pine and Oak, right after the corner—" She'd watched his face closely. He hadn't had to think at all; it came out spontaneously, like your own name is supposed to.

"Did you ever go to the Bijou movie-house, down on Courthouse Square, when you were there?"

This time there was a time-lag. "There wasn't any Bijou when I was there," he said blankly. "There were only two, the State and the Standard."

"I know," she murmured softly, looking down at her own hand. "I know there isn't."

Her hand was shaking a little, so she dropped it below the table. "What street is it where the iron foot-bridge crosses the railroad tracks—you know, to get from one side to the other of the ditch they run in?"

Only those who were from there, who'd lived there half their lives, could have answered that.

"Why, it doesn't cross it at any street," he answered simply. "It's in an awkward place, midway between two streets, Maple and Simpson, and if you want to cross it you've got to go along a cat-walk till you get to it. People've been kicking for years, *you* know that yourself—"

Yes, she knew that herself. But the point was he did.

He said, "Gee, you ought to see your own face, it's getting all white too. That's how I felt before, myself."

So it was true, and this freak number had come up.

She sat down, arms stiff against the chair-arms, and when she could speak again, she whispered: "Do you know where I lived? Do you want to know where I lived? On Emmet Road! You know where *that* is, don't you? Why, that's the next street over, after Anderson Avenue. It isn't cut all the way through. Why, the backs of our two houses must have been facing one another, even if they weren't directly opposite! Did you ever hear of such a thing?" Then she stopped and wondered, "How is it we never knew one another back there?"

"I came here a year ago," he computed.

"And I came here five."

"We didn't move into the Anderson Avenue house until after my Dad died, and that's a little over two years ago now. Before then we were on a farm we had out around Marbury—"

She nodded quickly, happy the enchantment hadn't been shattered by cold cartography. "That's what it was then. I'd already come away by the time you moved into town. But maybe right now, at this very minute, my folks already know your folks back there. Sort of backfence neighbors."

"They must," he said, "they must. I can see them now. Mom was always a great one for—" Then he stopped, and remarked with more immediate relevancy: "You haven't told me what your name is yet. I've already given you mine."

"Oh, haven't I? It already seems like backing up a long way, doesn't it? I'm Bricky Coleman. My real name's Ruth, but everyone calls me Bricky, even the family. Gee, I hated it as a kid, but now—I sort of miss it. They started it—"

"I know, on account of your hair," he finished it for her.

His arm crept out along the tabletop toward her, palm extended upward; little hesitantly, as though ready to withdraw again if it were ignored. Hers started out from her side, equally hesitantly. The two met, clasped hands shook, disengaged themselves again. They smiled at one another embarrassedly across the table, the little act completed.

"Hello," he murmured diffidently.

"Hello," she acknowledged in a small voice.

Then the brief glazing of formality evaporated again, and they were both fused once more by common interest in the bond they'd found between them.

"I think they must have met by now—back there—don't you?" he suggested.

"Wait a minute—Williams, that's a common name—but have you got brother with a lot of freckles?"

"Yeah, my younger brother, Johnny. He's only a kid. He's eighteen."

"I bet he's the very one been going around with my niece, Millie. She's only sixteen or seventeen herself. She's been writing me off and on about some new heart-throb of hers, a boy named Williams, everything perfect about him but the freckles and she's hoping they'll wear off."

"Hockey?"

"On the Jefferson High team!" She squealed the answer. "That's Johnny. That's him all right."

They could only shake their heads together, rapt with amazement. "It's a small world!"

"It sure is!"

Now she was the one doing the looking at him, boy how she was looking at him, studying him, learning him by heart, seeing him for the first time. Just a boy, a dime-a-dozen boy, plain as calico, nothing fancy about him. Just a boy from next door. *The* boy next door. There was one in every small-town girl's life. And this was he. Here was hers now. The one who should have been hers; who would have been, if she'd stayed, waited a little longer.

Nothing to him. There never was anything to the boy next door. He was too close to you to see him clearly. Nothing dashing, nothing romantic. That always came from a distance. But he was *clean-cut*, that was the point. How had she missed seeing that at the mill, even when he first walked in, even before she knew? Well, when they

were just a ticket to you, and a pair feet, how were you going to see anything?

They talked about it, their home town, for a while, voices
low, eyes dreamily lidded. They brought it close, in through
the window, into the very room with them. They pushed
New York, hanging around in the night outside, back, far
back and away. The Paramount clock, riding the night sky
somewhere beyond the window, receded, and instead they
could almost hear the steeple bell of the little white church
down by the square softly, sweetly, tolling the hour. Saying,
"Sleep. I'm looking after you. You're home where you belong.
Sleep. You're safe, I'm keeping watch over you—"

They talked about it for a while; slow in starting and
self-conscious at first, awkwardly. Then faster, more fluent-
ly as they warmed to it, and forgetting who they were and
what they were; not talking any more for one another but
each one for himself. Till there was just one running stream
between them, just one flow of reminiscence into which they
dropped their neatly-interspersed memories with rhythmic
alternation.

"That plank sidewalk in front of Marcus' Department
Store, with the board that used to tip up if you walked too
close to the edge; I bet they haven't fixed that yet!"

"And Pop Gregory's candy store, remember? The names
he used to think up for his specialties—'De Luxe Oriental De-
light Sundae'—"

"The Elite Drugstore, down on lower Main, that was another great one—"

"Morning glories on the porch-sheds—"

"Hammocks on all the front porches in the summer, in
the evening, swinging lazy, and a glass of lemonade on the

floor under you. With you was it lemonade? With me it was always—"

"And at night no music. A hush. You could hear a pin drop."

"And Jefferson High, all spick and span, spotless granite and a block long. I used to think it was the biggest building in the world. Did you go to Jefferson High?"

"Sure, everyone goes to Jefferson High, I guess. Those polished stone bevels alongside the front steps, I used to slide down them standing up every time I came out."

"I did too. I bet you had Miss Elliott. Did you have Miss Elliott in Advanced English?"

"Sure, everyone has Miss Elliott in Advanced English. You have to."

Something hurt her a little bit, for a minute. The boy next door, and I've met him two thousand miles away and five years too late. The boy next door, the boy I was supposed to know and never did.

"Folks saying good morning to you from all the way over on the other side of the street, even if you'd never set eyes on them before in your life, and they never had you."

"And no music, after dark came. No slide-trombones that go in and out, and bray. Only crickets and things like that. No music. No music, ever."

"Thick, deep, fluffy snow in the winter, topping everything like marshmallow—"

"But in the spring—! Oh I could skip it in the winter, in the fall, and even in the summer. But in the spring! Those pale pink things used to come out in the trees, and you'd walk down the street like through a whiff of Dorothy Gray's apple-blossom stuff—"

"People that knew you from the time you were a kid, all up and down the line. People that took an interest in you. That stopped at the door with jellies if you were sick. That would have gladly lent you money, when you got a little older, if you happened to be broke—"

"And look at us now." Her head dropped into her folded arms on the tabletop as suddenly as though her neck had been broken.

Twice, three times, her fist struck lightly at the tabletop, in futility "Home," he heard her say smotheredly. "Home, where I belong—I want to see my Mom again—"

He was standing over her when she looked up again. He hadn't touched her, but she knew he'd started to, he'd put out his hand and tried to when she wasn't looking, and then didn't know how to go ahead, had given the idea up. She could tell by the lame way he was holding his hand.

She smiled and tried to blot her eyes by blinking them, to keep him from seeing they were wet.

"Give us a cigarette," she said huskily. "I always have one after I cry. I don't know what got me. I haven't cried for company like that in years."

He wasn't having any of that. He didn't give her the cigarette, to help her pretend she was tough again. "Why don't you go back?" he said. He seemed again a little older. Maybe now it was that she'd grown a little younger in turn. The city made you old. Home, you stayed young at home. And even when you thought of home, that made you a little younger, for a little while.

She wasn't going to answer. He came back to it again. She saw that he had a one-track mind when he once got started on anything. "Why don't you? Why don't you go on home?"

"Don't you think I've tried?" she asked him sullenly. "I've priced the fare until I know it backwards. I've been down there so many times to inquire, I know the bus schedule by heart. There's only one through once a day, and that leaves at six in the morning. There's an evening one you can take, but you have to stop overnight in Chicago. And overnight—in Chicago or anywhere else—you lose your nerve; you'd only turn around and come back again. I *know*; don't ask me why, I *know*. Once I even got as far as the terminal, had my bag all packed next to me, sat there waiting for them to open the gates. I couldn't make it; I backed out at the last minute. Turned my ticket in, and dragged myself back here."

"But why? Why can't you go, if you want to that bad? What's holding you?"

"Because I didn't make good. I didn't make the grade. They think I'm in a big Broadway flash-production. I'm just a taxi; just a hired duffle-bag you push around the floor. See that piece of paper there, with nothing on it but 'Dear Mom'? That's part of the reason; the stuff I've been writing home to them. Now I haven't got the courage to go back and face them all and admit that I'm a flop. It takes plenty, and I haven't got enough."

"But they're your folks, they're your own people; they'd understand, they'd be the first to try to make it easy on you, to buck you up."

"I know; I could tell Mom anything. It isn't that. It's all the friends and neighbors. She's probably been bragging to them about me for years, reading my letters, you know how it goes. Sure, Mom and the other girls would stand by me, they wouldn't say a word; but it would hurt them just the same. I don't want to do that. I always wanted to go back and make them proud of me. Now I've got to go back and make them feel sorry for me.

There's a big difference there." She looked up at him, shook her head. "But that's only part of the reason. That isn't the main reason at all."

"Then what is?"

"I can't tell you. You'd only laugh at me. You wouldn't understand."

"Why would I laugh? Why wouldn't I understand? I'm from home too, aren't I? I'm here in the city just like you."

"Then here it is," she said. "It's the city itself. You think of it as just a place on the map, don't you? I think of it as a personal enemy, and I know I'm right. The city's bad; it gets you down. It's got a half-nelson on me right now, and that's what's holding me, that's why I can't get away."

"But houses, stone and cement buildings, they haven't got *arms*, they can't reach out and hold you back, if you want to go."

"I told you you wouldn't understand. They don't have to have arms. When there are that many of them bunched together, they give off something into the air. I don't know fancy language; I only know there's an intelligence of its own hanging over this place, coming up from it. It's mean and bad and evil, and when you breathe too much of it for too long, it gets under your skin, it gets into you—and you're sunk, the city's got you. Then all you've got to do is sit and wait, and in a little while it's finished the job, it's turned you into something that you never wanted to be or thought you'd be. Then it's too late. Then you can go anywhere—home or anywhere else—and you just keep on being what it made you from then on."

This time he just looked at her without answering.

"I know that sounds spooky to you. I know you don't believe me. But I know I'm right. I've *felt* it, I tell you. There's a brain, something that thinks on its own, hanging over it. Watching you, playing with you, like a cat does a mouse. It'll let you go a little ways away from it—like it did me, to the bus terminal—and then just when you think you've made it, you're going to get away altogether, it'll reach out after you and haul you back again. You think it's your own free mind, but it isn't; you think you changed your mind, but you didn't. It's the vapor, the fumes—there's a certain word, see if I can remember it—the miasma given off by the city, that's got into you already, that does it for you. Or you could say it's like a whirlpool. If you sit quiet in the middle of it, don't *try* to get away, you don't feel anything. But when you get too near the outside, trying to work your way out, is when it sucks you back again. I know what I'm saying. There've been times I could almost feel the *pull* of it. Like when you're in swimming and an undertow gets you. You can't see anything, but you can feel the drag of it. You're the only one that knows it's there, but you're the only one that has to. It's you it's hauling under. You can't break that by yourself; now do you see what I mean?"

She swept her hand out, brushed aside what he hadn't said, but what she'd thought he might. "Oh I know. There are thousands of them like us come here every year. They shoot right up to the top. They're in every walk life. *All New York came from somewhere else*, is what they say. But that doesn't kill my point, it only proves it all the more. The city's bad. If you're the one out of the thousand who's a little weaker than the rest, a little slower, needs a little extra help, a little boost over the hurdles, that's when it jumps you, that's when it shows its true colors. The city's a coward. It hits you when you're down and only when you're down. I say the city's bad, and if it's good for everyone else, I'm me, and that still makes it bad for me. I hate it. It's my enemy. It won't let me go—and that's how I know."

"Why don't you go back?" he said again. "Why don't you?"

"Because I'm not strong enough any more to break the grip it has on me. I thought I just got through telling you that. I proved it to myself that early-morning when I sat waiting in the bus terminal, I saw what it was then. The lighter it got outside, the stronger the pull back got. It sneaked up me calling itself 'common sense'; it sabotaged me. When the sun started creep down from the tops of the buildings, and the people started to thicken along the sidewalks on 34th Street, it kidded me by trying to look familiar, something I was used to, something that wouldn't hurt me, I didn't need to be afraid of. It whispered, 'You can always go tomorrow instead. Why not give it one more night? Why not try it one more week? Why not give it one more tumble?' And by the time the bus-starter said 'All aboard,' I was walking like a sleepwalker, with my bag in my hand, going the other way; slow and licked. No kidding, when I came outside I could hear the trombones and the saxes razzing me, way up high around the building-tops somewhere. 'We've gotcha! We knew you couldn't make it! Hotcha! We've gotcha!'"

She planted her head against her hand, stared thoughtfully down at nothing. "Maybe the reason I wasn't able to break the headlock it has on me because I was all alone. I wasn't strong enough alone. Maybe if I'd had someone going back home with me, someone to grab me by the arm when I tried to back out, I wouldn't have weakened, I would have made it."

His face tightened up. She saw that. She saw the imaginary boundary line he stroked across the table with the edge of his hand. As if setting off something from something else; the past, perhaps, from the present. "I wish I'd met you yesterday," she heard him say, more to himself than to her. "I wish I'd met you last night instead of tonight."

She knew what he meant. He'd done something he shouldn't, since yesterday, and now he couldn't go back. He wasn't telling her anything; she'd known all along he had something on his mind.

"Well, I guess I better clear out," he mumbled. "Guess I better go."

He went over toward where his hat was. She saw him lift up the edge the pillow a little. She saw the half-start his other hand made, toward his inside coat-pocket, as if to take something out without letting her see him.

"Put it back," she said metallically. "None of that." Then her voice mellowed a trifle. "I've got the fare, anyway. I've had it put aside for over eight months, down to the last nickel for a hamburger at the stop-over. Like a nest-egg. A nest-egg that's so old it's curdled already."

He came back to her, his hat on his head now. He didn't linger at the table any more. He went on toward the door, not fast, not purposefully, at a sort of aimless trudge, and let his hand trail over her shoulder as he passed her, in a parting accolade that expressed mutely but perfectly what it was intended to convey: mutual distress, sympathy without the power of helping one another, two people who were in the same boat.

She let him get as far as the door, with his hand out to the knob. "They're after you for something, aren't they?" she said quietly.

He turned and looked back at her, but without any undue surprise or questioning of her insight. "They will be, by about eight or nine this morning at the latest," he said matter-of-factly.

HE TOOK his hand off the knob, came back to her again.
He didn't say anything. He turned back his coat, fumbled
with the lining down toward the hem. He unpinned a slit
that looked as though it had been made intentionally with
a knife or razor blade. He worked something free through
it, with agilely probing fingers. Suddenly a deck of rub-
ber-banded currency was resting on the table between them.
The topmost bill was a fifty. He shifted to the other side of
the coat, opened up a matching suture there. A second tablet
of banknotes joined the first. This time the top-most denom-
ination was a hundred.

It took him some time. He'd had them evenly inserted all
around the hem of his coat, so that their bulk wouldn't betray
itself in any one particular place. He'd had others in his various
pockets. He'd even had one fastened at the side of his leg, under the garter. When he was done there were six of the banded
sheaves arrayed there on the tabletop, and the debris of a seventh that had already been sundered and partly dissipated.

Her face was expressionless. "How much is it?" she asked
tonelessly.

"I'm not sure now any more. It must still be over twenty-four hundred. It started out to be an even twenty-five."

Her face still showed nothing. "Where'd you get it?"

"Some place I had no right to."

After that, neither of them said anything more for a few minutes. It was as though the money weren't in sight there between the two of them.

Then finally, without any further urging, he began to talk about it. Maybe because she was from his own home town, and he had to tell someone. She was the girl next door, the one he would have told his troubles to, if they were both still back there. He wouldn't have had anything like this to tell her, back there, but he had it here, so he told it here.

"I had a job as an electrician's helper until just a short while ago. Sort of an apprentice or assistant, whatever you'd want to call it. It wasn't much, but it was something. We did a little of everything, repairing radios, converting them from one current to another, electric flatirons, vacuum cleaners, putting in new wall-outlets or extra lengths of wiring in people's homes, fixing doorbells—you know, all that sort of thing.

"It wasn't what I'd come here for, but it was a darned sight better than the first few weeks had been, when I'd slept out on park benches. So I wasn't complaining.

"Then about a month ago, I lost it. I wasn't fired, it just folded up under me. The old guy got a heart-attack and was told to take it easy, so he quit business. He had no one to take over for him, I was no kin of his, so he just closed up shop. I was left high and dry again, like I'd been before. I tramped around by the hour, and I couldn't get myself anything else. Nothing that was halfway permanent, anyway. Either in that line or any other. Stints at washing dishes in greasy-vest joints, or busman in one-arm hash-houses— Things are tight in this town, and nothing else was open. 1939's a tough year, you know that yourself. When I saw that I was heading for the ash-heap again, I should have gone back home while I still had the price of the fare on me. Or written the family for money; they'd have sent it. But it was like with you, I guess. I hated to admit I was licked. I'd come here on my own, and I wanted to make good on my own. Smart guy, me."

He was pacing slowly back and forth now, while he spoke to her; hands shoved deep into his pockets in dejection, head bent, looking down at his own feet as he moved them.

She just sat there, listening intently, sideward on the chair, hugging her own waist.

"Now I've got to go back and mention an incident that happened last winter, several months before I lost my job. This is the part that's going to sound shady, that you won't want to believe, but it happened, just the way I'm telling you. We got one of these custom-made jobs, that came our way once in awhile. The shop was on Third, but it was right on the edges of the Gold Coast; you know, the swanky zone, the east side Seventies. My boss had been in business there a long time, and he had a good reputation for thorough, methodical work, and you'd be surprised how often these people would call him in for something in their homes. We got to see the insides of lots of the swellest homes in the city.

"Well anyway, this particular call was from a swanky private home over on East Seventieth. The guy had bought an ultra-violet ray sunlamp, to keep himself fit through the winter instead of going to Florida, and it needed a special outlet rigged up for it on the bathroom wall so it could be plugged in.

"The name was Graves. Mean anything to you?"

She shook her head.

"It didn't to me either. It still don't, as far as that goes. My boss claimed they were in the society columns a lot, very old and well-known family. Not that he read the society columns himself, but he seemed to know all about them. The job itself was easy enough. It took us three days, but that was because we only worked at it for an hour or so at a time each day, in order not to inconvenience them too much.

"We had to chop a hole about the size of a fist part way through the bathroom wall, then hook up a wire with one that was already inside the wall, leading into the room beyond, and bring it through, to take the lamp-connection. Well, it was an old house, and the walls were good and thick, I never saw them so deep. One time, when I was chipping away there by myself—my boss wasn't with me at the moment, he'd gone back to the shop to get something—I struck wood offside to me. I didn't know what it was, but I shifted further over to avoid it. After that, it didn't give me any more trouble.

"Then the next day—I think it was—somebody stepped into the next room from where I was working, it was a sort of library or second-floor study at the back; he was only there for a minute or two, and then he went out again.

"I heard a slight disturbance in the wall right next to me. The doorway between was open, and I leaned my head back and glanced out. There was a mirror opposite, and I could see him in that; he was standing on the other side of the same wall I was working at, just a little further over. He'd opened sort of a wooden panel—the whole wall in there was panelled about halfway up—and he was turning a little dial on a safe-lid built-in behind it. It wasn't a very big one, oh about two by four, one of these baby-sized safes, like they have in rooms sometimes. He swung out the lid, and slid out a shallow drawer, and I saw him take out some money; then he shoved it back again. "I didn't even wait to watch any more. I went back to my work. I wasn't interested. All I'd wanted to know was what the vibration was I could feel right next to me in the wall. Afterwards I remembered about hitting wood the day before, so I figured it must have been the back or the side of the wooden lining the safe was set into that I'd grazed. And I let it go at that, I didn't think any more about it from then on. I don't ask you to believe that; I don't blame you if you don't."

All she said was, "I didn't believe you when you said you were from the same town I was, at first, either. If that was true, why shouldn't this be?"

"Then what I'm going to tell you next is even harder to believe. I don't know myself how it happened; I only know it did, and I had nothing to with it. They had a little table, downstairs by the door as you came Several times, without meaning anything, I'd left my kit standing open it, while we were busy upstairs. It had things that we'd found out we didn't need, after we'd once got the job lined up; I guess it was more absent-mindedness than anything else, though. Then when we were all through and went back to the shop for the last time, I emptied it out and I found something in it that must have got mixed up with my tools and wiring and things by mistake. Either somebody had dropped it in by mistake, or I'd swept up off the table with my own hand without noticing, when I was putting things back in the kit. There was a dopey-looking sort of a maid answered the door for us once or twice, she might have done it when she was dusting around the table, thinking it was part of my equipment. All I know didn't do it purposely, I swear to you I only saw it for the first time when got back to the shop. I don't know yet how it got in there."

"What was it?" she asked.

"It was the latchkey to the front door of the house, that I'd brought away with me by mistake in my tool-kit. Or at least one of the latchkeys to front door."

She just looked at him, long and hard.

He said again, "I don't know how it got in there. I only know I didn't do it, didn't know about it till I saw it." Then he let his hands fall limp at sides. "That I don't expect anyone to believe."

"An hour ago I wouldn't have," she admitted. "Now I'm not so sure anymore. Go ahead, finish it."

"The rest don't need much telling, you can guess it from here. I should have told my boss about it, turned it over to him. I would have, but he wasn't there any more; he'd already gone home and left me to close up shop. Then the next best thing was, I should have gone right straight back there myself and returned it to them. But it was late and I was hungry and tired; I wanted to eat and take it easy, I'd been working all day. So I left it where it was overnight, and I meant to drop around the next day and turn it over to them without fail. I didn't do that either. I was kept on the jump from eight the morning until the last thing at night, and I didn't have a chance. By day after that, it had already slipped my mind. First thing you know, I'd forgotten about it completely.

"Then the job folded, like I told you, and I was left stranded. My money all went, and— Well, to make a long story short, yesterday I got out my kit and looked it over, to see maybe if I could borrow something on it at a hock shop. I'd already hocked about everything I owned that I could get anything on.

I dumped it out, taking inventory, and there was the key. I saw it and remembered where it had come from.

"I put it in my pocket, and I groomed myself up a little, and I went back there with it. All that was in my mind was that maybe they could put me the way of doing a little work, even if it was only tightening a lamp socket.

"I got there, and I rang the bell, and no one came to the door. I kept ringing away, and no one answered. This was in the early part of the afternoon. I started to leave, but I didn't make a clean break of it. I sort of loitered around outside the place, wondering what to do next. Then a delivery boy came out of one of the other buildings close by, and noticed me looking up at the place still waiting for an answer, and without my asking him he came out with there was no one in the house, they'd all gone to their country place for the summer the week before. I asked him how was it they hadn't boarded up the door and lower windows, the way they usually do in such a case. He said he understood one member of the family had stayed behind a few days to finish up some business; probably the house would be closed up proper when he got through and was ready to follow the rest. I asked him if he had any idea when would be the best time for me to find this one person in. He didn't know any more than I did about it, but he suggested what my own common sense should have told me without asking: to try in the evening.

"So I went back to my room and I waited for the evening, and it was while I was waiting that the idea first started in to grow. You know; I don't have to tell you what it was."

"I know," she acquiesced.

"It grew without my noticing it, and those kind of growths are bad ones. They're like weeds, they're hard to rip up once they get a start on you. And everything helped to—to water it, you might say. I was down to my last dime, I couldn't get any supper. When you're down to a dime, you can't spend it, not even on coffee and a cruller; you might need it more the next day than you do right then—you're afraid to let go of it. I'd been dodging being put out of my room for over two weeks past, and that's about as long as you can stretch that; *that* was going to come any minute. Well, the thing sprouted like a stinkweed, while I sat there on the edge of my bed all afternoon long, throwing the key up and down in front of me with my hand.

"Around seven, just a little past dark, I went out and headed for there a second time." He smiled at her bleakly. "Now the excuses stop, and you can listen to the rest of it without making allowances. I came to the corner below, and stopped a minute, and this is what I saw from there. There was a light on, coming from the lower windows, so I'd come back in time—if that was what I'd come back for, to catch this one person in. And there was a taxi in front of the door, standing waiting for someone. Right while I was looking, the light went out, and a minute later a man and a woman came out of the door, on their way to the taxi. I had plenty of time to catch them before they got in. They took their time, they weren't in any hurry. I could have run up to them from where I was, or hollered to them to attract their attention, and they would have stood and waited a minute.

"My feet just took root there and wouldn't let me move. I stood there quiet, watching them go, waiting for them to go. I didn't know which of the two belonged in the house, and which had stopped by for the other. But I could tell they were going out for the evening, they were going to be gone for hours. She had on a long dress and he had on a tux, I could see it from where I was. And when people dress like that they're not coming back right away, inside the next hour or so.

"They got in the cab and they went away, and I went away too. I walked around the block, with my hand in my pocket feeling the key, fighting the idea. I came back to it again from the other side, and I turned and walked around the block again, in the other direction. I fought hard, all right, but I guess I didn't fight hard enough. My stomach was empty, and you don't fight so good that way. I hadn't brought my kit with me, but I did have a couple of lightweight tools in my pocket, just about what I'd need. This time you don't have to strain your imagination; they didn't get separated from the rest and get into my pocket by accident, I'd picked them out and put them there myself.

"Once I even tried to drop the key into a rubbish can that I passed, to kill the temptation. But it wouldn't work; inside of two minutes I'd weakened, and gone back, and picked it out again. Then I hurried up after that, came back around the corner, and marched straight up to the door without any more dillydallying. Well, I'd lost the bout. And at first it felt awfully good to lose too, don't let them kid you about that."

He sounded a note of laughter, without joy. "The rest you don't need a blueprint for. You can take it from there yourself. I rang the bell one last time, for the look of it. I knew there was no one in there now any more. Then I stepped inside the vestibule and got busy on the inner door with the key. It opened right up at touch; they'd never even changed the lock, the dopes. Maybe they'd never even missed the key, I don't know.

"I didn't need the lights to find my way around. I went right up the stairs, like my boss and I had so many times before, and into that study or whatever it was at the back of the second floor. I lit up the bathroom, because it was safe there, it had no outside window that could give the light away. I took out the couple of little things I'd brought with me, and I went at the safe from behind. I reopened the hole we'd made in the bathroom wall, only this time I aimed it straight at the back of the safe, instead of over to the side. And I made it bigger than the first time too, big enough to pry away one of the wooden panels the safe was imbedded in.

"It was the jerkiest kind of safe I ever saw. Only the lid and the frame were steel; the rest of it was just a wooden lining. And when you ripped out the back panel, it was all open; you could reach in and pull the drawers out backward into the bathroom. I guess it was tough enough to crack from the front, but you weren't supposed to get at it from behind like that.

"It was cluttered up with papers and stuff, but I didn't bother with anything but the cash. I cleaned that out, and left all the jewelry and heirlooms and securities they had in it just the way they were. Then I slipped the cash-drawers back in again, and tidied up. I cleaned all the chipped plaster and mortar up off the floor, and I swung the shower-curtain around on its rod a little, so that it covered up the great big gaping hole I'd made. If he—I guess it's he that lives there—goes in there when he comes back late tonight, he probably won't notice anything wrong. He won't find out about it until tomorrow, when he swings the curtain around him to take his morning bath.

"Well, that was all there was to it. To that part of it, any-way. I put out the light, and I came down to the door again, and I watched from behind it for a minute or two until I was sure there was no one around to spot me. Then I came out, closed it behind me, and walked quickly away from there.

"And right away, I started to pay for it; boy, how I paid for it. Before I spent a nickel of it or got a block away, I was already paying for it through the nose. Until now, I'd owned the streets. That was about all I'd had, but I'd had them, at least. I was hungry and broke and jobless, but I looked everyone square in the face, I went anywhere I damn pleased on them, the streets were mine. Now all of a sudden, the streets were taken away from me, to stay on them too long became dangerous. Faces coming toward me, if they seemed to look at me too closely, became something to watch out for. And people walking behind me—my shoulder would twitch, as if I expected a hand to drop on it.

"But the worst part of it all was, now that I had it, I didn't know what I wanted to do with it any more. Half an hour before I'd known a hundred things I'd wanted so bad I would have given my right arm for them. And now I couldn't remember one of them any more.

"I'd thought that I'd been hungry, and matter of fact I hadn't been eating right for a week or more past, but now I found that I wasn't even that any more. I went into the swellest restaurant I could find, a real swell one, and I ordered everything straight down the list, like I'd always dreamed of doing some day. While I was still ordering, it sounded great, but when the stuff started to show up—something went wrong. I couldn't seem to swallow right. Every time they brought something and put it down in front of me and I tried to dig in, somehow I'd find myself thinking 'This is your own future you're eating, years and years of it,' and it would gang up and stick in my throat.

"After awhile I couldn't stand it any more; I peeled off a five-dollar bill and I left it on the table, and I got up and I got out, without waiting for the rest of it. And when I came out, I couldn't help remembering that when I only had a dime of my own to spend, a dime that really belonged to me, I didn't have any trouble swallowing the coffee and the cruller that

that bought me. In fact, my throat stayed wide open long after it was gone and there wasn't any more on the way down, just waiting to see.

"I don't know, I guess you're either honest or you're crooked by nature, and you can't change yourself over that suddenly from the one thing to the other without a lot of growing pains. I guess you have to do it slowly, it takes years, maybe.

"Then afterwards, I was walking along the streets again, in that new way I had now, leery of faces in front of me, shying from steps in back of me, and I heard music coming from a row of open windows across the street. There was a guy I hadn't liked the looks of the last couple of blocks, he seemed be coming along behind me too steadily, so when he wasn't looking, I over and jumped in there. It seemed a good place to stay in for a while, keep out of sight and off the streets. I bought a whole carload of tickets, make sure I'd have enough to last me for a while, and then I looked around and the very first girl I saw—" he ridged his forehead at her deprecatingly—"was you."

"Was me," she repeated thoughtfully, running her hand slowly along edge of the table and back, slowly along the edge of the table and back.

They fell silent. He'd been speaking so steadily, just now, that the silence seemed longer to both of them than it actually was, by contrast. It was probably only a moment or two.

"What are you going to do now?" she said finally, looking up at him.

"What's there I can do? Just wait, I guess; just wait for them to finally catch up. They always do. He'll find out about it by nine or ten, when he goes in there to take his bath. And probably that errand boy'll remember seeing some fellow ringing the doorbell there the afternoon before. Then old boss'll tell them who I am and where I lived last. It won't take long. They'll know me, they'll get me. Tomorrow. The day after. By the end the week. What difference does it make? They always do, they never fail You never stop to think of that before. You think of it after. It's after for me, now, and I'm thinking of it."

He shrugged hopelessly. "It's no use trying to run out of town, hide somewhere else; that never works either. Not for little guys like me, that are new at it. If they're going to get you, they'll get you wherever it is, whether here or some place else. They've got a long reach, and it's no use trying to away from it. So I guess I'll just stick around and wait." He sat there staring down at the floor with a puzzled, defeated smile on his face. As if he was wondering how the whole thing had come about in the first place, couldn't quite make it out.

Something about that look got to her. There was some sort of a helplessness about it, you might say a resigned helplessness, that did something her. The boy next door, she thought poignantly. That's who he is, that's all he is. He's no crook, no dance-hall shark. He's just that boy on the porch you waved to when you went in or out your own gate. Or that sometimes leaned his bicycle against the fence and chatted with you over it a while, a big wide grin on his face. He came here to do big things, to lick town, but now instead the town had licked him. He'd kissed his mother or his sister goodbye, at the trainside or at the bus one day, and she'd be willing to bet anything he'd felt a little like crying, for just the first minutes after leaving them, though of course he hadn't shown it.

She knew, because so had she. And then the golden glow came on, effacing that; promise of great things to be, the aura in which youth sallies to the wars. Probably before the first hour was done, all his plans were made, his castles reared; fame, fortune, happiness, all the things that were to be had taken shape. She could have read just what the thoughts in his mind were, that first day of departure, because hers had been that too. Back home they, the one or two of them who were particularly his, thought he was swell, they thought he was wonderful. And the funny part of it was, they were right and the rest of the world, that didn't, was wrong. Back home they probably read from his letters across the back fence to the neighbors, bragged about how well he was doing. Her folks did too.

And look at him now, look at him here, in this room with her. She didn't know, any more than he, why it had gone wrong, why it had turned out like this. She only knew he shouldn't end up like this, furtive, hiding, hunted up and down the streets, never knowing when a hand was about to drop to his shoulder and hold him fast. The boy next door, the grinning, puppy-friendly boy next door.

She raised her head at last from the hand that had shaded it. She hitched her chair forward, as if some invisible dividing-line it crossed in doing so marked the boundary between passive auditor and active participant, slight as the adjustment was. She stared at him closely for a moment, not so much in discernment of him as in contemplation of what she herself was about to say. "Listen," she said finally. "I've got a proposition for you. What do you say we both go back where we belong, back home there where we come from? Get our second wind, give ourselves another chance? Both get on that six o'clock bus that I was never able to make alone."

He didn't answer. She was leaning across the table now,

to press her point more strongly home. "Don't you see it has to be now or never? Don't you see what this place is doing to us? Don't you see what we'll be like a year from now, even six months from now? It'll be too late then, there won't be anything to save any more. Just two other people, with our same names, that aren't us any more—"

His eyes flicked aside to the packets of money on the table, then back to her again. "It's already too late for me now. Just a few hours too late, just a half night too late, but that's as good as a lifetime." He said again what he'd said before. "I wish I'd met you last night, instead of tonight. Why couldn't I have met you *before*, instead of after? It's no good, now. They'd only be waiting to grab me when I got off the bus at the other end. They'd know by then who I was, where I was from; they'd look for me there when they couldn't find me here. I'd only drag you into it, if I went with you. The people back there, the very ones I would want least of all to find out about it, they'd see it happen right under their eyes—" He shook his head. "You go. You've still got your chance, even if I haven't got mine. Go by yourself, go right tonight. You're right about it, it's bad here. Go right now, before you weaken again. I'll go with you down to the bus if you want me to, I'll see you off, to make sure you get away—"

"I can't; haven't I been telling you that? I can't make it by myself. The city's too strong for me. I'd only get off at the first Jersey stop and come back again. I can't make it without you, just like you probably can't any more without someone like me. It'll take our combined strength. You're my last straw, and I'm yours; we've met, and we know that now. Don't let's throw this chance away. It's like dying when you're still alive—" Her face was puckered in desperate appeal, her eyes holding his by their intensity.

"They'll only be there waiting for me, I know what I'm saying. They'll collar me before my foot's even off the steps—"

"Not if nothing's missing, if nothing's been taken. What would there be to arrest you for then?"

"But something has. It's right here in front of us."

"I know, but there's still time to undo it, that's what my proposition is. Not to go with *that*, not to take *that* with you. What would there be to run away from then? We'd be bringing the badness of the city back home with us."

"You mean you think I could—?" A scared look was peering from his face, as if he was longing to hope but scared to let himself.

"You said he's there alone in the house. You said he went out all dressed up and won't be back until late. You said you didn't think he'd find out until he gets up in the morning—" She was speaking without pause for breath. "Have you still got the key, the key to get in with?"

His hands went to his pockets, darting from one to the other quickly now, as quickly as she had spoken. The tempo of hope was accelerating. "I don't remember throwing— Unless I left it in the door—" He rose from his chair to gain better clearance for his movements. Suddenly a terse breath gushed from him, signalling the finding of the key before it had itself appeared to view. "I've got it." Then he brought it out. "Here. Here it is, here."

They marvelled over the fact of its presence for a brief moment.

"It's funny I should hang onto it like this, isn't it? It's like a—a— Some sort of a—"

"Yeah, it is." She knew what he meant, though not the word they both needed.

He repocketed it. She jumped to her feet in turn. "Now if you can get back there before he comes home— Just in and out, long enough to put it back where you got it, that's all you need to do. Nobody's going to come after you just for chopping a hole in the wall, as long as nothing's been taken out—"

She was hastily gathering up the scattered packets, evening them together into one cube to give to him. The same thought struck them both at once, and they stopped to look at one another in dismay. "How much have you blown already? How much have you taken out?"

He pasted the flat of his hand to his forehead for a moment. "I don't know. Wait a minute, see if I can— Five dollars for that meal I didn't eat. And I must have bought about fifteen dollars' worth of those tickets up at your place— Twenty, altogether. Twenty bucks. It can't be more than that."

"Wait a minute, I've got it here," she said crisply. "I'll put it back in for you."

She jumped up, ran over to the cot, dismantled it by pulling up the bedding at the side. Then she tilted the mattress along its edge, thrust her hand into some unsuspected slit lurking along its underside, extracted a small quantity of paper money bedded there in tortured shape, like some sort of a flower pressed flat within an album.

"Oh, no," he started to protest. "I don't want—I can't let you do that. It's my worry, why should you make good the difference?"

She put on her best dance-hall armor, cut her hand at him frontally. "Now listen, I'm doing this, and I don't want to hear any arguments. All of it has got to go back; if there's even a dollar still out, it's technically a theft and you're open to arrest. Besides, what's the difference? Call it a loan, if it'll make you any happier. You can pay me back after we get home and you've started working again. I've still got enough left here to take care of both our bus tickets. You can square that up too, later on, if you want to." She thrust it into his hand. "Here, you hang onto it for us. It's *our* bankroll now, yours and mine."

He gave her a look that was like a pause in the flurry of their preparations for departure. "Gee, I don't know what to say—"

"Don't say anything." She flung herself back into the chair she'd originally sought out when she first entered the room. "The main thing is to make sure we both get out of this town tonight. Wait for me a minute, till I get my shoes on—throw a few things into my bag—there isn't much to take—" Then as she saw him make a tentative move toward the door and look at her inquiringly, "No, stay right in here with me, don't even wait outside—I'm afraid I'll lose you, and you're my one chance of getting home tonight—"

"You won't lose me," he promised almost inaudibly.

She jumped up again, settled her feet into their gear with a slight downward stamp of each one. "It's funny, but I'm not tired any more—"

He watched her throw things headlong into a battered suitcase she had hauled out from under the cot. "Suppose he's back by the time I get over there?"

"He won't be. We've got to keep saying that, praying it. It's the only way. You weren't caught when you went there to take it, why should you be caught when you go there to put it back? He's stepping out some place with that girl you saw leave with him— there's an even chance he won't get back till half-past three or four; till he sees her home to wherever she lives herself and—"

She went over to the window, raised it and leaned out. Not in the center of it, but slantwise, over in the far corner, looking off at an angle. "Look, we've still got time. You can still make it, you've still got a fighting chance."

"What's that out there you're looking at?"

She drew her head in again. "That's the only decent thing in this whole town. Every night it let me off when I thought I couldn't hold out another minute. It never tricked me, never gypped me, and I know it won't tonight. It's the only friend I've got, the only one I've ever had since I first came here. It won't let us down. It's the clock on the Paramount Building, all the way over; you can see it from here, if you look the right way, where there's a chunk cut out between two of the buildings— Come on, Quinn, it says we still can; and it never steered me wrong yet."

She latched down the lid of the valise. He reached for it, and she passed it to him. He held the door wide for her a moment, after she'd already passed through to the hall. "Got everything? Sure there's nothing else?"

"Close the door," she said wearily. "I don't want to look at it again. Leave the key in it, I won't be needing it any more."

They went down the rickety stairs one behind the other, he with her weatherbeaten valise in his hand. It didn't weigh much; it had hardly anything in it—just busted hopes. They trod softly, not so much in fear of inmates around them as with the instinctive hush that goes with night-departure.

At one place he saw her put out her hand to a star-shaped gash shattering the tinted plaster of the wall, hold it pressed there for a moment. "What'd you do that for?"

"That used to be my lucky spot," she whispered. "I'd touch it on my way out, every time I left here. A year or so ago, when I was still going around to casting offices and such. You get that way, you know, when luck's against you. It's been a long time since I touched it last. It never paid off. But maybe it will to-night. I hope it does. We need it tonight."

He'd gone down several steps beyond it, in her wake, while she spoke. He stopped for a moment, hesitated. Then he turned, went up again the step or two it took to reach it, put his hand to it as she had. Then he followed her down once more.

They stopped for a moment behind the street-door, side by side, before going on. Then she put out her hand to the knob. He put out his at almost the same instant. His hand came to rest atop hers. They stayed that way for a second. They looked at one another and smiled, artlessly, without coquetry, like children do. He said, "Gee, I'm sort of glad I met you tonight, Bricky."

She said, "I'm sort of glad I met you too, Quinn."

Then he took his hand off and let hers open the door. It had been her house, until just now, after all.

Outside the street stretched still and empty—

THEY CAME out into the slumbering early-morning desolation, flitted quickly past the brief bleach of the close-at-hand street-light, and were swallowed up again in the darkness on the other side of it. The street-lights, stretching away into perspective in their impersonal, formalized, zig-zag pattern, only added to the look of void and loneliness. There was not a single one of those other, warmer, personal lights to be seen anywhere about, above or below, denoting human presence behind a window, living occupancy within a doorway.

It was like walking through a massive, monolithic sepulchre. There was no one abroad, nothing that moved. Not even a cat scenting at a garbage-can. The city was a dead thing, over here on its margins, and like a dead thing it was stark and clammy, it frightened them a little. They drew closer in together even as they moved forward; suddenly without noticing she was hanging on his arm and he had drawn his arm protectively closer against his side, pressing her suppliance to him. They were not walking now as they had walked the time before, coming over here; spaced and self-sufficient. They were huddled together shoulder to shoulder as they moved. Their footsteps echoed hollowly in the exacerbated stillness, as though the street were one long plank bridging a hollow space beneath them.

He raised his hat in mock leavetaking, which only imperfectly covered up a very real trepidation. "Goodbye, Manhattan."

She quickly sealed his mouth for a minute with a sort of superstitious intensity. "Sh, not so loud. Don't tip our hand to it ahead of time. Don't let on to it. It'll cross us sure as you know."

He looked at her and grinned a little. "You really take that halfway serious, don't you?"

"More than you know," she said sombrely. "And I'm more right than you know, too."

At the corner he stopped, put down the valise a second. Here along the avenue there was motion, in contrast to the side-street they had just issued from, but it was cold, jewel-like, and it had thinned since before. It was as though the string holding the red and white beads had broken, and the last lingering few were rolling off into the distance.

"You better go down and wait for me at the bus terminal. I'll go over alone about—the other thing, first, and then I'll meet you down there."

She tightened her grip on his arm convulsively, as if afraid of losing him. "No, no. If we separate, we're licked. The city'll get its dirty work in. I'll think, 'Can I trust him?' You'll think, 'Can I trust her?' And before you know it— No, no. We're staying together, every step of the way. I'm going right over there with you. I'll wait outside the door while you go in."

"But suppose he's gotten home by now? You'll only— They're likely to pick you up for complicity."

"That's a chance we'll have to take. You'd be taking it even without me, so we're going to take it together. See if you can see a cab anywhere around; the longer we take getting over there, the more dangerous it'll be."

"On your money?"

"This reformation is on me," she answered.

They got one finally, by a process of walking slowly north, and stopping and throwing up their arms in unison whenever a pair of the lighted beads raced close enough past to seem likely to see them. One pair swerved in as if about to leap the curb and run them down, swelled larger, stopped, and turned into a cab. They ran for it without waiting for it to correct its discrepancy of halting place, and clambered in one at the other's heels.

"Take us up to the east side Seventies," he said. "I'll tell you where to stop when we get there. Go fast. Go up through the park, that's quicker."

It raced north with them, and then over through the classic fashionableness of Fifty-seventh, and then in at the Seventh Avenue entrance, stopping only when it had to, for the red disks that seemed to multiply perversely so that one leaped up to bar them at every crossing. Then after that it didn't have to stop any more, though the roadway used up some of the gain by becoming curved and indirect.

Once in the cab they hadn't spoken until, at one of the halts, he asked her: "What're you sitting way over in the corner, keeping your head back, like that for?"

"It's watching us. It's got a thousand eyes. Every time a street goes by, it's like there was an eye hidden deep back along it somewhere, an eye that we can't see, keeping tabs on us, giving itself the wink. We haven't fooled it any. It knows we're trying to run out on it. It's going to trip us yet if it can."

"Gee, you're superstitious, aren't you!" he commented indulgently.

"When you've got an enemy, and you're wise to it, that don't make you superstitious, that just makes you canny."

Then later she peered rearward through the edge of the cab-window. Back toward the west side skyline, now that their passage through the park was giving it depth enough of perspective; towers rearing like menacing black cacti against the reflection-lightened sky.

"Look. Don't it look cruel? Don't it look sneaky and underhanded, like it was just waiting to pounce and dig its claws into someone, anyone at all—?"

He chuckled a little, but only with moderate conviction. "All cities look like that at night, kind of shady and dim, tricky and not very friendly—"

"I hate it," she said with whispered vehemence. "It's bad. And it's alive, it's got will-power of its own, no one can tell me different."

"It's never done me any favors," he admitted. "I feel about like you do, I guess. Except I never thought of it as just one person, like you do; I thought of it more as—conditions, breaks."

Ahead of them a new skyline was looming, to take the place of the one that had dropped down out of sight behind them by now. The great gap in the middle of the city made by Central Park closed up again and they entered the East Side. New York, from Fifty-ninth Street to One Hundred and Tenth, is not one city but two; everyone knows that but few stop to think of it. Two widely-separated cities, more far-apart from one another than St. Paul is from Minneapolis or Kansas City, Missouri, from Kansas City, Kansas.

The famous East Side, the Gold Coast, the Butterfield-8 Exchange, that thin veneer of what the Victorians used to call elegance, and what moderns call smartness, spread very thin, not more than three blocks deep anywhere along its entire extent, Fifth to Park or so, and then behind that all the rest of the way to the river, pretty much the same drab huddle as anywhere else in the town.

The driver brought them out at Seventy-second, tacked to correct the unavoidable discrepancy the park-outlet had imposed, and went down Fifth a couple of blocks. Quinn stopped him at Sixty-ninth, a block past, so that he wouldn't be able to identify their destination too exactly. "We'll take it from here," he said to him clippedly.

They got out and paid him and put the little valise down between them, like a sort of dry-land anchor, and then just stood waiting for him to get out of the way. He stepped on the gas and went down Fifth again, toward where there was more life and better chances.

As soon as he was safely gone they walked as far as the next corner, Seventieth, and turned it, but no more. Then as soon as they were safely within the sheltering shadows of the side-street just beyond the corner, they stopped again briefly and made their arrangements to separate.

It was their first separation since they'd been one in purpose. She didn't like it. She would have rather there weren't to be any at all, not even such a brief one as this. But she didn't urge him to let her go right in with him, because she knew he wouldn't have heard of it. It *would* make the attempt more of a blind risk, at that. This way she could serve as a sort of look-out. But she didn't like it; still and all, she didn't like it.

"You can see it from here. It's on this side, on the even-numbered side, just past the second street-light down there," he said guardedly, looking all around to make sure they weren't observed. "Don't come any nearer than this, just in case. Wait here with your valise. I'll be back in no time. Don't be frightened. Take it easy."

She was already, but she would have died rather than let him know. It wasn't in the way he meant, anyway. He meant: don't be frightened for yourself. She wasn't. She was something she'd never been before. She was frightened for someone else. She was frightened for him.

"Don't take any chances. If you see any lights, if it looks like he's gotten back already, don't go all the way in—just drop the money inside the door. Let him pick it up from there in the morning. It doesn't have to go right smack back in the safe. And be careful—he may even be in bed already, with the lights out, and you won't know it."

He gave his hat brim a determined tug, moved away from her down the silent street. She watched him go. Watched his figure getting smaller all around the edges, shrinking down to half-size and even less. She didn't move a muscle; she was like some sort of pointer, except that she had no paw raised from the ground. Her heart was putting on more steam than it needed just for her to stand still like that.

The second light hit him a glancing blow, just on one side of him, then he darkened up again. She saw him glance cautiously around, and she knew he was up to it. It was just a skinny slice of stone from here, sandwiched in among the rest, with a stoop running down from it. He turned aside, went up that to the entrance. A pair of swinging, glass outer doors flicked out, then flattened back again.

He went in.

The act of restitution was under way.

The moment he had entered, she picked up her valise and started moving slowly down that way after him, in spite of his cautioning her to stay where she was. She wanted to be as near him as she could. She kept rooting for him as she edged along.

Her lips moved soundlessly, like a Sicilian warding off the evil eye. "If it catches on it'll do something to interfere, do something to throw a hitch in it; try to keep him the crook it just about had him ready to turn into."

It was always the same "it" with her, the same enemy. The city.

She looked down at the fingers of her free hand, and without her knowing it two of them had crossed themselves rigidly, held themselves pressed that way into her flank.

She addressed a sultry warning to "it" through baleful, half-parted lips, meant to frighten it off as she frightened too-intrusive customers at the mill. "Let him alone now, hear me? You keep out of it. Let him go through with it."

It leered somnolently back at her down the long tunnel-like vista of sooty gray and dark-blue and out-and-out pitch-black that were the colors of the night palette.

She'd reached the house now herself. She continued on past it, in order not to attract attention by stopping in front of it. The entryway, the vestibule between the outer glass doors and the inner one, the one that was the real bulwark, showed empty by the reflected street-light as she glanced in with elaborate dissimulation on her way by. He'd gone all the way in, into the depths of it, closed the door after him.

But suppose that one particular member of the family who was known to have stayed behind was upstairs asleep in there right now? Suppose Quinn didn't catch on in time? He'd cut off his own retreat, closing the door after him like that. Suppose the inmate woke up, discovered him—

She tried to shut the terrifying thought away. Nothing had

gone wrong the first time, when he entered on a dishonest errand. Why should anything go wrong this time, when he entered on an honest one?

The city. That would be just like the city, though.

"Let him alone now, hear? Now let him alone, do you get me?"

She was well past it now, in the other direction. She stole a look back. Nothing had happened yet; no outcries, no sudden brightening of upper-story windows, so he hadn't been discovered yet.

Her fingers were lame, they were so tired from being crossed so tight. She was like some sort of a slow-motion sentry posted out here to protect him. Like a picket, keeping the city out. Staunch, defiant, with no weapon but a lightweight valise swinging at her side. And after awhile she needed the courage for herself as well.

She was trying her best to be calm, but there was a tumult going on all around her heart as she sauntered along so dilatorily, so aimlessly. He was taking longer than he should, wasn't he? Even without using light, it shouldn't be taking him that long just to get upstairs to the second floor of a house and down again. He should have been out again by now. He should have been out *before* now.

It was still breaking and entering, even to return the money. And if he was caught returning it, how could he prove he *was* returning it, and not just removing it for the first time? He had to get out of there and in the clear, before the restoration held any virtue in it. Maybe Quinn should have mailed it back, instead of coming back in person with it. He and she hadn't thought of that; she wished now they had.

A figure suddenly materialized at the lower corner ahead,

on the opposite side from her. It didn't move out very far, just detached itself slightly and then stood still. It was just barely visible beyond the building line, standing with its back to her. A patrolman on his tour of duty. She whisked herself quickly down into the shelter of one of the shadowed areaways at hand, valise and all. It would have looked too suspicious to be seen loitering about there on the sidewalk at such an hour, with a piece of luggage in her hand.

If he came up this way— If Quinn should happen to come out while he was still down there at the corner— Her heart wasn't just beating, it was swinging from side to side and looping around in a complete circle like a pendulum gone crazy.

Metal clinked faintly as he opened a call-box to report in. That's what he was doing, standing there like that with his back to her. Even the blurred sound of his voice reached her in the stillness of the night air. She caught: "Larsen reporting in, two fifty-five," something like that. The box clashed shut again. She shrank back against the sheltering base of the stoop that walled one side of the little quadrangular hollow she was in. She was afraid to look to see which way he'd go now, afraid he'd come up this way, past her. She heard the very faint scrape his footsteps made, crossing over the mouth of the street down there, to this same side she was on. Then it faded, slight as it had been, and wasn't any more.

She peered infinitesimally out, and he wasn't in sight, he'd gone on past along the avenue. She let her breath out slowly, stepped up onto sidewalk-level again. Now she knew what it meant, what he'd felt, Quinn, when he kept looking behind him on the way over to her place from the mill earlier tonight; insecurity was awfully contagious.

She drifted back the other way, eying the inscrutable house-front apprehensively as she neared it. What had happened to him in there? What had gone wrong, to hold him so long? He should have been out ages ago.

Just as she came abreast of the near end of the house, the vestibule-doors up above parted noiselessly and he appeared between them. They fell to again behind him but he didn't move at once. He stood there looking down at her as though he didn't see her. Or as though he did see her but didn't know her. Then he moved to the rim of the steps and started down.

But there was something the matter with the way he was coming out of there. It wasn't *fast* enough. It was both too slow and something else besides; stupid, that was it. He was coming out too slow and stupid. As though he didn't know where he was. No, that wasn't it. As though—this was it—as though it didn't matter whether he came out or stayed inside.

Twice he broke his uncertain descent to stop and look behind him up at the doorway he'd just come through. He was almost staggering with a sort of lassitude.

She'd reached him with a quick questioning step or two. She got to him just as he got to the bottom.

She stood a smattering of inches from him now. Even in the gloom, she thought, his face looked white and taut.

"What's the matter? What're you looking so frightened about?" she whispered hoarsely.

He kept staring blankly at her in a sort of dazed incomprehension. She couldn't get it right out of him. Whatever it was had log-jammed in him. She put down the valise and shook him slightly by both shoulders.

"You've got to tell me. Don't stand there looking like that. What happened in there?"

It had a hard time coming, but it came. Her slight shake had dislodged it. "He's been killed in there. He's dead. He's lying in there—dead."

She gave a shuddering intake of breath. "Who, the—the man that lives there?"

"I guess so. The man I saw going out early this evening, the one I told you about." He passed his hand across his brow, under his hat brim.

For a moment, of the two, she was the more stricken one, the more frustrated at any rate, for she knew who their adversary was, he didn't.

She leaned against the stone side-arm of the stoop, wilted. "*It* did it," she said dully, her eyes sightless over the top of his head. "I knew it would. I knew it wouldn't let us square it. It never does. It's got us now good, better than before. It's got us just where it wants us."

Apathy only lasted a moment. *It* teaches you how to fight, too. It teaches you a lot of bad things, but it teaches you one good thing. It teaches you how to fight. It's always trying to kill you, so you learn to fight just to live at all.

She made a move, a sudden turn, as if to go on up the steps.

He reached out and caught her, held her tightly gripped, tried to turn her around again the way she'd been. "No, don't *you* go in there! Stay out of there!" He tried to pull her down to the sidewalk, from the step or two she'd gained above it. "Hurry up, get out of here! Get away from in front of this house! I shouldn't have let you come over here with me in the first place. Go down there, get your own ticket, climb on the bus, and forget you ever ran into me at all tonight." She struggled passively against his hold. "Bricky, will you listen to me? Get out of here, beat it, before they—"

He tried to push her before him a step or two along the

sidewalk to start her on her way. She only swerved around in a loop and came back to him again, in closer than before. "I only want to know one thing. I only want you to tell me one thing. It wasn't you, was it—the first time you were in there? *You* didn't, did you?"

"No! I only took the money, that was all. He wasn't there. I didn't *see* him at all. He must have come back since. Bricky, you've got to believe me."

She smiled sadly at him in the semi-darkness. "It's all right, Quinn. I know you didn't. I know. I should have known even without asking. The boy next door, *he'd* never kill anyone."

"I can't go back now," he murmured. "I'm finished. Cooked. They'll think I did it. It knits in too close with what I did do. They'd only be waiting to get me at the other end, when I got there. And if it has to happen, I'd rather have it happen here, than there where everyone knows me. I'm staying, now. No use bucking it. Let it happen. I'll wait. But you—" And again he tried to jostle her on her way. "*Please* go. Will you, Bricky? *Please.*"

This time she was immovable, he couldn't even budge her. "You didn't do it, right? Then let me alone, don't push me any more, Quinn. I'm going in with you."

She drew herself up defiantly beside him. But her defiance wasn't of him; she looked out, and around them, at *it*. "The city, the city," she breathed vindictively. "We'll show it. We're not licked yet. The deadline is still good. We still have until daylight. No one knows yet, they haven't found him, or the place'd be full of policemen by this time. No one knows; only us—and whoever did it. We've still got time. Somewhere in this town there's a clock that's a friend of mine. I know that it's saying right now, even if we can't see it from where we are, that we've still got a little time. Not as much as we had before, but some. Don't quit, Quinn, don't quit. It's never too late, until the last second of the last minute of the last hour."

She was shaking him again, by the arms, imploringly. But this time to put something into him, not to drag something out of him.

"Come on, we're going back in there and see if we can figure this thing out. We've got to. It's our only hope. We want to go home; you know we do. We're fighting for our happiness, Quinn; we're fighting for our lives. And we have until six o'clock to win our fight."

She could hardly hear him. But he'd turned toward the flight of steps, leading up, leading in. "Come on, battler," he said softly. "Come on, champ."

Her arm unconsciously slipped through his going up the steps, both to lend courage and to borrow; it was a case of mutual support. Strangely formal promenade, slow and frightened and very brave, into the place where death was.

IN THE coffin-like confinement of the vestibule the misappropriated key shook a little as he fitted it unlawfully into the door for the third time that night. Her heart shook in time with it. But that was bravery, that slight shaking of his hand, and no one needed to tell her that. He was going *in*, not *out*; toward it, not away. And the man who says he's never been afraid is a liar. So she admired the shaking of his hand; that was honest, that was brave.

He got it straight at last and a latch-mechanism recoiled and freed the door. They went in. His off-shoulder hitched a little, she could feel the gesture transferred to her, and the latch-mechanism bedded softly back into its groove again. The door was closed now at their backs. A blurred grayish oval remained, that was the street-light, dun and smoky as it was, struggling to come in after them all the way and giving up after it reached that far. It receded, grew smaller, to the size of an ox-eye, as step by step they felt their way forward.

The hall—they were in some kind of a hall, she surmised—had the stuffy air of a place closed up all day. She tried to visualize the house by her unaided sense of smell. She was no expert in scents, but over and above its stuffiness the place had an expensive leather-and-woodwork aura to it. Not distinct, that was just the sensory impression. No mouldiness of decay or disrepair, no cookery taints, no sachet of feminine occupancy. Impersonal, austere maybe, but not cheap.

"He's in the back, on the floor above," he whispered. "I don't want to light any lights down here. They might be seen from outside."

Again a transfer of motion told her his hand had gone into his pocket for something. "No, don't use matches either," she cautioned. "You lead the way, I'll be able to follow. I'll keep my hand on your sleeve. Wait, let me put this down here somewhere first."

She groped her way to the wall, set her valise down close against the baseboard of it, where she could find it again readily. Then she moved back to him, took up her position of telepathic accompaniment, hand to his coat-sleeve. They toiled forward in a sort of swimming darkness that was almost liquid, it was so dense.

"Step," he whispered presently.

She felt him go up. She raised her foot, pawed blindly with it, found the foremost step with her toe. The rest of them followed in automatic succession, were no trouble at all. The staircase creaked once or twice under their combined weights in the stealthy silence. She wondered if anyone else were in the house, anyone still alive. For all they knew, someone might be. Many a nocturnal murder isn't discovered until the following day.

"Turn," he whispered.

His arm swung away from her, to the left. She kept contact,

wheeled her body obediently after it. The stairs had flattened out into a landing. They made a brief half-pirouette together, like a couple executing a ghostly cotillon in the dark.

She felt his arm go up again, after the brief level space. She found the new flight, reversed in direction to the old. Finally they too had leveled off, there weren't any more. They were on the second floor now.

"Turn," he breathed.

His arm crowded in against her, around toward the right this time. She corrected her own direction accordingly. They were moving along an upstairs hall now.

The leather-and-woodwork aroma became a little more personal. The ghost of a cigar lingered in it somewhere or other, too evanescent to be trapped. Something sweeter was in it too, that was not even a ghost, that was a memory, it was so far away, so long gone by. A single grain of powder, perhaps, in—who knew how many cubic feet of sterile air? Or the exhalation of a single drop of perfume that had passed this way—a year ago, a night ago? She *thought* of perfumery, remembered it from other places, other times; she did not actually detect it *now*.

She felt herself go over a wooden door-sill, only slightly raised, not high enough to impede.

The air changed subtly. There was someone in it besides themselves, yet there was no one in it. They say you can't smell death, at least not recent death. Yet there was a *stillness* in it, a presence in it that was more than just emptiness.

She was glad they weren't going forward any more. His arm had stopped. She stopped alongside it. He reached behind them and did something with his other arm, and she felt a slight current of air as a door swept by. She heard it close gutturally just in back of them.

"Get your eyes ready, here go the lights," he warned.

She shuttered them protectively. Electricity flashed on with unbearable brilliance after the long pilgrimage in the dark. The dead man was the most conspicuous thing in the room; it seemed to form a halo about him.

The room itself was an amalgam, a blend, a sort of all-purpose room. There were books in it to a moderate amount, two or three short rows of them on shelves built into the wall, so that it was a library to a limited degree. There was a Sheraton desk in it, so that it could be termed a study, also to a degree.

There were a number of comfortable, leather-covered club-type chairs disposed about it, a liquor cabinet, ashtrays, so that it was perhaps more than anything else a masculine variety of sitting-room. An upstairs living-room, pertaining more to one person than to the house in general. What had been once, in an earlier society, known as a den.

It was not masculine to a sophomoric extent, its character was not blatant. It was first and foremost a room, the rest was insight on the part of the beholder.

The walls were lime-green, but so pale that in the electric light they appeared white. It was only when actual white was placed in juxtaposition with them, as if say a square of paper were held up against them, that their faint tint became perceptible. The woodwork was walnut. The carpet and chair-backs were a dark, earthy brown. The lampshades, of which there were two, were parchment.

It was oblong, lengthwise to the direction from which they had entered. The two short side-walls were blankly unbroken. The one at their backs held, of course, the doorway by which they had entered. The one facing them held two doorways, one leading into a bedroom, the other, at a spaced distance from it, into a bath. Quinn left her side to go into the former. She could see his indistinct figure, in the gloom in there, drawing heavy, sheltering drapes together over the windows, to keep the light from showing through to the rear of the house. This room they were in had no outside openings, no windows, whatever.

He didn't bother with the bath, so it evidently had none either.

She was aware of him, of his movements, but only dimly, as of something beyond her immediate ken, something on the perimeter of her mind.

She'd never seen anyone dead before. That thought kept turning over and over in the turmoil of her mind, like some sort of a powerful cylinder. She stood there staring down, but it wasn't with a feverish, unhealthy interest, it was with a stricken, thoughtful awe. So this is that thing we're all so afraid of, ran the current of her thoughts. This is that thing that has to happen to all of us, to myself, to Quinn, so young, so agile in there, to everyone else, some day. So this is where all my dancing leads to, and all my scraping of pennies; all my snarling and clawing at my annoyers, all my hanging onto my ideals of person. All those rolls I take out of the slots at the Automat day after day, I'm only fooling myself, they can't keep this away— So this is it. So this.

She thought she'd seen everything, known everything, but this was one thing she'd missed. One night a girl, right out on the middle of the floor at the mill, right in the middle of *Begin the Beguine*, she suddenly crumpled, went down like a shot. They said, afterwards, she'd taken something, but nobody knew for sure. All Bricky knew was she'd come in the long way, upright, and moving all over;

she went out flat, and not moving, just twitching a little. They all rushed over to the windows in a mass and peered down, no matter what the manager said, how he berated them. They saw her down on the sidewalk, being shovelled into the ambulance, looking awfully small, awfully flat, on the white stretcher. She didn't come around next night. She never came around again.

But even that, that was just *before* it happened. This was *after*. She'd never seen anyone dead before.

She looked at his face, tried to reconstruct it, tried to fill it in. It was like reading a page on which the writing has already grown faded, blurred, distorted. It was like an ink-written page on which it has rained. Everything was still there yet, but everything had moved a little out of focus. The lines that had been facial characteristics were seams now. The mouth that had been either strong or weak, bitter or good-humored, was a gap now, a place where the face was open. The eyes that had been either kindly or cruel, wise or foolish, they were just glossy, lifeless insets now, like isinglass stuck into yellowish-gray dough.

His hair was well-cared for and full of life and light yet, for it dies last, or rather it doesn't die when the body does, it grows on afterward. Even the death-shock and the fall had hardly disturbed a blade of it. Just one or two had fallen out of the furrows that his brush had trained them into through the years.

He had fine dark brows, like tippets of sealskin. Not grotesquely thick, but well-emphasized. And they were perfectly straight now, even; death had taken away perplexity and the need for bending them this way or that.

With all this, she couldn't make out much what he'd been

like. He looked as though he'd been about thirty-five or so. But the ages of men are trickier to calculate than those of women; he might have been thirty or he might have been forty. He must have been facially good-looking until an hour ago, or whenever it had happened—the putty mask that was left behind told her that—but then that's the least important attribute a human being can have. Angels and devils are good-looking, both.

He'd liked life, in its pleasanter recreational aspects. Even in death he was still immaculately attired in evening clothes, the starched bosom of his shirt scarcely rumpled at all, the gala flower in his buttonhole still in place.

The underparts of his shoes were faintly glossy with floor-wax, so he'd danced in them not long ago, and their rims weren't nicked or marked in any way, so he'd been a competent dancer, avoiding others and seeing that they avoided him on a crowded floor. What good did it do to know that now? He wouldn't dance any more.

Quinn had come back to her again. She was aware of him standing beside her, without looking, and she was glad to have him there. Their shoulders touched lightly, and it felt good.

"Shouldn't we close his—? They seem to be watching you when you're not looking at them, and then when you look, they're not."

"No, don't touch them," he whispered. "I don't know how to, anyway, do you?"

"I guess you just squeeze the lids together." But neither of them did it.

"Can you tell what it—was?" she asked with bated breath. "What it was done with?" She crouched slowly downward toward the floor, as if drawn by an irresistible compulsion. He remained erect an instant longer, then he crouched with her.

"It must be on him somewhere."

He saw her hand arch timidly above the button holding the two sides of the jacket together across the form's middle. Her fingers spread as if trying to undo it without coming into too close a contact with anything but that.

"Wait, let me do it," he said quickly. He scissored his own fingers deftly, and the two sides of the jacket sprang open.

"There it is." She drew in her breath.

A small reddish-black sworl was revealed, marring one armband of the white piqué vest. It was a good deal below the armpit, however, almost dead center above the heart.

"It must have been a gun," he said. "Yeah, bullet. It's round and frazzled. A knife would make a slit."

He undid the buttons of the vest and parted that. Underneath it repeated itself, but it was far more spreading in its secondary results. The shirt had absorbed it like a blotter, all down the side, and a little bit over to the front in a random offshoot or two. He tried to keep her from seeing too much of it by holding the vest wings upward like a screen. Then he folded them back over it again.

"Must have been an awfully small one," he said. "I'm no expert, but it's a pretty tight little hole."

"Maybe they're all that way."

"Maybe." Then he admitted, "I never saw one before, so I can't tell."

She said: "Then one thing we can be sure of, there was no one staying in the house but him right now, or they would have heard it go off."

He was scanning the room. "They took it away with them; there's no sign of one lying around."

"What'd you say their name was again—the people that live in this house?"

"Graves."

"Is this the head of the family, the father?"

"There is no father; he's dead about ten or fifteen years. There's the mother, she's a well-known society woman, I think. Then there's two sons, and a daughter. This is the older son. There's another one, still a student, away at college somewhere. The daughter's one of these, what they call, debutantes; you know, they write her up in the papers a lot."

"If we could figure out why, if we could get at the motive—"

"In a couple of hours. When it takes the police weeks sometimes. And they know all about these things."

"Let's start with the easy ones first. He didn't do it himself, because then the gun would still have to be lying around the room somewhere, and it isn't."

"I guess that's safe enough," he said hesitantly. But he didn't sound any too sure.

"Robbery or burglary is about the commonest reason. Was anything taken out of the safe, that had been in it the first time, when you went back to it just now, the second time?"

"I don't know," he admitted. "I came in without using any lights, you know. I stumbled over him and went down on my hands and knees."

She sucked in her breath sympathetically.

"It was like a third rail poking into your heart. So, after I'd lit a match and seen what it was, I just staggered over to the safe—I mean around behind it—tossed the money back into it, and got out fast without stopping to look."

She struck her uptilted kneecap, poised a foot above the floor. "Then let's look now. Do you think you'll be able to remember, if there's anything gone that was there the first time?"

"No," he said frankly. "I was pretty steamed-up even the first time, don't forget. But I'll try, and see if I can."

They left their crouched positions and turned their backs on the body for the present. They went into the bathroom, Quinn in the lead because he knew where the light-switch was.

It exploded into a dazzling flash of white tiling at his touch. The mirrored surface of a wall cabinet at the other end gave them a disconcerting impression of other people stepping in from there at the same time that they were stepping in from here. Who were those frightened kids, looking so young, so hopeless, so helpless?

She didn't waste time on that, though.

The most conspicuous thing was the square opening he had hacked into the plaster, to their right as they stepped in and just behind where the safe was in the outside room. It seemed incredible that walls, inner walls in a house, had once been made so thick.

He'd had the shower-curtain arranged the first time to conceal it; artificially draped and panoplied so that it fell over that way. He'd told her all about that. But in returning just now in his fright and haste, he'd cast it aside once more and then left it that way. It was pushed back, "dented" in, you might say, and within this sagging loop was where the wall-fracture lay exposed.

He'd done a neat job, but she took no pride in that, and she knew he didn't either. She could tell by his face. It was almost as though he'd used a ruler to outline it, it was so straight. No more than a thin pencil-line of the white plaster-fill was exposed around the gums of the aperture. The tinted surface of the wall was scarcely cracked around this, it was so little disturbed. A flake or two threatened to peel off, that was all. He must have scuffed the fill he'd taken out, away from sight under the tub with the edge of his foot. She didn't ask him, but there was none in sight on the floor, and the tub was one of these old-fashioned kind, raised above floor-level and supported by claw-feet, she saw.

At the back of the opening, plaster-whitened wood peered faintly. He reached in and caught at it around the edges with his fingers, in some way that he already knew of from having done it before, and presently he'd brought it out and set it down. It was the rear section of the lining, of the wooden casing or chamber within which the safe bedded.

Then slowly after this he drew out the steel cash-box rearwards, until he held it slanted across both his arms. That was all the safe consisted of: an ordinary steel cash-box, without even a lock to it, inserted into a wood-lined cavity built into the wall. It was true that on the opposite side, fronting the other room, it had a steel lid or plaque to cover the entire thing, that worked on a combination. But from the rear it had been like cutting through butter to get at it.

"Not much, is it?" she remarked.

"I suppose it was built years ago, when crime wasn't as expert as it is now. When they didn't expect it to come right into their homes with them—"

Then he stopped, and his face colored up a little. He was

ashamed of it now, she could see, of what he'd done. He *was* crime himself, at least he had been as far as this particular safe was concerned. He was ashamed at the recollection of his own former act, his instincts were against it. That was all to the good; that was the way the boy next door should feel about having done a thing like that.

He hooked forward a three-legged enamelled bath-stool with the curve of his foot and they rested the heavy box on that and opened it up to examine its contents.

The money was right there on top, the money that he'd just restored. They cast that aside, went burrowing through the shoals of papers. Yellow, incredibly old, most of them older than he and she were themselves.

"Here's a will—d'you think that could have anything to do with it?"

"I hope not—if it does that's not the kind of thing we could work out in time."

He went ahead dredging, while she stopped to read snatches here and there. "It's the will of the father. He was made executor—" She flicked her head toward the outside room. "Isn't that his name, Stephen?" Then dipping into it a little further, "I don't think this had anything to do with it. Everything's left to the wife, Harriet; the children don't get it until her death. And *she's* not the one who's been murdered, the son has." She repleated it, flung it aside.

"That's not the motive we're working on now, anyway. It's robbery."

"You said there was some jewelry in it. Where is it, I don't see it?" For a moment her hopes were raised.

"That's in a second compartment, behind this first one. The lid bends back in sections, I'll show you. It's not very valuable, anyway. I mean, it *is* valuable, in a way, but it's not diamonds or anything like that."

He laid bare the second compartment. They took up a number of old-fashioned plush boxes, of various shapes, all faded alike now to a dingy gray-tan. A rope of pearls. A necklace of topazes. An old-fashioned brooch of amethysts.

"These pearls must be worth a couple thousand."

"Everything's still there that was there the first time," he told her. "I saw all these things. Nothing's been taken out, since I—"

Again he stopped, and though he didn't flush this time, he dropped his eyes for a minute.

She wasn't pleased; their hopes, in this, were gauged to work in reverse. "Then it wasn't robbery," she said soberly. "It's going to be something harder than that for us to—"

They started putting everything hastily back again. The money went in last of all. He gave it a look of hatred, this time. She knew. She didn't blame him.

They closed the box up, and he hoisted it and shovelled it back inside the wall-rent. He didn't bother trying to cover it over with the shower-curtain any more. She knew what he was thinking about that too. With a dead man inside lying in full view, what good was it trying to cover up this lesser trace of another, different guilt in here? No use trying to keep them separate any more. One would simply swamp the other as soon as it was found out.

"Well, that's out," he said discouragedly.

They went inside again. He killed the lights behind them, in the place where they'd been.

They stopped and gave one another a helpless look. What was there to do now?

"There are other motives, just as simple," she said. "Only more personal, maybe, that's all. Hate, and love— The next thing we'll have to do is—"

He knew what she meant. He walked resolutely over beside the body, dropped down by it once more.

"You haven't yet—have you?" she asked.

"No, I just lit a match, after I fell over him, and crawled back and touched him on the forehead to see, but that was all."

She conquered her repulsion, came over beside him, dropped down in turn. As close as he was, every bit. "Well, then we'll have to empty them out now," she said. "I'll help you."

"You don't have to reach in. I'll take the things out. You can look them over as I hand them to you."

They smiled at one another bleakly, to pretend they didn't dislike what they were going to have to do.

"I'll start up here," he said. "That's the highest-up pocket on anyone's suit." The breast-pocket. There was nothing in it but a fine linen handkerchief, pleated up into a sort of fan-shape, so that a little of the top edge would show above the pocket-mouth.

She opened it, then said: "Look, the bullet went through this. The way it was folded, it just made one little hole, down near the bottom. Then when you open it up, it makes three separate ones, a sort of design. Like when you cut papers, and make them into lace-patterns." They didn't smile about it; it was too gruesome a parody.

"That's all for in there. Now the one on the left side, on the outside. He's on it a little, the coat's caught under him." He had to raise the figure a little, pull the coat out, give it more slack.

Then when he had—

"It's empty, there's nothing in it, not a scrap." He pulled the black satin lining out after him, left it reversed to show her.

"Now the right-hand one."

He pulled that inside-out too. "Nothing, either." They made two little black balloons, half-deflated, at the figure's hips. Like a pair of midget water-wings. He left them that way for the time being.

"Now the inside jacket one."

This time his forearm had to coast along the dead chest to get in. His face didn't show anything. There was a layer of stiff-shirting between, anyway.

"Take out everything," she breathed, "no matter what it is."

She made a sort of audible inventory for him as they went along, passing things from pocket, to his hand, to hers, to floor beside her.

They resembled, grotesquely, two overgrown kids playing with their pails in a sandpile, or making mud-pies or something. The way they were huddled over, knees cocked up. He didn't say anything, but she could tell by his face he was thinking they didn't have a chance—not in the little time there was left to them.

Behind them on the book shelf there was a clock. They both kept from turning to look at it by sheer will-power alone. But they could hear it. It kept chopping up the silence fine. It kept going *tick-tock, tick-tock,* so mockingly, so remorselessly, so fast. Never stopping, never letting up, *going, going, going—*

"Cigarette case. Silver. Tiffany's. Given to him by somebody with the initial B. 'To S from B.' Three cigarettes left in it. Dun-hills." *Snap.* She closed it again, put it down.

"Wallet. Pin seal, Mark Cross. Two fives and a single. Two

ticket stubs from tonight's show at the Winter Garden. C-112, 114. Third row in the orchestra, that must be. Well, we know where he was tonight from eight-forty to eleven, at least."

"Two and a half hours out of thirty-five years," he said morbidly.

"We don't have to go back through his whole life. We only have to go forward about two, two and a half hours, from curtain-time on. He wasn't killed at the Winter Garden; he was still alive when he walked out of there. That's already narrowed the evening down a lot, that's taken a big chunk out of it."

"Anything else in it?"

"Business cards. Stafford, whoever that is. Holmes, whoever that is. Ingoldsby, whoever that is. I guess that's about— No, wait a minute, here's something else, in this second little compartment here. A snapshot. A snapshot of a girl in riding togs, and himself, both on horseback."

"Let me see it."

He scanned it, nodded. "That's the one I saw him leave the house with, early tonight. She's also inside there, in the bedroom, in a silver frame. I saw her when I went in before. Signed Barbara."

"Then she didn't do it. If she had, she wouldn't still be in there in his bedroom in a silver frame. Just the frame might, by itself, but not her any more. That's ordinary common sense."

"That's all for that pocket. Now I'll take the four in the trousers, two side, two rear. Left rear, nothing. Right rear, spare handkerchief, nothing else. Left side, nothing. Right side, his latchkey and a gob of change."

She counted it over listlessly, as if realizing how immaterial it was. "Eighty-four cents," she said, and planked it down.

"That finishes the pockets of his clothing. And we're still no further than before."

"Yes we are, Quinn. A good deal. Don't say that. After all, we didn't expect to find a piece of paper with 'To whom it may concern: So-and-so killed me,' written on it, did we? We've pulled a name out of thin air— Barbara—and we know what Barbara looks like, and that she was out with him in the early part of the evening tonight. We also know where it was they were together. That trims the blank down to just the couple of hours before and after midnight. I think that's a whole lot for just one set of pockets to tell us."

Tick-tock, tick-tock, tick-tock—

She looked down at the floor. She reached out and pressed her hand down atop his for a moment, as if to steady, as if to encourage him. "I know," she said almost inaudibly. "Don't look at it, Quinn. Don't look around at it. We *can* do it, Quinn. We *can*. We can make it. Keep saying that." She got to her feet.

"Shall I put this stuff back?" he asked.

"Leave it there for now. It doesn't matter much." He got up after her.

"Let's take the room next," she said. "The room around him. We've tried him, now let's tackle the room, see what we can do with that." They separated, with the corpse for an axis. "You start over there. I'll start over here."

"What are we looking for?" he said dully, with his back to her.

I don't know, she felt like wailing. Oh, God, I don't know myself!

Tick-tock, tick-tock, tick-tock—

She dropped her eyes, to miss seeing its dial, even as she passed right in front of it. Like an ostrich with its head in the sand, she told herself. It wasn't easy to do, either; it was over there on her side of the room, staring her right in the face. The books on one shelf had been parted in two to receive it in the middle.

"*Green Light,*" she murmured aloud, as her feet slowly side-stepped along. "*Oil for the Lamps of China, Personal History—*" Then dropped her eyes.

Tick-tock! A moment gone, a moment out of their scanty store.

Then raised them again on the right-hand side of it. "*North to the Orient, The Tragedy of X—* He wasn't much of a reader," she commented.

"How do you know?" he asked curiously from his side of the room.

"It's just a hunch of mine. When a person's a heavy reader, all the books on his shelves would be pretty much alike, I mean pretty much of one type. This is just a smattering; one of this kind, one of that. He probably only read one maybe once in six months or so, when he had a wakeful night or something."

She was the one who first came to it, and stopped.

Then after a thoughtful moment she called over to him, "Quinn."

"Yes?"

"A man that's a cigarette-smoker—and we found that case in his pocket—would he also go in for cigars, as a rule?"

"He'd be apt to, yes. Plenty of people smoke both. Why, did you find a cigar-butt over there?"

"Well, would he be apt to smoke *two?* Alone, by himself? There are two butts on this tray here—"

He came over to her and looked at it.

"I think he had somebody up here with him," she said.

"Some man. You can't tell which of these two chairs the stand goes with, it's out where it can be reached from both. One butt's in one notch of the tray, and the other's in another notch, around on the other side from it."

He bent down and looked more closely. "He didn't smoke both. Those are two different brands, and nobody does that. There was somebody up here with him, all right. Here's another thing. They were having an argument of some kind, too. Or at least, one of them was worked up about something, even if the other one wasn't. Look at the butt on this side. Smooth at the mouth-end; a little soggy, but still intact. Now look at the one over here. Chewed to ribbons at the mouth-end; *fringe*. One of those smokers was all steamed up over something. That tells it." He looked up at her. "This is the best thing we've had so far. This is the best of the lot."

"Which was the keyed-up one and which the calm, though? Graves or the other man? We don't know."

"No, but that doesn't matter so much. It does show us that there was another man up here, and that's what counts for us. The mere fact that there were two different brands of cigars shows that the interview wasn't a friendly one. One of them refused the other man's offer of a cigar—or else it wasn't even made—and smoked his own. They smoked at the same time, but not together, if you see what I mean. There was a strain, a row or an argument of some kind, going on."

"It's good, but it's not good enough," she agreed. "It doesn't tell us who the other man was."

He moved around to the wall-side of one of the chairs; not that they were pressed close up against the wall, but to the side away from the middle of the room, which their own bulk had kept screened until now.

"Here's the drink of one of them, put down on the floor close up against his chair."

"Is there one for the other?" she asked quickly, jealously protective of his theory of ill-will.

He moved over to the inside of the second chair, looked down. "No."

She drew a quick breath of relief. "Then that proves they weren't on friendly terms. For a minute I was worried. It also shows us that this must have been Graves, sitting over here, where the empty glass was. He was the host. He helped himself to a drink, but didn't invite the caller. Or else did, but the caller, because he was sore, refused."

"Yeah. That's not a hundred proof, but it's reasonable enough. It could be the other way around, but most likely it wasn't. A host feeling unfriendly toward you wouldn't ask you to have a drink, and then show his unfriendliness by not joining you. He wouldn't offer in the first place. So let's call it Graves, over on this side, and let it go at that."

"It's not *where* he was sitting," she muttered frustratedly, "it's *who* he was sitting with."

"Wait a minute, here's something—" His hand drove perpendicularly downward into the seam between chair-arm and seat, of the second chair, the one they had decided the visitor had occupied. Both their faces dropped a little when he'd brought it up.

"Match-folder," she said, crestfallen.

"I thought it might be something else, for a minute," he admitted. "I saw it peeping up out of there. Graves had his own on him; I took them out when we were over there. These must be the other guy's. Slipped down there, I guess, in his excitement."

He flipped open the little folder, fitted it closed again, made to cast back where he'd found it. Then he quickly brought it back toward him again, opened it a second time. He frowned at it.

"Whew! He sure must have been excited. Look how many he used up, just on that one cigar. Can't you see him lighting one after the other, through the whole conversation, and maybe even forgetting to use half of them, the cigar going out every other minute by his forgetting to draw on it, he was talking so fast?"

"The folder could have been half used-up before he began on it," she tried to suggest. "It didn't have to start out brand-new, even with the cigar."

But he'd already gone on past that point, evidently. He made no rejoinder. He was still staring, for far more than the object was worth in the ordinary course of events.

"Come here a minute," he said, without taking his eyes off it. "What does this tell you? I want to see if you get what I do."

"Chew Doublemint Gum?"

"Not the cover. The match part itself, inside."

Her head was down close, beside his. They were holding it like some sort of a precious talisman. "Wait a minute, there's usually twenty matches come to one of those things. Two rows of ten each, front and back. There's—get your thumb out of the way—five left, two in front, three in back. That means he used up fifteen separate lights just on that one cigar, is that what you mean?"

"No, you still don't get what I mean. All right, look. The five left are the end ones in both rows, over to the right."

"Oh, sure—" she said belatedly. "I saw that from the start."

"Now, wait. Here. Here's a folder from my own pocket." He passed over to her. "Tear one off and strike it and blow it out. Don't stop to think what you're doing. Just strike a match, like you would at any other time. You're lighting the ring under the coffee-pot. Go ahead, don't stop now."

She struck one, blew it out, then quirked her head at him with a sort of charming uncertainty.

"Look at it now. See where that came off of? The right-hand side. Every man, woman, and child that uses one of these things starts at the outside, on the right, and works their way along the line, match by match, over to the left. *His* folder was worked in reverse. Now do you get what I mean? *The guy sitting in this chair facing Graves tonight was a left-handed guy.*"

Her mouth opened into a soundless oval of sudden perception, and stayed that way.

"I don't know who he was, what he looked like, if he killed him or not. But I do know these things about him: he was all steamed up or rattled about something, whittled away fifteen matches to one cigar and mangled it to ribbons between his teeth; he was on bad terms with Graves; and he was left-handed."

She'd reached out for it, the folder, and he'd relinquished it absently to her; this was several moments before. He caught a strange look in her face now.

"I'm sorry, Quinn," she said with an odd air of compassion.

"What do you mean?"

"The whole thing just fell all to pieces."

This time he did the strange-looking. "Why? How?"

"It was a woman."

She took his hand first, and held it. Then planked the folder down into it with her other. "Smell this," she said laconically. "Just hold it about even with your upper lip, that's all."

He wanted to argue before he'd do it. "A woman chopped that cigar into spinach?" He gestured violently behind him. "A woman sat in that chair?"

"I don't know anything about the cigar or the chair. All I'm asking you to do is hold that steady up by your lip for a minute."

"Sulphur and stuff, like matches always—"

"Give that a minute to clear away. That's the stronger of the two, it tops the other. *Now.*"

His face gave in with a disheartened grimace. "Perfume," he said wryly. "Faint perfume."

"It came out of somebody's handbag. It's been carried around all day in a handbag. A handbag that stinks of perfume. Just being in it skunked the cardboard. Just the opening of the bag, once or maybe twice, while she was in here, gave the air a shot of it. I noticed it out in the hall, in the dark, when we were coming in. There's been a woman here in this room tonight."

He didn't want to give in. He had to, but he didn't want to. "What about the cigar? Who smoked the two cigars, one strong, one weak? One calmly, one all riled up? You mean he did, at one and the same time?"

"Maybe there was a man here *before* she was here. Or maybe he was here *after* her. Maybe they were both here at the same time."

"Nah, they couldn't," he said arbitrarily. "The cigar-butt shows the man was in this chair, facing him. The matches show a woman was. They couldn't have both been in it at one and the same time."

"If his nerves were all frazzled, and he'd used up all his own matches, he might have had to borrow hers from her. He was in the chair here talking away to Graves, and she was across the room somewhere, listening to them."

He killed it with a pitch of his head. "That don't hold together. Graves was smoking away right opposite him, much nearer than wherever it is she was supposed to be. There's no third chair handy. He would have borrowed from him instead."

"But if they were bawling each other out, or burned up?"

"A match doesn't count as a favor. It's not like the drink or the smoke. He would have almost reached without asking. Anyway, for him to borrow, there'd have to be a discarded folder around without *any* left in it, the one ahead of the one he borrowed. And there isn't." He bounced one bent knuckle off the top of the chairback. "They weren't here together."

"All right, they weren't here together. But that don't help much. Which came first? Because whichever is the one that came last is the one that did the killing."

"We're gaining ground backwards by the minute," he said gloomily.

Tick-tock, tick-tock, tick-tock—

They both looked down at the floor, over the other way, away from it.

They were standing there close by those two chairs. The whole thing had taken place by those two chairs.

Maybe it was because they were looking down avertedly like that, trying to avoid the sound of the clock. It must have been a difficult thing to see. The carpet itself was brown.

Suddenly she followed her own look down. Went all the way down, half-prone, on the point of one knee and the palm of one hand. Her hand thrust a little ways under the chair, the second chair, of the folder and mangled cigar-butt, came out again. She straightened up, holding her palm upturned now, poking at something in it with one finger.

"Don't tell me something else—?" he gasped incredulously.

"Well, look at it for yourself," was her answer.

It was small; the exact size of a half-dime. It was brown. It was half-moon shaped; rounded on the outside, straight down the middle. It had two little holes in it, intact, and the remnants of two more indenting the straight edge. A corkscrew of brown thread still dangled from the two that were intact.

"Broken button," he breathed almost reverently. "Vest?"

"No, cuff. Those ones that you don't use, on the outside of the sleeve. I mean that we don't. Too small for anything else."

"It must have been split for some time, maybe from the last dry-cleaning his coat got, and it finally dropped off tonight in the chair. Maybe he moved his hand too much, gesturing or with that cigar."

"How'd it get *under*, though?"

"Fell down over the side, I think. And then maybe in getting up angrily, he gave the whole chair a shove over a little, and that put it below it, where it was already lying."

"How do we know it isn't Graves'? It may have been kicking around here on the floor for days."

"Well, we'll try matching it up right now, settle that point before we go any further. That's one thing we *can* do, thanks be! It's got to be from a brown or tan suit. I don't have to be a man to know that blues or grays don't have brown buttons. And he's lying in a tux right now, it's not from that."

She went into the bedroom, flung open the clothes-closet, pulled on a light-cord. "Windows all right?"

"Yeah, I covered them up." His eyes widened ingenuously, peering forward over her shoulder. "Will you look at that! How can a guy live long enough to wear all that many—"

They both thought the same thing, without saying it: well, he didn't.

The browns and their offshoots were in a minority, as they are for some reason in almost any grouping of men's clothes, whether large or small. "Here's a mustard-color thing it could have gone on." She took the hanger down, turned up the bottom of one sleeve, then the other, ran her fingernail rapidly down the line of vest-buttons. "All on." She put it back. "Here's a brown." She took that down in turn, went over it.

"Don't skip the back trouser-pocket," he cautioned. "The one on the left usually buttons down—at least it does on mine."

"Nope." She put it back again. "That's all. No, wait, here's an extra jacket, hanging up there on a hook all the way back, must be old as the hills. That's a brown, sort of." She tried it, hung it up again. "Wrong type buttons; solid, with an eyelet in back, instead of pierced through. None gone, anyway."

She tweaked the light-cord, closed the door. "So it's not his. It's from the man who came, and chewed the cigar, and was sore at him, and may—or may not be—left-handed."

They went back inside again, swiftly striding. "We know two things more about him now, Quinn. D'you realize that?

He's got on a brown or tan suit, and there's one button either gone or half-gone from one of the sleeves of his coat. My God, if we were professional detectives, d'you know what we could do with all that? With only half of all that?"

"But we're not," he said, tasting something imaginary—and not very pleasant—on his own lip with the tip of his tongue.

"We're going to have to be, tonight."

"This is the biggest city in the world."

"That may make it all the easier for us, instead of making it harder. If it was a little place, if it was a village, like back home, they'd know the risk of discovery was so much greater they'd lie low, they'd take precautions, we'd *never* be able to— Here it's so big they may feel safe, it may give them a sense of false security, they mayn't bother even to hide or keep out of the way—" She stopped and eyed the expression on his face. "Well, that's one way of looking at it, isn't it? That's one way."

"Ah, it's no use, Bricky," he moaned. "What's the use of kidding ourselves? It's like one of these fairy-tales for kids, where a magic spell would have to be used to make it come true—"

"Don't," she said in a choked voice. "Don't, please. Don't make me do all the work for the two of us—" Her head went down.

"I'm yellow," he said. "I'm sorry."

"No, you're not yellow, or I wouldn't be here in this room with you."

Tick-tock, tick-tock, tick-tock—

"I'm going to turn and look at it in a minute, and so are you," she said. "And it may take real guts *then*, once we do. But before we do, let's get the thing lined up. There are two people. Two shadows, but still and all they're real. One of them, but not both, killed him. We've got to find the one that did, we've got to know, or that'll make it *you*—"

He started to say something.

"No, let me finish, Quinn. I'm lining it up like this as much for myself for you. In other words, we have to go out of here and track them down, find out where they went to, and go there after them, and break them down some way, shake it out of them. That's the job. That's the job we've got facing us. And all the time we've got is, while it still stays dark in New York tonight. At daylight, at six, there's the bus that leaves for home. The *last* bus, Quinn, remember that, the *last* bus. I don't care what the schedule says, for us it's the last bus there is, the last in the world."

"I get you. They'll keep running—but not for us. We've got to be out of here by daybreak."

"Now, the job," she nodded. "We can't both take both of them."

He got what she was driving at. He looked aghast. "I thought you said we should stick together in this? That was the whole reason you came over with me, instead of going down to the term—"

"There isn't time now any more! We *have* to split it two ways, whether we like to or not. Look, here's how it is. We have these two possibilities now, a man and a woman who both came here tonight at separate times. One of them's innocent, one of them killed him. The thing is which? We haven't time for hit or miss stuff; we *can't* follow them up one at a time. We have to follow them both up at the same time. That gives us our only chance. We can only be wrong once, and if we're both wrong together, we're cooked, we're finished. If we separate, and one goes after one, and the other goes after the other, that gives us our fifty-fifty chance. One of us is sure to be on wild-goose chase, but the other one won't be. That's where our hope lies, right there. You take the man. I'll take the woman.

"Now listen close, because we haven't darned much to go by, and we have to make the most of what we've got. *You* have to look for a man in a brown or off-brown suit, with one button on his cuff broken, who maybe is left-handed or maybe is not. And that's about all you've got. *I* have to look for woman, who is left-handed for sure, and who uses a kind of heavy perfume. I don't know what it is now, but I'll know it when I get it again."

"You haven't even got as much as I have," he protested. "You haven't got anything."

"I know, but I'm a girl, and that evens it up. I don't need as much, our minds can do more with less."

"But how *can* you do anything, even if you do track her down? An unarmed girl like you, with nothing but your bare hands? You don't know what you're likely to come up against!"

"We haven't time enough left to be afraid. We only have time enough to wade in and go through with it, right or wrong. Now here's how we'll work it. We'll meet back here—yes here in this house where he's lying—no later than a quarter to six, with them or without them, empty-handed or successful. We'll have to, if we want to make that bus at six." She moved over toward the body, stooped for something, came back again. "I'll use this latchkey, that was in his pocket, to get in with. You keep the first one."

She took a deep breath. "Now turn, and let's look—"

Tick-tock, tick-tock, tick-tock—

"Oh, God," she grimaced whimperingly. "Three hours—!"

"Bricky!" he said hoarsely, his courage recoiling for a minute. But she was already out at the head of the darkened stairs.

He went out after her.

She was already halfway down them. "Bricky—"

Her voice came up softly. "Put out the lights." He went back and put out the lights.

He went down after her.

She was already at the street-door. She had it open, waiting for him. She was standing there by it.

"Bricky—"

"What was it you wanted to say?"

"Just—" He stopped a second. "How game you are, how spunky you are—that's all. We'll make it. If there's a star that looks out for a little fellow and a little girl, and there must be one somewhere—we'll make it."

He moved on a step or two from her, to go out. Then he stopped and came back again.

"What is it?"

"Bricky, I don't suppose—would you want to kiss me, just for luck, like?"

Their lips touched fleetingly for a moment, in a sketch of a kiss. "Just for luck, like," she murmured.

As they parted there in the darkness, just inside the front door, to slip out into the street one at a time, the last thing she said to him, in a pleading whisper, was: "Quinn, if you should get back first, before I do—wait for me, ah, wait for me, don't leave me behind. I want to go home tonight, I want to go home."

So HE left her, and he struck out down the night-charred street, thinking: Oh, this is hopeless. It's no use. Why not admit it, why not recognize it? If he'd been alone in it, he would have gone over to the park and planked down on a bench and waited for the daylight to come around, and for it to end that way. Or maybe he would have even beat the daylight to it by getting up again in a little while, after a reflective cigarette or two, and walking around to the nearest police station and marching himself in.

But she was in it now, so he didn't. She was in it now, so he kept going. So she was helping him by that much at least: she was keeping him going. They do that to you. For you. Sometimes, as now, even in spite of you.

He was sorry he'd dragged her into it. It wasn't right, it wasn't fair. He was almost sorry he'd gone up there to that dance-hall at all earlier in the evening. But gee, that would have meant— not knowing her. He couldn't be sorry for that, he couldn't make himself that unselfish.

All right, he said to himself. Get started. I'm *him*, now.

I'm leaving there, where I've just killed a guy. He's lying back there behind me, and I've just killed him. Where do I go? What do I do?

He stopped short, held his forehead. I've never killed anyone, so how do I know? That's the whole trouble, I've never killed anyone, so how do I know *what* I'd do? *What* they do?

He shook his head. Not in negation, but violently, as if to clear it, to get any loose preconceptions out of it.

Take it up again. Take it from where you left off.

I've just killed someone, and he's lying back there. Now what do I do? He was at the corner by now.

Which way do I turn?

There's a cab. Do I get in one? A bus-line stops here. Do I get on one of them? Two blocks over, on Lexington, there are subway steps. Do I go down them? Three blocks over, on Third, there's the El. Do I climb the stairs of that? Or do I just keep walking, do I steer clear of all those things and just keep using my own two feet, as the safest and best way? Or maybe I didn't even come this far. Maybe I had a car of my own waiting up the street, just a door or two away from the place where I killed him. Maybe I got in that.

Six choices. And splitting each into its two possible main directions, uptown and down, that made twelve altogether. An even dozen. A maze of getaways, and I'm lost in the middle of all of them. And even if I picked the right one, what good would that do? I still wouldn't know where it led to, what the destination at the end of it was.

Don't keep doing that, don't keep giving up. You wouldn't want *her* to think you were that kind of a guy, would you? Start over. Start over fresh. Now.

I've just killed a guy, and I'm at the corner now, I've come as far as the corner. Never mind about what did I do, this time.

How did I feel, try it that way. Maybe the emotional approach will get you there quicker.

Well, how *did* I feel? I'm shaky all over, I guess, inside and out—unless I'm a pretty hard case. The nervous reaction has caught up with me, along about here; the anger is gone, or whatever it was that made me do it, and I'm getting the after-effects.

I'm shaky all over, pretty well shot.

Wait a minute, there's a drugstore over there, still lit up. It's got a little sign in the window, it says "Open all Night." If it's still open now, it was surely open then.

Well, if I'm shaky all over, inside and out, maybe I go in there and ask for something to steady me up. Gee, that'd be dangerous, wouldn't it, right after killing a guy in the immediate vicinity? The druggist would notice my condition, he'd remember it later and tell them about me. I wouldn't go into such a place, right after killing a guy. But maybe I'd have to, maybe I'm so shaky I wouldn't stop to think of all that, I'd go in anyway.

He'd remember and tell about me. That's it, right there. Let's see if he does. He went in.

There was only one man in the place. He was behind the prescription-counter, at the back. Quinn went up to it, and just stood there.

He took such a long time to bring it out, that finally the prescriptionist said, with a sort of impersonal asperity. "What can I do for you, young man?"

He brought it out slow. He'd been rehearsing each word, and he wanted to keep them the way he had them arranged. "Mister, look. Suppose I walked in here, and I was—well, kind of upset, shaky all over, nerves shot, what would you recommend?"

"Best thing I know of is a little spirits of ammonia in half a glass of water." Quinn came out with part two.

"That what you usually give?"

The pharmacist chuckled with a sort of tart geniality that seemed to be a characteristic of his. "Want to be sure what you're getting before you take it, eh? Sure, I usually give that."

Quinn held his breath.

It came. "Matter of fact, I already gave that to one fellow, couple hours or so ago. You're the second one tonight."

Quinn let his breath out, soft and slow. As easy as that. As simple as that. He couldn't believe he'd actually hit bull's-eye like that, at the very first shot.

Wait a minute, he cautioned himself. Take it easy. Find out a little more about it first, before you go jumping to conclusions. It mayn't be it at all. It's too good to be true, too pat, too easy.

"Somebody else was in my fix, hunh?"

He got a nod on that; that was all that one got. "Well, do you want me to give you some?"

"Yeah, you can." He had to have some excuse for staying in there and talking to him.

The prescriptionist went behind the fountain and shot a little water into a glass. Then he dumped something cloudy into it from a large bottle and stirred it a little. He took the spoon out and handed it over to Quinn. "Try that," he said. "Ten cents, please."

It didn't smell bad, but it looked like soapy water. He wondered how it was going to taste.

"Don't be afraid of it, drink it down."

He wasn't afraid of it. It was just that he wanted to make it last as long as he could.

The druggist was eying him shrewdly. "You don't act very jumpy. Fact you act sort of absent-minded."

Quinn dipped his tongue in, hauled it out again in a hurry. He quickly blocked the verbal opening that had been made by shoving his foot into it. Again verbally, "Maybe his grief wasn't mine. He acted sort of jumpy, hunh?"

The prescriptionist chuckled again in that tart way of his, this time reminiscently. "He sure had ants in his pants. He couldn't stand still. He kept going from here over to the entrance, looking out into the street, coming back again. He couldn't stand still, the guy."

Quinn made an ingenuous discovery. He said, "Hold on." He looked up at the topmost row of bottles on the shelf, to make it more plausible. He said, "That sounds like someone I know. Just like someone I know." He wetted his tongue in the mixture again, without allowing its quantity to diminish any.

"What'd he look like?" he said artlessly.

"Worried," the druggist chuckled.

Quinn threw in a name gratuitously, to act as a stimulus. "I bet it was Eddie. What'd he look like?"

This time it paid off. The druggist fell for it, it had been woven into the fabric of the conversation so dexterously. "Thin sort of a guy. Little taller than you are."

Quinn nodded raptly. He would have nodded if he'd said he was an Eskimo. "Little taller than me. And—" He made a pass up toward his own hair, but left out the color-adjective that the ear expected to hear accompany the gesture.

Automatic response did the rest. The druggist supplied it without realizing he was filling a void. His tongue tripped; he thought he was just corroborating, not making a unilateral statement. "And sandy hair."

Quinn said it after, not before him. "And sandy hair." He nodded in completely hypocritical confirmation. Then he added quickly, "Did he have on a brown suit?"

The druggist said, "Come to think of it, he did. Yeah, he did, he had on a brown suit."

"That's Eddie all right," Quinn said. He took a deep breath. Now he was going good. Now he was on the beam. Now he was coming in for a landing, he told himself. "Yeah," he repeated. "That was Eddie." And to himself, unheard: Eddie, hell. That was Death.

He'd milked that for all it was worth. There didn't seem to be anything more he could get out of it.

Suddenly something more came. Like a left-over drop dripping from a faucet after it's already been turned off.

"He acted like he was having some kind of a chill," the druggist said.

"Shivering, hunh?" Quinn said.

"No, but he was holding his coat up close, like this, the whole time he was in here." The druggist grasped both his coat-reveres with one hand to show him and drew them together up under his chin.

"Maybe he was coming down with flu," the druggist said. "It ain't cold out tonight, you couldn't ask for a milder—"

It is if you've just committed a murder, thought Quinn. It's fourteen below. "Then what'd he do, go out again?"

"No, he asked me to break a dime into nickels for him and he went back there." He motioned to an alley leading back, off-side to the counter. "To use the phone, I guess. He took the ammonia-water with him."

"Did you see him go out again?"

"No, as a matter of fact I didn't. Busy waiting on someone else by that time, I guess. But he must've, without my noticing."

Quinn handed back the glass. He'd drained it and he'd never even known he had, he was so steamed up. But it had been worth it. Even if it had been prussic acid, it would have almost been worth it, the way he felt.

The druggist was still a mile and a half behind him. He thought they'd been carrying on a desultory, aimless conversation. "Guess you're looking for him, is that it? You sure must want to see him bad."

"I do," Quinn said. "Bad." He turned away. "I guess I'll go back there myself."

He turned into the little dead-end aisle and passed from the druggist's sight.

There were two booths there, both on one side. There was a rack on the other side, with the directories in it. One had been up-ended, opened, was lying there flat. The others were still underneath in their grooves.

The glass was standing there, the empty glass, on the exposed directory-page. He'd forgotten to take it back with him again when he left.

Page-finder for murder.

Quinn looked at it first, the way you do a sudden unexpected apparition. Almost as though afraid it would disappear again if he put his hand on it. His, all right.

For a moment an ambitious idea occurred to him. Fingerprints. It must still have his prints on it. Wrap it up and turn it over to the police.

Then it deflated again. No, that was no good. Take too long. The night would be gone. The bus would be gone. Besides, who was to turn it over to them? They were looking for him himself. Or soon would be. It wouldn't prove this unknown to be the killer anyway. *This* wasn't the scene of the crime. The house around the corner was. That was where they'd have to be found, not around here outside a telephone-booth.

So I've followed him this far, he mused, and now I've lost him again. He's gone up in smoke, here at the back of this drugstore, leaving behind an empty glass reeking of spirits of ammonia.

He called someone, though. He came back here to call someone. Whom did he call? He stepped inside the first booth, without closing the front after him. Ah, if the slots on that little wheel could only speak. He sat down on the little ledge, put his hand to his forehead, tried to think.

Whom do you call after you've just killed someone? That depends on who you are, what type you are. You call and say: "I've done as you told me to, boss; it's all taken care of." That was one type. Or you call and say: "I'm hot, pal; I'm in trouble, I'm in a jam, you've got to help me out." That was another type. Or maybe you even call someone and don't say anything about it one way or the other; call some-one and say: "I've got that dough I owe you, never mind how. I'm ready to settle up, you can turn off the heat." That would be still a third type. And then there was even an-other, more hideous to contemplate. Calling and saying: "I know it's late, baby, but how about me dropping over for a little while and lifting a few with you? I feel like a little relaxation."

But he wouldn't be that last type. Not if he'd had to go into a drugstore for a dose of something to settle his nerves.

He turned his head and looked out of the booth, over at the glass. It was directly sideward to him. The pages it stood on were cornmeal-yellow. It was the Classified.

He got up and crossed quickly over to it and peered down. The heading at the top of the page was "Hospitals-Hotels." He looked straight down through the center of the glass, using it as a sort of sight-finder. This is what he saw through the transparent bottom:

> "Sydenham Hospital, Manhattan Ave—
> York Hospital 119 East 74
> Hospitals—Animal—See Dog and Cat—"

Hospitals. He hadn't thought of that. That was one type of call you made after murdering someone, if— He remembered something the prescriptionist out there had said just now. "Holding the front of his coat up like this, as if he was having a chill." That wasn't from any chill, that was from something else.

He jumped back again into the booth he'd just been in, struck a match, floated it all around just over the surface of the floor. Nothing, just the usual debris of phone-booths. Tinfoil from chewing-gum, the masticated end-product of the same, a cigarette-husk or two. They all came floating into the matchlight, floating out again, as he circled it.

He whipped it out, turned, jumped into the second booth, the one he hadn't been in until now. He struck another match and paid that around, turning the floor tawny-pale.

There it was. A gorgeous blob of clue. Right there in front of his eyes. Four big dark glistening polka-dots on the floor, close together, making almost a four-leaf clover pattern the way they had dropped. And there, in the corner, was what he'd been using to staunch it. A wad of ordinary paper facial tissue, two or three ply thick in this case, crumpled tight and thrown away. It was clotted, mired with blood. Only one edge of it still showed white.

He'd probably replaced it with a fresh one while he was in

here, and it was during the process that those four drops had
escaped.

So that was why he'd hugged his coat tight over his chest.
And that was why the tell-tale glass stood atop the hospi-
tal-page of the classified directory. That was the type of
post-murder call he'd made. He'd killed Graves, but not before Graves had—

It couldn't have been a very large wound, for him to remain on his feet like that. But the one on the side of Graves'
head hadn't been either, and it was probably the same gun.
Maybe just a flesh-wound or a nick.

He straightened, went back to it again. This time he lifted the glass, set it aside. It had served its purpose well, it
had betrayed him. He was at some hospital in the city at this
very moment, getting treatment. They had to report gunshot
wounds. Would he be willing to run that risk? He must be,
or he wouldn't have telephoned in ahead of going there. No
doubt he had some trumped-up story he'd give them, to account for it. It mightn't be a gunshot wound at that, there
was no absolute certainty that it was; Graves might have in-
flicted some gash on him, struck at him with something,
even though there had been no evidences of a struggle visible
up there. In which case he'd be that much safer in presenting
himself for emergency-treatment.

The thing was, which? Which one had he called? Which
one had he gone to? There were so many, from A to Y. The
position of the glass meant nothing; he must have set that
down at random, to rid his hand of it, after having already
ascertained the number of his choice.

But then, why phone ahead? Why not just go there? That
part he couldn't understand. But again—there was no actual
proof that he had phoned. True, the bloodied waste was in

one of the phone-booths, but he might simply have gone in there to change improvised dressings and not touched the instrument itself. Simply looked up the address that he wanted in the book, opened his coat a minute to apply fresh staunching-tissue, and then gone on outside again.

The glass? Should he make use of that, concentrate on the ones that had appeared through its bottom? But that was childish, that was sheer mumbo-jumbo. Why not go by accessibility, then, nearness to this immediate neighborhood? There was no time to go through the entire list, he had to have some short-cut.

He chose that one. He ripped the entire page bodily out of the directory, folded it and stuffed it into his pocket, for quick reference. Then he strode on out.

The prescriptionist looked up, from a small supply-room at the back of the counter to which he had retired, as he heard him pass. "Steadier now?" he called after him.

Quinn couldn't integrate the remark for a minute; he'd forgotten his own invention on entering a few moments before.

"A lot steadier," he replied across his shoulder.

He went up the entrance-steps with the leg-spread of a runner taking a hurdle-jump. The ground-floor corridor was coolly dim and the flooring shiny. He went over to the receptionist seated within a lighted alcove at one side, only her head and shoulders visible.

"Did a man come in here for treatment, within the past couple of hours?"

"An ambulance case?"

"No, walking in by himself."

"No, there hasn't been anyone like that all night."

"Wearing a brown suit. Holding himself like this." He gripped his coat together to show her.

"No—" she started to say.

He turned away, reached for the torn page from the directory within his pocket.

"Oh, wait a minute—" she called after him abruptly.

He turned and went back again, so swiftly he nearly skidded on the floor.

"I think I know who you mean." She gave him a weazened smile. "You'll find him on the fourth floor. He's waiting up there to get in—" Then she called after him: "To your right as you get off the elevator. Turn this way." He went over to the car and got in.

He got out at the fourth and turned this way, the way she'd said. Another of those long coolly dim corridors stretched before him. No one in sight along it. He passed doors, but kept going. He followed it to the end, and then made still another turn, that she hadn't told him about. It broadened into a sort of waiting-room, or at least a place with a couple of benches, and he didn't have to go any further. There he was.

He saw him from the distance, and he knew him right away, before he'd even come up to him. He hadn't been admitted yet. He must have just gotten here after all, to be still outside like that.

He was huddled there on a bench against the wall, disconsolate and in distress. He was still holding himself there where he'd been shot. Or at least holding his coat convulsively clenched over it. It must be hurting him a lot. His head was way over, tilted back against the wall, as if he were staring straight up at the ceiling. But he had his free hand pasted over his face, hiding his eyes. Or holding them or something.

His mouth was a little open, and he was doing his breathing through that. There was room on the bench for two, and Quinn sat down next to him.

There was silence for a moment, just the heavy sound of Quinn's own breathing after his fast hike along the corridor.

The man beside him didn't look at him right away. Too much pain or too much misery or something. He didn't care who it was next to him, didn't even want to know.

Quinn reached for a cigarette and took one out and lit it. Then he blew the smoke straight at the side of his face, to attract his attention. Straight into his ear almost. It was calloused in a way, that occurred to him even at the moment of doing it. But he wanted him to know he was there. He said to himself: That'll get him. That'll make him turn. Watch.

The hand came down off his face, and then the face itself came down to a level, and he turned around and looked at Quinn.

Quinn thought he'd never seen such hopeless misery in his life. A sort of shock went through him. But not on that account. Some strange feeling of kinship got to him, and he couldn't understand why, at such a moment. He didn't look like a murderer. He looked like—just anyone at all you sat down next to. Quinn thought: Why, he looks like me, almost. At least, he looks like I *feel* I look like. Sort of harmless, and helpless, and he's no older than me. Why, it might be me sitting there, looking back here at where I am, with a bullet in my chest.

He looked down and he saw a paper tissue there on the floor, bloodied up.

Like the one in the booth.

He spoke first. He said to Quinn: "Can I have one of those?"

Quinn let him have one. He said drily, "Yes, I guess a guy like you, he needs a smoke pretty bad."

The man beside him gave him a wan sort of smile back, and he said: "Does he? He sure does."

Quinn waited for him to light the cigarette, but instead he aimed it toward Quinn's own and ignited it from the tip of that. Quinn let him. He thought: This is the closest I've ever come to a murderer yet. Some of the other's smoke-laden breath got in his face.

He spoke again. He said to Quinn: "Are you here for the same thing I am?"

"No," Quinn said grimly. "Just the opposite, about. Just the reverse."

He waited a moment. Then he said: "You ran out of cigars, I guess."

The man said: "Yes, I did. I only had one left, and I used that up hours—" Then he got it. "How'd you know?" he said.

"I found it up at Graves' place, chewed to ribbons," Quinn said quietly. The man just looked at him. It was beginning to sink in now.

Nothing more came, so Quinn spoke again. "Did the spirits of ammonia make you feel any better? The dose you had at the drugstore over on Madison near Seventieth?"

The man's face was starting to go a funny color. The profile of his throat joggled a little. "How did you know?" he breathed.

"I found that too; on the directory, outside the phone-booths at the back."

The cigarette Quinn had given him fell to the floor. He hadn't wanted to discard it, his mouth got too loose to hold it, and it fell out before he could catch it.

Quinn kept looking at him, looking at him, and he kept looking back.

Quinn said: "Does it hurt you very much? There where you're holding it?" And he ran his bent knuckle past the up-ended reveres without actually touching them.

"Did you lose a lot of blood?" he said. Then he took the man's hand and disengaged it forcibly, but still trying not to jar it too much, trying to be gentle about it.

The coat peeled open and there was nothing, just blank whiteness, unbroken whiteness all the way down to his belt.

Quinn sat back with a jolt on the bench.

The man said: "I haven't any undershirt on. I came out this way, with my coat on my bare back."

He tightened it up again, with a gesture that must have become almost second-nature by now.

Quinn leaned forward again. "So he didn't get you," he said. "I thought he did. Then where was the blood from?"

"From my nose. Any time I get excited it does that. All night off and on, it's been—"

"That's a bad combination," Quinn said. "A killer with a chronic nose-bleed. That puts a strike on you."

The man's jaw hung slack. "What?" he said idiotically, as though he hadn't heard him right.

"You know you killed him, don't you? You know you left him up there dead behind you? You know that, don't you?"

The man tried to get up off the bench. Quinn put his hand lightly on his shoulder, and then bore down a little. "No, stay here," he said with deceptive unconcern, "don't try to get up right away. Stay where you are a while."

The whole lower part of the man's face was dancing now.

"Graves, I'm talking about," Quinn said. "Where you chewed the cigar to ribbons, remember? Seventieth Street."

"Sixty-ninth," the man quavered. "And he said his name was—I don't remember what it is now myself. But it wasn't Graves. He has the flat under me, and I only went down there and smoked a cigar with him for ten minutes because I was too nervous to stay by myself— If somebody killed him, it happened after I left there."

The man's face was stunned. It was like slow ripples spreading outward over it, and freezing as they went. He said, "I don't like the way you're talking. I'm going to get away from you."

"You're wrong about one of those two things," Quinn said stonily. "You bet you don't like the way I'm talking, but you're not going to get away from me."

This time the man got up off the bench, taking Quinn's hand on his shoulder along with him. He tried to get rid of that, so Quinn came up after it, and put the other one on him, got a good tight hold on him with that.

"Get out of here, now," the man kept panting hysterically. "Get out of here." They started to thresh around and stagger to and fro in a locked embrace.

They hit the edge of the bench, and it squealed and jumped a little along the floor.

"It was you, wasn't it," Quinn said through his clenched teeth. "It was you, wasn't it. Graves—Seventieth Street—I'll get it out of you if I have to—"

"Haven't I been through enough for one night— Look, see what you did?

It's starting in again, after I had it quieted down—"

A thin line of red started to edge down from under one nostril. The man wrenched one arm free, clawed at his pocket, brought out another fistful of paper tissue. He slapped it violently against his own face. Then he removed it again, looked at it. The sight of the red on it seemed to enrage him; he stopped being just passively resistant in Quinn's grasp. He swung out at him violently, missed, followed it up with another panicky punch.

The door opened suddenly and a nurse stood glaring out at them. "Here! What's going on out here?" she said sharply. "Stop it! What's the matter with you two?"

They both became reluctantly quiescent, still hanging onto one another and breathing laboredly.

She gave them a black look of reproof. "The idea. I never heard of such a thing. Which one of you is Mr. Carter?"

"I am," the bedraggled individual in Quinn's grasp heaved. The red line had reached his chin now; a second one was beginning to venture downward parallel to it. His coat had been wrenched open by Quinn's continuing hold on it. His thin, unclad stomach was going up and down like a bellows.

"I've got some news for you. Don't you want to hear it?" she said disapprovingly.

"What is it?" he quailed.

"You've got a son."

She turned quickly to Quinn. "You better hold that man up a minute. I think he's going to faint. These prospective fathers give us more trouble than the mothers *and* the babies do put together."

"WHERE TO, lady?" He swung the door open.

She closed the door again, remained outside. "I wonder if you can help me. Have you been on this corner all night?"

"From twelve, off and on. I come on at twelve every night. I haven't been here steady, but this is my reg'lar stand. I start out from here and come back to it again each time."

"Did you have a woman fare, by herself, from this corner anytime after twelve tonight?"

"Yeah, I did have one. A couple hours ago." Then he asked, "What are ya trying, to find someone?"

"Yes, I am."

"Well, if you tell me what she looked like, maybe I can help you."

"I can't tell you what she looked like."

He shrugged, hitched the edges of his hands up off the wheel-rim, then back again. "Then how am I gonna help you, lady?" he demanded not unreasonably. He waited a moment. "Well, is it something serious? Why don't you try the cops?"

"No, it's nothing serious. Just a personal matter." She thought a moment. "Look, when they pay you off, do you notice it pretty closely?"

He smiled cheerlessly. "When they pay me off, that's all I do notice, mostly. Just how much, and just how much over."

"No, I don't mean that. I mean— You remember where you took her."

"I remember where I took her."

"And you remember what she paid you."

"I remember what she paid me."

"But when she did pay you, do you remember— Look, I'm her now, a minute. Just watch me like you did her. Did she pay you like this—?" She handed him an imaginary sum through the cab-opening with her right hand. "Or did she pay you like this?" She handed him an imaginary sum with her left hand.

"I don't get it," he said. "Try it again." She tried it again.

He shook his head. "All I saw was her hand. With the money on it. I picked up the money off it, and that left just her hand. I handed her back what was coming to her. And then she handed me back what was coming to me out of that. And that left just her hand again."

"You don't remember which side her thumb was on?"

"Nah." He bucked his head disgustedly. "I didn't look for it. What did I care which side her thumb was on? I did notice she had a ring on her hand, if that's any good to you."

"No, that isn't any good. What kind of a ring was it?"

"Just an ordinary everyday wedding-band, no different from any of the rest of them. One's like the other."

She closed in a little against the cab. "It was on the hand she gave you the money with?"

"Sure, how else would I know she had it on?"

"Then she did pay you with the left hand."

He acted immensely surprised. "Is that what you've been trying to find out? I didn't get what you meant."

She opened the door and got in. "Take me where you took her."

He took her down Madison almost forever it seemed, then when he'd hit Madison Square and there was no more Madison after that, he turned west and took her along Twenty-third as far over as Seventh. Then he turned south again and took her down that until they were coming close to Sheridan Square. Suddenly he stopped short, at one of the minor streets just above Fourteenth. She thought it was for a light, it was so unexpected, but there was a green on when she looked ahead. He turned around.

"This is it."

"This? But your fender's out past the corner. Which side was it on, which building—? She didn't give you any number?"

"She didn't give me any number. She stopped me just like this, just like I am now. She tapped and said, 'Let me out here.' Look, I'm doing it over for you just exact. She climbed down right where you're standing now yourself, right on the curve of the curb, right over that grate. I'm practically over my same oil-drippings from before. I can't do it any better than that for you."

"But which way did she—?"

"I didn't look at her any more after that. As soon as her money left her and landed in my hand, I looked at that instead. Then I looked ahead of me down the street to make sure it was clear. Then I went."

"But wait—don't leave me stranded here like this! Don't go!"

But he already had. His machine gave her a Bronx cheer out

of its exhaust pipe, and she was standing there alone, with four corners around her.

She looked them over. Going clockwise, they went like this:

On the first corner, before which she stood now, was a cigar store. It was locked and dark. On the second was a barbershop; closed up also. On the third was a filling station, blunting the corner with a cement runway, a dim light or two peering fitfully over it. On the fourth was a laundry; that was dark too.

To stop the cab where she had, shaving the corner, she must have gone into one of those four places. The barbershop was out entirely, the filling station scarcely more likely. It was the cigar store that was the likeliest. It was the nearest to where she'd alighted, and it was plausible that she'd felt the need of a cigarette after what she'd been through. But Bricky had no choice in the matter in any case; since the filling station was the only one available, she went over to that.

She said to the attendant: "Have you been on duty here all night?"

"Yeah, I'm on the night-shift."

"Did you happen to notice a girl get out of a taxi by herself, over there on that other corner, see where I'm pointing, within the last hour or so?"

He looked over. "Yeah," he said. "Yeah, I did. I seen her go into the cigar store."

"You didn't see her come out again?"

"No. I didn't keep watching that long."

She turned away. She'd traced her an inch further, that was all. Just from the curb to the cigar-store entrance.

She went back over there and stood where she had before and looked around. There was a narrow gash of light seaming the sidewalk about five or six doors back along the same block on whose outer extremity she stood perched. Conspicuous because it was rare at this hour.

At least it was something that was open. She started toward it. *She* might have come this way. She started to be hopeful again. It only lasted for a few paces.

The casing through which the light was escaping widened slowly as perspective brought it up toward her. "Delicatessen" slowly spread out on its surface as the window-space expanded.

Food after a murder? It was only a degree less likely as a stopping-place than that barbershop back there. She'd come up abreast of it now. She went in anyway simply because there was no other resource left to her. She knew she was only wasting her energy.

"I'm looking for someone. Have you seen a girl, a blonde, in here the last hour or so? She was by herself."

"With deposit-bottles?"

"No." You don't bring back deposit-bottles from a murder.

"I should know." He let his hand fall heavily back on the counter.

His assistant chimed in: "I think I know who she means. That fussy one. You know, the one I had to say to her, 'Lady, don't scratch lines on the bread with your fingernail to show me how thick you want it sliced, if you ain't going to buy the whole loaf. Maybe somebody else after you wants to buy it too.' For ten cents worth of salami and pumpernickel, she takes up the whole loaf like this." He picked up a loaf to demonstrate, stroked his nail down the soft underside of it, powdered white. "It's got to be just so."

"You're doing it yourself," his employer pointed out.

"Well all right, but I work here."

The proprietor remembered now, if vaguely. "Oh *her*, you mean. Yeah, that's right."

Bricky was leaning avidly across the counter at them. "You couldn't tell me her name, could you?"

"That I don't know. She comes in here all the time. She lives next door there somewhere." He negligently speared a thumb toward the wall behind him. Toward a row of catsup-bottles on a shelf, to be more exact.

"Oh," she said flurriedly. "Oh." She started to back away. "I'll look for her, then. I didn't know—I'll go there right now and look for her."

"Just next door," he repeated.

She went out faster than she'd come in. It had paid off. She'd gained a yard on her this time.

She looped around and plunged into the flat-entrance immediately adjoining.

Six letterboxes in a row, on her left. Six more, on her right. Which was the one? Even if this was the "next door" of the delicatessen-keeper—and he'd carelessly thumbed down this way, instead of up the other—which of the doors within this all-embracing "next door" was it? How was she to know? She didn't know the name. She didn't know the face. The taxi-man was gone now. The trail had ended imbedded head-on in a slab of salami between two chunks of pumpernickel. That was the mocking windfall at the end of the treasure-hunt.

Miller, Carroll, Herzog, Ryan, vacant, Battipaglia. She bent low, eyes eight inches from the wall, scanning them. Some were in crooked, had to be read on the bias. One wasn't in all the way, the "ia" of Battipaglia projected on the outside of the slot-frame. She was blonde, that was the name least likely to be hers of the lot. Still it was not an out-and-out impossibility; by marriage, by the peroxide-bottle—

She turned to the other side, ran her eyes along there at astigmatism-distance. Newmark, Simms, Lopez, Kirsch, Barlow, Stern.

It ought to be one. It couldn't be all. It mightn't be any. One chance out of eleven to be right. Ten chances to be wrong. Eleven, considering that it might not even be this building at all. "Next door" was elastic, could mean two houses down, three, any number as far as the first intervening crossing.

Ring one, any one at all; suppose they did scowl or snarl at her, what was that? She might be able to find out from them. No, she didn't want to do that; she might be giving herself away. The floors, the walls, might have ears. The only way to strike and hope to succeed was suddenly, without giving any warning.

She went over to the inner door, to see if she could get in beyond where she was, even though the eventual flat remain anonymous. The knob was brass and it was kept well-polished. This seemed to be a conscientiously cared-for building, even though in the lower-rental brackets. She just stopped her hand in time, from pressing on it and turning it.

It was such a small thing, such a faint thing, such a nothing really. The contact of her hand, no matter how light, would have surely obliterated it. It was a miniature smudge upon the glossy, satin-surfaced brass, but in white. A sliver, a paring of a fingerprint, the ghost of a crescent scallop. As if someone whose fingertips had lately touched chalk had turned this knob before her.

"My pumpernickel-customer." The delicatessen-man's voice. "The machine don't cut it thick enough to suit her. She takes her finger like this and shows me how wide she wants it cut." Pumpernickel, a bread dusted with stubbornly-adhesive flour.

"She came in this door," she said to herself. "She's somewhere in this house." The eleven chances to be wrong had shrunk to ten.

Go on in, you fool, go on up, go from door to door; you know now. She shook her head, stayed where she was. Strike suddenly, strike unexpectedly, otherwise you might lose everything.

A tiny piece of paper on the floor. In this entryway that was otherwise so meticulously clean, so it must have fallen only recently. A little fingernail-length tatter, that was all it was actually. It lay under the six letterboxes on the right-hand side as you came in, but under the whole row of them in general, not under any one in particular. For it was too far below, and out a little too far, to be attributed to any one of them individually.

She picked it up and looked at it carefully. It was so small, her two fingers almost hid it even as they held it. It was too much to expect it to have writing on it, there wouldn't have been room for any, even had coincidence been willing to vouchsafe her that freak of good fortune; and there wasn't. It was just a little nick of white.

But everything can tell you something. Her fingernail pried at it, and it came open, in flap-shape. It had been doubled in thickness. There was a neat, machine-made seam bisecting it now.

In other words, it was from a letter. It was a minute sliver torn from the top of an envelope, where the flap folds down, in hasty finger-opening. All the rest of the way across, the envelope had simply erupted into unsightly tatters. This one microscopic section, however, had been amputated by the violence of the process, had fallen off entirely.

What good was it to her even then? To be opened in here, the letter had come out of one of those boxes. One of the six on the right-hand side. Well—and? Well, to come out of one of those boxes, the box first had had to be opened. They opened downward, like little brass gangplanks. In opening them, the letterbox-key alone would be touched by the fingers. But in closing them up again, wouldn't the natural, the quicker, the more dexterous thing to do be to use the tips of the fingers, to press them back flat again?

On the knob of the door was a tiny white sworl.

She peered close this time, even closer than the eight-inch gauge she'd used before. She looked all up and down the glass inset in each one, and the brass trim around it, not just at the name on the card beneath the push-button. She looked so close her breath steamed each one, and then it cleared again as she passed on to the next. Newmark, Simms, Lopez, Ki— She stopped short, went back a step, in a double-take of her entire body, not just the eyes alone.

There it was, a sketchy scar of white flecking the outside of the box, right up against the seam. A blemish that was so trivial, had not her mind been prepared ahead of time to see it, her eyes would surely have not seen it even then. And the name above it, Kirsch. The second-floor flat, on the right-hand side of the stairs as you went up.

The six chances had collapsed into one. The one was not a chance now any longer, it was a positive certainty.

Little things, the little things that are all around you, if you only know how to use them, The little things that can destroy you, if you don't stop and think of them in time, guard yourself against them. And who could, for you don't even realize they are there until it's too late.

The nick of a nail across a loaf of pumpernickel, to show how thick it is to be sliced. The closing up, by thoughtless fingermotion, of a letterbox-flap within which there had been a square of white peering waiting. A bill, perhaps an advertisement, almost certainly nothing important. The hasty ripping of it open; what else is one to do with a letter? Finally, the turning of a knob to gain entrance within a building. How else is one to go inside to where one lives? Little things. And the sum-total of all of them? Catastrophe. Identification, confrontation, and accusation, for a thing thought safely buried miles away from here, and unseen by living eyes.

She pushed the ground-floor one on the other side. They wouldn't have to shout down an inquiry through the core of the house then. The door retched several times on inner pushbutton-control, to show the latch had been lifted, and she swung it open and went in.

A man stood looking inquiringly through a crack of the inner door on her left-hand side as she made for the stairs. She flashed him a placating smile as she went hurrying past without stopping. "I'm sorry, that was a mistake. My hand must have slipped."

He was too sleep-riddled for his perceptions to be very acute. He blinked vacantly and the door-crack closed up again. She was already nearly at the top of the first flight, and climbing fast.

A swing around the turn, and there it was looming in front of her. Coffin-size. The door through which death had come home a little while before. It looked just like all the other doors here. But it wasn't. There was death pulsing from it, in unseen waves. She could almost feel them on her face, like a vibration.

Her outthrust foot had fallen to a halt, toe inches away from the bottom of it.

Her other foot lingered further behind.

She listened. For a moment nothing, because she had caught it in a moment of silence. Then suddenly there was the sound of a plate going down on a table. Quick footsteps going away. Quick footsteps coming back again. The sound of another plate going down. This time the sound of a plate going down on another plate. Or more likely, of a cup going down on a saucer. Quick footsteps going away again.

She shuddered in spite of herself. Death had come home to an early-morning snack.

Quick footsteps coming back again. A paper bag rattled noisily as something was taken out of it. Pumpernickel bread, sliced thick.

Quick footsteps going away again. Gee, they were so busy, so chipper, happy almost. They wouldn't be in another second or two. Death didn't know she had an uninvited guest about to join her.

She knocked.

The footsteps died a sudden death. She knocked again, fast and insistent.

The ghost of the footsteps came toward the door. "Who is it? Who's out there?"

She was a little frightened, you could tell it by the voice. People didn't challenge in quite that breathless way, no matter what the hour of the night.

"A lady to see you."

"A lady? What lady?"

"If you'll open, you will see." She kept threat out of her voice, to try to cajole the final obstacle out of her way.

The knob pivoted undecidedly, she saw it go around, but the door didn't open. "It isn't you, Ruth, is it?"

"Just let me speak to you. It will only take a minute."

Trust this once, and you're undone forever; trust this once, and you'll never trust again.

A latch-tongue shot back, the door broke casing.

She was about twenty-eight. Well, it was hard to say; twenty-six, then. She was blonde, and her hair was short and curly. It was a natural blonde, though it may have been given some slight abetment. Her sandy eyebrows and almost white lashes told that. Her face was hard, and yet it wasn't. It wasn't the hardness that comes from within, it was rather a protective coating, a crust, it wore. Beneath, still lurking in the eyes and along the seams that caught tautly at the corners of its mouth, was a child-like trustfulness, that was afraid to come out too far, it had been rebuffed so often. It had learned its lesson not once but many times; it tried to hide itself away from the world now.

Her cheeks were thin, there was a hollowed spot in each. She had too much rouge on them, and over too great an expanse, and it gave them a fevered look. She had on a cheap cotton dress in a design of thin pencil-stripes. They ran diagonal; on one side of an invisible center line, they ran down one way, on the other, they ran down the opposite way.

She was a little frightened by this intrusion, but she was hoping to be reassured.

All this in an instantaneous snapshot taken by the eyes, to be assembled later as the minutes went by.

"I want to see you."

That forepointed foot was in the way now; the door couldn't close any more.

She hadn't looked down, so she wasn't aware of this yet. "Who are you?"

"You'd better let me talk to you about this inside, for your own sake as well as mine. Don't keep me standing out here."

She pushed by her and was in. One of them closed the door, neither one of them was sure at the moment which of the two had done it.

It was a small living-dining room in a cramped furnished flat. Neat enough, but shoddy-cheap in every aspect. A window cast its foreshortened square of light upon a gray wall an arm's span out from it. A skimpy length of cranberry velour drapery hung down on either side of it. A card table had been erected, and dishes and the things she had brought from the delicatessen stood upon it, waiting to be partaken of. A newspaper was even on it, a pale green tabloid, furled and held flat between two of the dishes, waiting to be taken up and read. A package of cigarettes, still unopened, lay waiting there too—she must have brought them in with her just now—and a furbished ashtray to go with them, and even a folder of matches. A paper napkin was spread over the sandwiches to keep the dust off them until she was ready.

A doorless opening beyond, with light coming through, must have led into a bedroom.

She saw all this, but it didn't matter. Even death has a home-life, it doesn't strike out suddenly out of nowhere.

"What're you up to, anyway? I don't let strangers in on me at this time of night. I don't like the way you're acting."

She gave it to her without any embroidery. "You got in a taxi at the corner of Seventieth and Madison, around one. You'd been paying a call on someone around the corner from there. Right?"

The woman's face answered for her. It was starting to get white. "The man you were calling on is dead now. Right?"

The woman's eyes curdled. The outside of her face died a little. It wasn't pretty to watch.

"You killed him. Right?"

"Oh my God." She said it soft and low. Her eyes rolled; the pupils were carried upward under their lids, out of sight. She was all white eyeball for a minute or two.

The corner of the bridge-table kept her upright, she found it with her hands, sight unseen.

She started to cry; it came up only as far as her eyes, then she changed her mind. Not enough tears formed to push their way out. They stayed in, giving the eyes a glassy coating.

"What are you, a policewoman?"

"Never mind what I am. We're talking about you. You're a killer. You've killed someone tonight."

The woman's hand went to the base of her throat for a minute, trying to ease it. A sob that was more like a cough sounded in it. "Let me get a drink of water a minute, I'm all— It's all right, there's no other way out of here."

"And get your things while you're in there," Bricky said mercilessly.

She went in through the lighted opening. She had to hold onto one side of it to steer herself through it.

Bricky stood there looking down. She was listening, not thinking. A glass tinked. Her ears didn't tell her. Some wire-fine instinct, jangling to an unseen current, told her. She took a quick step forward, went in there after her.

"*Don't drink that!*" Bricky swung backhand at her face. The glass was knocked away from her parted lips. It didn't break, it was cheap and thick. It just thudded to the floor, rolled over, spewing a thin watery trail after it.

It was only after she'd completed the act that her eyes roamed around and saw the bottle standing uncapped on a shelf above the sink. Brown glass, "Lysol" on the label.

The woman was gripping the edge of the sink with both hands, as though it were unsteady and liable to get away from her.

"So you've as good as told me, haven't you?"

The woman was silent. Her hands, on the sink, were shaking a little, that was all.

"You didn't have to. I knew it anyway." The woman was silent.

"You're coming back there with me now. You're coming up there—where it happened."

The woman exploded into a strangled bleat. "No. You can't make me. I don't know who you are, but you can't make me. I'll kill you first. I don't have to die twice. Once was enough."

Her hand shot out into some sort of a rubber rack hanging to one side of the sink. Something flashed in the light, and a short, sharp-bladed kitchen-knife reared back over her shoulder, about to slash forward at Bricky.

There was no time to get out of the way, the place was too cramped. She flung herself forward upon her instead. Her hand caught the death-dealing arm at the wrist, tried to hold it off. Their other two arms threshed and clawed at one another, and finally riveted themselves together and stalemated one another.

The woman had the strength of desperation, of suicide. Bricky had the strength of self-preservation. An equipoise was established, that had to break sooner or later. They swayed slightly, moving very little, scarcely leaving the rim of the sink at all. Once they both bent over it together; again, they both bent outward the other way. Their hair came down. They didn't scream, didn't shrill. This wasn't a cat-fight over some fancied slight; this was a fight to the death between two human beings. And death abolishes sex.

They rotated a little, then they went back again the other way. In the silence you couldn't hear anything but their strident breaths. They had frozen into a tableau of exhaustion, Bricky too spent to ward off the knife, the other too spent to drive it home altogether.

A key fumbled at the door, on the outside of the other room. Suddenly, with crazy irrelevancy, their roles had reversed.

The other woman was desperately trying to fling the knife away, rid herself of it, discard it. Bricky, still not understanding, held her wrist in a vise, choked off its power of motion. The fingers opened and the knife fell to the floor. The woman's foot darted out, kicked it out of sight under the sink. There was nothing to strive over any more. They released one another uncertainly.

The woman dropped to her knees beside Bricky, began pulling at the bottom of her dress in agonized supplication.

"Don't tell Harry. Oh my God, don't tell Harry. Have pity on me." The door in the other room was opening.

A voice called through cheerily: "Helen, you back yet?"

"Don't. I don't care what you do to me, but don't tell Harry. Not right away, anyway. I love him so. He's all I've got. I'll do anything you say—anything."

Bricky was bending over, trying to detach her importunate, kneading hands from the fabric of her dress. "Will you come back there with me? Will you come back quietly, like I want you to?"

The woman nodded, avid for reprieve.

His shadow was already coming toward the doorway. He must have stepped aside for a moment to sample a mouthful of the food waiting on the card table.

"All right," Bricky relented. "I'll play ball with you if you play it with me." The woman cowering at her feet only had time to whisper one thing more.

"Leave it to me, let me do the talking—" He was standing in the doorway.

Just a guy, to Bricky, a man. Only the eyes of love could change him into what he was for this other woman, and only this other woman had those eyes of love for him. So Bricky couldn't really see him as he was to her. Just a guy. A dime-a-dozen guy.

The woman kneeling at her feet seemed not to see him. She said, "The hem is too long on this side, that's what the trouble is. It makes the whole skirt hang uneven." She stopped as if she'd only then seen him. "Oh, hello, Harry," she said delightedly. "I didn't even hear you come in!"

He said, "Who's this? Who've you got with you?"

She picked herself up, went over to him and kissed him. He gave Bricky a stupidly inquiring look over her shoulder.

She stood aside. "Mary, meet my husband."

"Mary Coleman," Bricky said dutifully.

They nodded to one another reservedly. He glanced down at his own coat and trousers, then over at the bed; he was obviously tired. After a strained moment of triple silence, he turned on his heel and went back inside. "I'm going ahead in and eat," he said inhospitably.

They followed him in there. "Well, I guess I'll run along, now that your husband's back."

"Wait a minute, I'll go over with you and get that. You know, that pattern."

He'd sat down. He shoved the paper napkin into the gap between two buttons of his shirt, so that it fanned out from there. "At this hour?" he said. "Clothes at three in the morning," he grunted under his breath.

"I'll be back in five minutes. She lives just around the corner from here."

"Should I wait up for you?" he asked disgruntledly. "I'm tired."

"You go ahead and get to bed. I'll be back before you know it. I won't even take my coat."

"You'd better take your coat," Bricky said. "It gets a little chilly at this hour of the morning."

She went in and got it. Both their faces were a little pale, Bricky's and hers.

Bricky wondered if he noticed it.

He'd gotten up to come to the door with them, chewing on a mouthful of his sandwich. A sandwich that had cost so dear.

She kissed him again.

"And Harry, don't make a mistake and lock the door on the inside so that I can't use my key. I don't want to have to ring and wake you, in case you *are* asleep already."

"Don't stay out too long. I don't want anything happening to you." She kissed him a third time.

"You kissed me already," he said.

"Can't I kiss you an extra time if I feel like it?"

"Sure, if you feel like it," he consented.

His hand was already at the knot of his tie, and his mouth was stretching into a yawn, as he ushered them out.

She started to cry the minute the door was shut behind the two of them. Grimacing without sound. "I thought I'd break down before we got out of there. He was tired, or he would have noticed it in my eyes. I love him so much."

"Take it easy," Bricky said brusquely.

They went down the stairs, Bricky in the lead. They went out into the solemn blueness of the street.

Helen Kirsch glanced behind her at the doorway. "I won't be coming back again, will I?" She bit her lips. "I loved it there— with him. It wasn't much, but it had him in it."

"Then why didn't you stick close to it, while you had it?" Bricky said stonily. "Cut out the hearts and flowers. I carried out my part of the bargain, now see that you carry out yours." She thought: Life is like a see-saw. Every time one of us goes up, somebody else at the other end of the board goes down.

They walked as far as the corner.

"We'll take a taxi," Bricky said. "That's about the quickest way." The figure beside her cowered a little.

She hopes I won't find one, Bricky said to herself. Any little thing to delay us. She saw one and she shrilled at it, and it came over.

Bricky shovelled her hand invitingly toward her companion, as if to have the destination come from her unprompted, to hear what it would be.

"The exact—?"

"No, the nearest corner is good enough."

"The corner of Seventieth and Madison," Helen Kirsch said in a stricken voice.

Bricky nodded to herself in narrow-lidded confirmation, cracked the door to after them.

The cab wheeled about for uptown, the city began to pay off block by block. The street-lights roller-coastered in and out again, in and out again, through the windows at the sides.

Helen Kirsch's hands formed a bow-knot of despair at her mouth. "Who'll send his shirts out to the laundry for him? He'll never remember that; I've always had to do it for him."

Bricky didn't answer.

The blocks paid off. The street-lights flickered in and out.

"I wonder what he'll do with himself, without me, on Sundays. That was his only day off. Now he'll have the whole day on his hands."

Bricky looked the other way. "Why rub it into yourself?" she said gruffly.

A light stopped them, and in the stillness of the wait, the engine-throb was like somebody's heart going.

More blocks. More flickering street-lights seeping in. New York's such a long city, especially when you're riding lengthwise through it—to the end of all your hopes.

"You're so fast, you police," Helen Kirsch said. "I always heard you were, but I never believed it before, until now."

We police, Bricky thought sadly. We police is good. If she only knew.

She started to cry a little more, Helen Kirsch. "I can't believe it. He isn't really— He can't be—"

"He's dead," Bricky said flintily. "Dead as they make them. Dead as they come."

The sound of the word seemed to do something to Helen Kirsch. She crumpled forward suddenly above her own lap, as though she had a folding pain; covered her face. This time the tears came good; hot and heavy. "I didn't mean to!" she sobbed strangledly. "I didn't! Oh, I didn't, I tell you!"

"Were you alone there in the room with him?" She saw her head nod reluctantly in the gloom. "Did you have a gun in your hand?"

The nod came even slower, but it came once more. "Did you fire it at him?"

"It went off—"

"They always do. Funny how they always do, with girls like you. Always go off of their own accords, and with darned good aim too. Did he fall down when it went off? Answer me. Did he?"

"Yes." She shuddered at the recollection. "He fell, and he pulled me down with him. I couldn't get clear for a minute. I tore myself away from him, and I got up and I ran."

"But he didn't. Did he lie there after he'd fallen? Did he lie there still, or did he get up and chase you?"

"He—he didn't get up and come after me."

"You fired a gun at him. He fell down. He lay there. All your welshing won't change what that is. Little sister, you've got yourself a murder on your hands."

Helen Kirsch squealed like a stuck pig. Or like a puppy dog that's been accidentally stepped on. She burrowed her face rearwards into the corner seam of the cab, almost as though she were trying to squeeze her way out through there, burst it asunder. Her hand beat a reflex protest on the padding.

"I didn't mean to! Oh God, hear me! I didn't mean to! I didn't want to go to that party. This other girl, where I work, she talked me into it! I didn't want to go. I'd never done a thing like that before, behind Harry's back. Then when I got there and saw there were only four of us, just the two couples, I didn't like the way it looked, I didn't want to stay. And then the other couple slipped off somewhere, before I knew it they'd gone, and I was alone with him."

Bricky tried to buck her up, the only way she knew how. "What're you so afraid of anyway?" she said brusquely. "You'll never even do a stretch on it, probably. You've got the perfect defense. They always take the woman's word in a case like that. And this time, there *is* no other word but yours."

Her head didn't go up. It went lower, if anything, in utter prostration.

"It isn't that— It isn't that— How can I ever live with Harry any more, after? He won't have me."

"He'll forgive you for going to what you thought was just a harmless party."

"They never do, they never do—for that."

Suddenly Bricky understood, completely, devastatingly. "Oh," she said in a crushed voice. "You fired at him—"

"I fired at him *after*."

The cab slowed, came in for a stop.

Bricky paid him from the seat, then they got out. Bricky took her by the wrist, said, "Stand here a minute till the cab drives away."

They stood there motionless; the cab rolled off, leaving its ghost in blue exhaust-tracery on the night air. Its going tugged at their skirts and flared them a little. Then they stood there alone on the edge of the curb.

"What are you going to do to me now?" Helen Kirsch quailed in pitiful helplessness.

"Show me where you ditched the gun. That's what I want to know first. You lead the way."

Her hostage went down that street there, bearing east; Bricky close beside her like an upright shadow.

Bricky thought: "She went out of her way first, over this way, to discard the gun; then doubled back along the same street to the avenue once more and got into the cab there. That was an erratic thing to do." She didn't comment on it, went with her unquestioningly.

They crossed the arid grandeur of Park Avenue, with its double width and stepped-up wedges of safety in the middle; dead to the world, scarcely a light showing in a window along it for the twenty blocks or so that the eye could encompass. Most of the bedrooms along here were to the rear, anyway. The most overrated thoroughfare in the world.

They went on. They came to Lexington, narrower, more human, more alive at least. They still went on, toward Third. They crossed that, under the iron tracery of the El, went on toward Second.

Bricky said at last, "What brought you so far over?"

"I was going the wrong way. I didn't know where I was at first. I was, like dazed, when I first came out."

Yes, Bricky thought, anyone would be, immediately after taking someone's life.

The Kirsch girl spoke again in a moment or two. "It's in one of these alleys between the buildings along here. There was a row of ashcans standing there, waiting to be dumped. The first one had a lid on it. I lifted that and chucked it underneath." Then she said, "Maybe they've been emptied already."

"They don't come around until just before daybreak," Bricky said.

"I think that's the one. There it is, in there. See them? There's about six of them in a row."

"Stay with me," Bricky warned. "Come over next to me while I look."

All the other girl said was, "I'm playing the game. You played it back at my place."

They turned aside and the shadows of the inset blacked the two of them out. All you could hear were their voices, whispering guardedly. That and the faint clash of an ashcan-lid being removed.

"Got it?"

There was an accusing pause. Then Bricky slurred, "Are you telling me the level on this?"

"Somebody's found it! Somebody's taken it out!"

"Are you sure this is the right place?"

"It was in this alley, and no other. I remember how it looked, when you turned and faced the street from in here. Those windows across there with all the little white splits in their panes. And it was this first can here. It's full of coke-husks."

Silence from Bricky.

"I swear I'm telling you the truth. Why would I want to back out now, after bringing you all the way over here?"

"You sound like it was the truth, at that. Never mind, don't dig your arm all the way down through that stuff. It would be on the top if it was anywhere at all. Some night-scavenger must have come along right after you and found it. Maybe someone noticed you slip in and out of here."

They reappeared suddenly in the lesser sombreness of the sidewalk. "All right, now let's go there," Bricky said quietly.

The girl stopped short and looked at her pleadingly. "Do I have to?"

"You've got to go where it is. That's what I hauled you out of your place with me for. That's the main thing, not digging up the gun. The heck with the gun."

They started on the way back. They recrossed Third. Suddenly the girl had stopped again. She was shaking all over; Bricky could tell even in the darkness.

"Snap out of it," she started to say. "What're you balking for n—?"

Without a word the girl turned aside and went into the rancid entrance they had halted opposite. For a moment Bricky thought she was trying to elude her, make a getaway. Her arm started to reach out after her to pull her back. Then she let it fall, checked the exclamation that had risen to her lips. A curious, coldly-frightening sensation coursed through her for a minute.

She went in after her. "What're you doing, kidding me?" Her voice was unsteady.

In the dim light there was inside this hallway, this tunnel toward—who knew what?—she saw the girl look at her as if she didn't understand her, didn't know what she meant by asking that.

She waived the question. The girl went up stairs there at the back. She went at her heels. She couldn't have told which was the more frightened one of the two of them now. Her fright was a sort of sick dismay.

Halfway up the girl stopped again. "I can't— Why do I have to?"

Bricky motioned ahead of the two of them with a stab of her finger. "Keep going, wherever you're going," she said tersely.

Their shadows climbed the dingy walls beside them. They stood before a door now.

Harry Kirsch's wife looked at it, all around its edges four-square, as though it were insuperable.

"Open it," Bricky said, reading their destination in her antipathy.

She reached out and touched the knob as though afraid it would sting her. She gave it a quick turn and then snatched her hand back. It slanted open now.

"You first," Bricky said.

The other girl's face was that of a doomed thing as she went in before her. Bricky remembered something she'd said down at her own flat earlier. Yes, this was like dying twice, all right. But she wasn't dying alone, something in Bricky was dying along with her—had been ever since outside on the street before.

A light was on. First there was a narrow, prison-like hall. They went down that. They passed an open doorway, with the room beyond it dark. White-painted wood gleaming faintly in it. A kitchen, most likely. They passed a second one, also open, also dark. Then the hall opened frontally into a lighted room before it, and they went in there, and stopped.

It was a nondescript sort of place; it must have been rented just for the party, just for tonight, just for a place of assignation. Rented furnished as it was. It didn't look as though it had been lived in consistently, or was meant to be. Something about it.

There was no one in this room. There had been somebody in it before, plentifully in it, rowdy in it, raising hell in it, before. Glasses stood around haphazardly; only four of them to begin with, but multiplied four-fold, six-fold, in the many still-moist scars all around them, where they had been taken up and set down again repeatedly. A fractured phonograph record lay on the seat of one of the chairs. Bricky picked up a central fragment, bearing the label, and looked at it. "Pistol-Packin' Mamma." She winced at the malevolent appropriateness, chucked it aside.

The Kirsch girl stopped and pointed. Toward a doorless room-opening beyond. She was rigid there, rooted; she couldn't have been made to go on any further. Bricky went on alone.

She stopped at the threshold and stood looking in. There was no further place to go. There was no further need.

It had a window, but the shade was down over it, down firmly, down all the way. There were two more glasses in here. One was still full, as if it had been pressed on someone who quickly set it down untouched, in the face of some greater crisis looming.

He was lying there over on the far side, stretched out in disordered repose.

Inert, immovable.

Bricky went over close to him, bent down. Then she drew her head back sharply, averted it, fanned her hand in front of her face a couple of times. She got up, nudged her foot along the form here and there, as if with a sort of idle curiosity.

Then she went back to the doorway, looked out.

Helen Kirsch was standing there frozen, her face covered with both hands, in a pose of abysmal tragedy. Bricky just stared.

There was silence for a moment.

The other girl sensed her stare, slowly dropped her hands, met her look questioningly.

There was still silence.

Then, slowly, she discovered something on Bricky's face.

"What are you looking at me like that for? Why do you keep looking at me like that?"

"Come here a minute. I want you to see something." Helen Kirsch quailed, shook her head.

Bricky pulled her over against her will, held her, made her look into the second room.

Something grunted on the far side of it. The log-like figure was in flux now. Right while they watched it was struggling to pick itself up, with that floundering motion typical of the drunk who has lain comatose for a long while.

"He's not dead," Bricky said. "Just dead drunk. Even if he'd been dead, he'd have been the wrong dead man. There's the hole up there on the wall where the bullet went in."

A stifled scream from Helen Kirsch centered his wavering attention on them. He fixed a poached eye on her. He seemed to remember her vaguely.

"Whosh your friend?" he grunted. "Esh have another drink, you and me and her."

They both stood staring transfixedly at him until he was all the way up, like a bear on its hind legs. Then the tableau shattered.

"Let's get out of here," Bricky said tersely, "before the whole thing starts over."

Helen Kirsch would have stood there all night. She acted as though something had numbed her, robbed her of all power of motion. Bricky had to dislodge her, thrust her before her. She prodded her ahead of her, across the intervening room, along the hall, and out onto the stair-landing outside.

Behind them, something heavy fell back again into place, lay still. Bricky jerked the door to after them, for added safety.

"Come on," she had to tell her dazed companion. "Come

away from here. Don't stand there." All the way down the stairs they ran, armed together, the one in sobbing relief, the other in grim frustration.

They came spilling out into the open, in a sweep that carried them paces down the sidewalk before it slackened and died. Then Bricky stopped short, turned to her.

"You love that man downtown, that George or Harry or whatever his name is?"

Helen Kirsch shook her head, unable to articulate. Her eyes sparkled with a threat of tears again.

"Then what're you waiting for, you little fool?" She threw up her arm, as a brake to a passing cab. "Go back there. Go back there fast!" The cab veered up, stopped. "Get in."

Bricky closed the cab-door between them. A pale face looked mutely out at her for a moment. Bricky thumbed the driver on.

"You've got your happy ending now; don't crowd your luck. Stay with your Harry where you belong—and keep your mouth shut, your eyes to yourself, and your fingers off gun-triggers after this."

AND THEN he suddenly got this break. He was working his way back from the hospital, tail between legs, hands choking pockets, hat low over his eyes. He was coursing the bars now. They were easy to spot, even from a distance of two or three blocks away; they stood out like colored pins on a map, for they were the only places still open and lighted at this hour. He was working his way back at an extreme zig-zag, confining himself to a zone about six blocks wide from north to south, stretching between the hospital and the house. At each intersecting avenue he'd turn up about three blocks one way, combing it for bars, then reverse and go back about three blocks the other way, past his original starting point. Then come back to that again, and go on a block more westward, to the next intersecting avenue, do it over again there. They were all on the avenues, the bars, not on the side-streets linking them.

Some he entered, and stayed in for a moment or two, using his eyes. Some he just thrust his head into from the doorway, and then turned around and went out again. He wasn't drinking himself. That would have been fool-hardy;

that would have been too destructive both of time and of keenness of perception.

He could do it this way, because there were certain things to look for, certain tell-tale signs, hieroglyphs, call them what you will, that made it quicker, made for a short cut.

He told himself: If he's stayed in one of these places this long after, at all, then he'll be by himself, aloof, withdrawn. A person doesn't enter a bar, after killing someone, looking for sociability. A person enters a bar, after such a thing, to steady his nerves. Look for someone by himself, then, withdrawn, noncommunicative, separate from the rest of the customers both in stance and attitude.

That was one short cut. The first and foremost of them all.

He came upon this place, and he cased it quickly, first from the outside, without entering at all. It was small enough to stand for that without danger of omission of any pertinent detail. It was a store, an enclave, the width of half the usual shopfront. Its bar, instead of being something that belonged over with one side of it, bisected it mathematically down the middle. The aisle of clearance left on the outside, for the customers, was no wider than that left on the inside for the barman. Moreover, it had none of the usual adjunct of tables sheltered within booths or partitions, difficult to survey from out front where he was. He could look straight down the bartop, in central diminishing perspective, from the frontal window. And this is what he saw:

There were eight people paid out along it. They broke into about three groups, each self-contained, oblivious of the others, but he had to look close to tell where the divisions came in. Physical distance had nothing to do with it; they all stretched away from him in an unbroken line. It was the turn of the shoulders that told him. The limits of each group were marked by a shoulder turned obliquely to those next in line beyond. They were like enclosing parentheses, those shoulders. In other words, the end men in each group were not postured straight forward, they turned inward toward their own clique. The groupings broke thus: first three, then a turned shoulder, then three again, then another turned shoulder, then finally two, standing vis-à-vis.

No singles, no solitary drinkers there. He was about to pass on his way, then suddenly he looked again, something caught his eye, held him fast out there.

His eye had just run down the bartop, automatically checking the number of glasses against the number of people, and found something awry, out of true.

There were nine glasses, there were eight people. There was one more glass than there was a person to drink from it.

He counted both over again, to make sure. It was easy to tabulate the people; it was not so easy to tabulate the glasses, for there were hands continually dropping in and out amidst them, impeding his clearness of view.

Again they came out nine, even after he'd checked them for chaser-glasses, which would have been counted two to a drinker. There weren't any of those. Everyone in the place happened to be drinking beer at the moment.

Nor was the extra glass a discard. It stood, not before anyone, but by itself, at the far end, with only empty space before it where its user should have been. It was what he had been looking for: the aloof, solitary, removed symbol.

Only it was not a person, it was an inanimate glass mug.

The first hieroglyph. He went in.

He skirted all the others, he went down by the far end,

where it was, where all the eloquent empty space was. There was a gap of long yards there, between the last drinker and the wall. He moved in there, not directly in front of it, but very close to it.

He looked at it, and it paid off twice. Just a beer mug and yet it paid off by his very looking at it.

They had handles, as that type of receptacle always does; they were octagonal in shape, thick and bulky, with enormously indented bottoms, to the profit of the purveyors, and they had handles. The handles of all the others were in line, they pointed one way, away from the door, inward toward the back of the shop. The handle of this one and this one alone was in reverse, it pointed outward toward the street.

The second hieroglyph.

He bought a beer himself, to draw the barman to him, to lubricate the questions he was about to ask. The chase had suddenly come to a head again; landed in one spot, if only briefly, like the tormenting, buzzing, circling gadfly it was.

He said to the barman, "Whose is this?"

The barman said, "Fellow that just went back there a minute."

So he was still in the place. The quantity of liquid still in it, the fact that it was allowed to stand there undisturbed, had already told him that.

He didn't have much time; he slashed straight through to the next question, letting his informant like it or not as he chose. "What color suit'd he have on?"

"Brown," the barman said reservedly. The barman gave him a look. The barman didn't like it, but—"brown," the barman said.

The third hieroglyph. All at one time, all in one place, all out of a crass beer mug. Drinking isolated in a crowd, left-handed, wearing a brown suit.

He asked a third question. "How long has he been in here, 'd you notice?"

His ten cents was running out, evidently. There was a time-lag before he got the answer. He got it finally, but it came slow, like the last of anything. Or like when something's drying up, there isn't going to be any more.

"Two or three hours, I guess."

That took it back to about the right time. The fourth hieroglyph.

"Has he been on this stuff the whole time?"

This time it backfired. He would have had to be a rye-buyer to get any more answers.

"What are you doing, young fellow, taking a census in here?" the barman snarled, and he moved up the line, to where there was more profit and less interrogation.

He didn't have to ask any more; he couldn't have, anyway. A door broke casing somewhere unseen behind him, and the glass's owner was returning.

Quinn didn't turn his head. There was a strip of mirror-panel matching the bar straight before him. "I'll get him in that," he said to himself, and kept his eyes riveted front.

The mirror stayed blank for a minute, next to his own image. Then the mirror filled in next to that, took imprint. A face climbed up on it from the rear, that on the mirror-surface meant from below his own; steadied when it had gained the level of his own, stood still.

A tortured, beaten hat was down low over it, but not low enough to hide it. It was the face of a man about forty-five, but it had leaped ahead twenty years—perhaps in this one night?—to meet its own old age. Only the hair-coloring, the line of the neck, a few things like that, told that its owner was still young in years, that it, too, should have been still young. It was haggard and white with strain, silver in its whiteness where the electric light seeped in under the hat-brim and caught it.

There was something wrong with him. Quinn could tell that at a glance; anyone could have.

He didn't stand there upright against the bar. He crouched protectively against the wall, almost seeming to hug his whole right side to it, as if sheltering it, screening it from observation, there where the wall came across, ending the bar. It wasn't the inert lean of intoxication, it was the furtive, concealing lean of one seeking protection; very subtly expressed, but yet implicit in every line of his body. Even when he raised his hand, as now, and drank, he turned a little away, toward the wall. Very little, the slightness was one of attitude rather than of actual physical measurement, but he turned a little away, in mental hiding.

I've got him, Quinn said to himself. And this time it's something bad, no kid being born to a frightened father.

He drank again, and again he crouched a little like that, cowered. Only the left hand always came up; never the right was seen. The right was a secret between his guardian body and the wall.

The gun, Quinn wondered?

What did he see in his beer, dreaming into it like that? The ghost of a dead man, maybe? Was that why he couldn't take his eyes off it, his staring haunted eyes?

I'll try out his reaction, Quinn decided. I know already, but I'll give it the fifth hieroglyph.

He took his mug with him and ambled over and pretended to fool around with a cigarette-vending machine they had standing there. That way he had them all well out in front of him, in a straight line. He set the mug precariously down atop the machine, and then unnoticed gave it a little nudge off into space. It gave a shattering whack on the floor. Not terrifying, just, say, mildly startling. Eight heads turned and glanced casually around, then turned back again and went ahead with their own concerns.

But the ninth. His shoulder-blades had contracted into a vise, pinching his back together. His head had gone sharply down, as if to avoid a blow at the back of his neck. He didn't turn to look, he couldn't; shock held him in a strait jacket for a moment. And then as it slowly eased, Quinn could see his sides swelling in and out with his enforced breathing. And when he raised his hand a moment later its outline was all blurry even to Quinn's steady eye, it vibrated so.

Reaction: positive. Positive as to guilt. What else but guilt could make anyone cringe so, cower and quail into a lumpy bunched-up mass the way he just had? And, Quinn reminded himself, there might even have been more glaring symptoms he had missed seeing. If that bedded right hand, for instance, had half started out of the pocket that encased it, gun-laden, and then checked itself again, that was a give-away known only to the wall that faced it. Quinn had muffed it. And by the time he looked to see, he was too late, it was motionless again.

He drifted back once more to where he'd been, idly kicking aside a scallop or two of glass on the way.

But now awareness was ablaze between them, and a delicate duel of seeming non-awareness that fastened on every slightest move got under way.

The hat brim was down. Far down. But the sheathed sick-bright eyes under it, Quinn knew, were not looking at the counter-top they seemed to be directed at. Any more than his own, sighted forward toward the mirror, were merely concerned with the impersonal surface of the glass. It was as though each had unseen antennae, sensitively attuned to the other.

He senses something now, Quinn told himself. Not because of anything I've done; it's my very motionlessness, my non-awareness of him, that has tipped him off. I'm standing too still, for too long; I'm looking too straight ahead. He's on. I've got him afraid of me.

An invisible charged current was boiling from one to the other of them, and back again, recharged, and back once more, again recharged. Give and take of tension.

Lower and lower went the hat brim, defensively. Not a move otherwise. And blanker and blanker became Quinn's stare into the mirror, never diverging, never sidling over into forbidden surface offside. Until each of them could scarcely breathe.

And all around them the others drank and chatted, grinned and sometimes spat, all unaware. The two of them were like a still-life picture of two men at a bar, set down in the middle of a restless, murmuring real-life barroom scene, they were so different from the others. With their distance between them, of three or four paces. They were like inanimate markers, leaning against the bar.

There was no warning. Suddenly the glass showed blank beside Quinn. It was almost like a Faustian disappearance, only minus the puff of smoke. So much so that Quinn turned his head entirely the wrong way, to where the other had been standing first, and then continued it on around behind himself in a complete baffled half-circle, his body following, until at last he was facing toward the door, having reached it the long way around.

The other was just scuttling through it. Was a blur wiped off the glass as with a wet sponge, he floundered out so fast.

Quinn hadn't expected flight to be so overt, so unabashed. He'd expected, if anything, sidling dissimulation, gingerly-treading departure. This was open flight, before any hue and cry had even been raised. This was the whole scroll of guilt-hieroglyphs flung back in his face. *I'm guilty; I know it, so what need to wait for you to discover it? I fly from my own knowledge.*

He gave a choked cry of excitement and buckled after him, his mid-section lunging out ahead of the rest of him for a moment, before his arms and legs could take up their part.

He heard a muffled shout from the barman and he pulled something out of his pocket. Some sort of a coin, he didn't care what it was, and flung it up over his shoulder in a spiral. He was outside before it had even had time to hit the floor.

He was already in crazed flight down the street, the other one. Maddened was the only fit description for it. No one runs that fast unless he's touched with an insanity of fear. And yet he ran keeping that gun-bearing arm hugged close to him, still berthed in his pocket. It threw his balance off a little, gave the straight line of his running a slight sideward tilt.

He floundered around a corner and was gone. Quinn skittered around it after him and he was there again, distance between unchanged. He crossed over to the darker side of the street, the shadows had him, and he was gone again. Quinn crossed over after him, fusing into his very footprints before they'd had time to cool, and he was there again.

So they played hide and seek through the darkness, and the game had no laughter or mercy in it. He'll shoot, thought Quinn. I'd better look out, he'll shoot. But he kept on. Not through bravery; just through heat of the chase melting down all other fears.

He rounded another corner, the form ahead. Quinn rounded it after him, jerked him back into sight again. This time the distance between was less, was beginning to pull tighter. To run you need not only legs, you need the freedom of both arms, to buffet you through the air.

He was beginning to lose his head, the pursued. Around another corner, and gone. But then when Quinn rounded it, still gone this time. Yet when Quinn had already lost him, he gave himself back to Quinn again, out of his own fear. He flurried out of a doorway, that would have kept his secret for him if he'd only let it, as though mistrusting it at the penultimate moment, and the chase was on again. In reverse direction now, after Quinn had already overshot it. Fear rots the faculties.

And meantime, no one to stop them, no one to interfere. Why doesn't he cry for help then, if he's innocent, Quinn gloated? Why doesn't he?

He fled on before him in desperate, staggering silence, mute to the last.

It was nearly over now; Quinn was young, Quinn had purpose, he could have kept running straight through the night, straight through the city. The figure ahead stayed in sight full-time now, the corners couldn't save him, the doorways couldn't save him any more; they didn't come quick enough.

The pounding of his footfalls grew diffuse as they slowed, they burned themselves out to a standstill, and he leaned there, crushed for air. Sort of at bay against a wall. In a minute Quinn was up to him, then circled out a little, still afraid of that eloquently restrained arm, and came in on him from the outside instead of straight forward. Thus, too, whichever way he jumped, Quinn could jump with him.

He didn't jump, he couldn't.

His voice was a husky whisper, sand shaken through a sieve,

for lack of wind. "What is it? What do you—? Don't come any nearer."

Quinn's was sibilant with breathlessness too but gritty with purpose that nothing could have deflected, not six cartridges fired in a row. "I'm coming nearer. I'm coming right up to you."

He closed in and their faces were almost touching, breathing hot at one another. Both afraid, but one more afraid than the other. And the lesser fear was Quinn's. It was just a fear of being shot unexpectedly. But the other man was almost undone with his. He was palpitating with it. Like some sort of stuff pouring sluggishly down the side of the building he was backed against. Tar or thick paint. His mouth was open and some kind of wet stuff came out of the corner of it, in a funny long thread. Then broke off short, as though a scissors had snipped it.

The left hand moved before Quinn could check it. The left, not the right. If it had been a gun, it would have been too late. But it wasn't.

"Here. Is this what you want? Take it and let me alone." He kept pressing it on him.

"Take it. Take it. I won't holler. I won't—"

The wallet fell, and Quinn scuffed it offside with his foot. "Why'd you run?"

"What're you following me for? What are you trying to do to me? I can't stand it. Ain't I scared enough? I'm scared of the dark and scared of the lights, I'm scared of sounds and scared of stillness. I'm scared of the very air around me. Let me alone—" He screamed it out at him. Or past his shoulder, into the unheeding night.

"Pull yourself together, mister. What're you so scared of? Is it because you've killed someone? Is that it? Answer me. You've killed someone, haven't you?"

His head went down as though his neck were a matchstick that someone had broken in two.

"Plenty. Twenty. I don't know how many— I've tried to count them but I never can—"

"And tonight, one was—?"

He was crying like a baby. Quinn had never seen anything like it. "Let me go now. Don't make me stand here and face them— For the love of Christ, let me go—"

"What've you got there, a gun?"

He made a sudden brutal clutch at the inert right arm.

His fingers spiked into it too deep, to the very center bone, as though—as though there were nothing there to stop them. The whole arm leaped lifelessly up out of the pocket, but of his clutch, not of its own act. A roll of wadded newspaper dropped out of the empty sleeve. The sleeve hung there collapsed, flat as a board up to the shoulder.

"Yes, I did have a gun," he said in an oddly child-like voice. "They took it away from me. After it had done its work. And when I gave it back, I must have forgot to take my hand out of it. I've missed it ever since; every time I look, it isn't there any more. All the way up to here—"

The shock had needled Quinn straight through the heart. He was young and the puncture closed right up again. But for a minute it was enough to have dropped him in his tracks.

"I'm sorry, mister," was all he could choke out, and turn his head compassionately away. "What can I say?"

"Let me go now," he said, with a sort of docile mournfulness, like a small child helpless in the face of forces it can't understand or combat.

"This killing," Quinn said. "When was it? When did it happen?"

"In Spain, two years ago. Or was it just a few minutes ago, back there around that last corner? I can't tell for sure any more. The shells keep going off so bright and stunning me so."

Quinn picked up his battered hat from the street and brushed it for him, pityingly, tenderly, with lingering slowness. Over, and over, and slowly over again. There was no other way he could show him—

THE BRIEF shot of novocain that the easing of Helen Kirsch's predicament had vicariously given her wore off and the dull throb of her own dilemma came back again, twice as sore as before. The red back-light of the homeward-bound transgressor's cab petered out, and she was alone again. Out and around on her own again. With forty, maybe fifty good minutes smashed up, and as far from successful fulfilment as ever.

She was on East Seventieth Street already—bravura East Seventieth Street of the two revolver-shots in one night, one harmless, one murderous—so all she had to do to return to the Graves house was start walking slowly west along it. That was where she'd have to go now. She'd have to start out all over again, she had to start out from some place, and that was the logical jumping-off place for any new expedition.

She had the second key on her, the one they'd removed from Graves' person, so she knew she wouldn't have any difficulty in getting in again. She wasn't sure just what she could hope to gain by going in again; she was sure it would be taking a darned big chance. But there wasn't anything else she could do, now that her last lead had evaporated the way it had. Over and above all this, she was being drawn implacably nearer by the sort of irresistible fascination the scene of his crime is said to hold for the criminal. It was as though she were the murderer herself, the way she was being pulled back there.

She knew what it was; she wanted to see, she had to see, whether it had been discovered yet, whether there were any signs of police activity, any lights, anything to show that the secret reposing in it was no longer exclusively their own.

So she came back slowly, cautiously, not like anyone working against a time-limit, across Lexington, across Park. Nearer, ever nearer. From the middle of the Park-Madison block she could already see into the block ahead; see into it well enough to discern that it was still empty, still quiet, that outwardly at least everything was still under control. No cars drawn up anywhere around or near that doorway, no motionless figure of a cop posted outside it, no one coming in or going out. Above all, no light showing from any of the front windows. And window-lights can be seen far at night, particularly along such a lightless stretch as this was.

Or was this just bait? Was there some sort of trap down there waiting to be sprung? Oh, not a police-trap, not a trap set by men. They couldn't know she was coming back like this at just such and such a moment, or coming back at all. The other kind of trap, set by the real enemy. The city.

She'd reached Madison now. She looked over at the diagonally opposite corner from which she'd started. She'd made a complete circle, and here she was back again—empty-handed. The cab was gone, the one that had led her to Helen Kirsch and on a fool's errand.

A compact little aluminum-bodied milk-truck went

skimming by, one of the new kind they were beginning to use within the last year or so. As noiseless and as agile as one of those early electric cabriolets. The milk already. Daybreak was nearly here.

She crossed Madison and went on. It came nearer.

She'd never forget it, the face of that house. It was beginning to haunt her.

She'd see it a long time from now, a long way from here. Even if they tore it down, and the site was vacant and it was gone, she'd still go on seeing it. She'd still be outside it like this, some night in a dream. It would leap upright in her mind, and be intact again, be whole again, just the way it was tonight. And—if she was lucky—she'd wake up just as she was about to go in.

It already seemed like long ago that she had paced slowly back and forth, on the other side, in front of it, and he had been inside, putting back the money. It couldn't be this one same night, no night could last that long. But gee, how she wished she could go back to *then*, instead of it being now. For, as painful as it had been while that was going on, as frightened as she'd been then, as scared that he'd be caught, at least they hadn't known about it yet, they hadn't known what was waiting there inside for them.

She sighed. Her favorite dance-hall aphorism came back to her: what was the good of wishing?

She wondered where he was, how he was making out. I hope he's having better luck than I just had, she thought. She hoped he was all right, wasn't in any jam. Jam was good; what jam could be any worse than the one he was in, they were both in, already?

She was disgusted with herself. Aw, you with your hoping

and your wishing. Why don't you get a turkey wishbone and go up to the first cop you see and offer to pull it against him, and be done with it?

She came to a halt. It was directly opposite now. Funny, she thought, how a house with violent death in it doesn't look any different from any other sort of a house, when you're standing outside. It's only what you *know* that makes the difference.

She was going in. She felt it coming on before the first move had even been made. She didn't know why, she didn't know what good it would do; but then what good would it do to stand here at a loss on the street outside, staring over at it?

At least she made the brave approach. No slinking over, no sidling up. She cut straight over to it, razor-straight, and went up the stoop-steps. The other way was the more dangerous of the two, the more likely to arouse suspicion if caught sight of by some wandering eye.

The swinging storm-doors fluttered shut behind her, and the stuffy little cubicle of the vestibule—more like an upright coffin than ever—was around her once again. Most of her courage, or impetus, if that was what it was, seemed to have stayed outside, suddenly.

She'd gone in with him, the last time. It was more frightening going in alone. Suppose someone was lurking in it? Not the police or anyone legitimate like that, but someone whose presence couldn't be guessed at from out here, someone who wouldn't want the lights on or their intrusion made known any more than he and she did. Someone you wouldn't know about until it was too late.

She went ahead. What else was there to do? Backing out wouldn't have solved anything.

She put the key to the door. The dead man's key it was, too. She remembered how his hand had shaken when he did it, the time before. He ought to see hers now, he'd know what some real shaking was. Her forearm was practically bouncing around in its elbow-socket. And what a racket! To her own ears, at any rate, it sounded like tin cans jangling. She might as well have rung the doorbell and be done with it, the way she was telegraphing her arrival.

Aw, what was the difference, there was no one in there anyway. You hope, she amended in a minor key.

It opened. Silence.

She knew her way a little better now, from being in the time before. You just went straight, and then you hit the stairs. She closed the door behind her first of all, and then she started out. She had that slightly precarious feeling, as of being on a tight-rope, that moving ahead in complete darkness always gives, even when the sense of direction is fairly sure.

That smell of leather and of woodwork again.

How still it was. How *could* a house be this still? It was almost as if it were overdoing it, for treacherous purposes of its own.

She thought, Let's see if my valise is still where I left it, against the wall.

That ought to be sort of a clue as to whether anyone's been in here or not.

She knew which side she'd left it on, but naturally not just how far in away from the door. She turned and cut over to it. She found the wall, and felt down it with her palms. She got all the way to the bottom, to the baseboard, without anything impeding her.

Nope, not here. A little further on yet.

She moved out away from the wall a trifle, and went on again. She took about four more paces forward and closed in again and tried it there. This must be it, about here. It couldn't be any further in than this. She must be nearly all the way to the foot of the stairs by now.

Her hands came out again, palms front, to find the wall and pat themselves down it to about the level where the valise should—

The wall had changed.

It wasn't cool and smooth plaster any more, it wasn't flat. Her hand went into something yielding. Yielding up to a point only; that gave a little but then held finally of its own inner bulk. Something rough, and yet soft. Fuzzy, bristly. Nap. Nap of a coat. A coat, with a body behind it. A coat with somebody in it.

There was somebody standing there, flat against the wall. Pressed back against it, trying to escape discovery. And she'd stopped right in front of it, of him, and like someone in a ghastly game of blindman's buff—only this game was for keeps—had exploringly palmed her hands against him.

She could hear the sharp inhalation of breath coming from it, that wasn't her own, at moment of contact. Her own had stopped entirely.

There was someone right there in front of her, someone *alive*, but standing deathly still, pinned there by her discovery of him.

The darkness eddied violently all around her; it loomed up to a crest, like an obliterating wave about to break and dash all over her. It was like being in the surf; a bad surf of terror of the senses. She started to go over backwards, drowned into senselessness in the middle of it. A little moaning cry drifted from her, something not intended to be uttered at all.

"Quinn, help me—"

An arm lashed out about the curve of her waist; her awareness was too blurred for a minute to tell whether it was in succor or in seizure. It held her afloat, up out of insensibility.

Quinn's voice said, "Bricky! Hold it, Bricky!"

She went forward again, her head toppled inertly against his shoulder. She leaned there against him and couldn't talk for a minute.

"My God," he said, "I didn't know it was you. I've been standing here paralyzed, afraid to—"

She could still only pant, even after a moment or two. "If that doesn't kill me, nothing ever will."

He led her away from the wall in the darkness, both arms about her in a sort of barrel-staff hold. "Come over here and sit down on the stairs a minute, they're right over here—"

"No, I'm all right now. Let's go up, so we can put on a little light, get rid of this blame darkness. That's what did it, mostly."

They went up the stairs. It was all right now that she had him with her, she wasn't frightened any more.

"Funny we should both come back here like this, almost together. No luck either, hunh?" she surmised.

"Washed up. I came back to get a second start."

"That's what I was out for too."

They didn't ask each other about their experiences. They hadn't paid off, so there was no profit in repeating them. There was no time, either; that was the main thing.

When the lights went on, they scarcely glanced at the form on the floor, either one of them. They had gotten so far past that point now. Just a glimpse out of the corners of their eyes, of something black with a white shirtfront, was enough, so long as it showed them it was still there. She thought, How quickly you get used to the presence of death in a room. That's why those people who sit up with them all night never turn a hair. She'd never been able to understand their ability to do that until now.

It was the first one she'd ever seen, and yet all the awe had already worn off. She already found herself moving about the room and unconcernedly deviating a little from that particular place each time, no more. As one would to avoid treading on a sleeping dog or cat.

They were at a loss. They'd hit rock-bottom. They were blocked. They could read the knowledge in one another's eyes as they looked at one another, but they tried to keep from saying it, from admitting it aloud. His evasion took the form of moving restlessly about, as though he were accomplishing something, when they both knew he wasn't. He went to the bedroom-entrance, put on the light in there, stood looking about, as though desperately trying to discern something that was not there to be discerned. Then he came out again, went to the bathroom-entry, lighted that up, did the same thing there.

It was no use. It was hopeless, and they both knew it. They'd squeezed the last drop of muted testimony out of this place that there was to be had from it. They'd squeezed it dry.

Her sense of frustration took a more passive form. She stood still. It revealed itself only in the fingers of her hand, resting on the back of one of the chairs; those kept rippling like the fingers of a typist upon an unseen typewriter.

Suddenly something happened to the silence. It was gone, and they hadn't done it.

"*What's that?*"

Fright was like an icy gush of water flooding over them, as from some burst pipe or water-main; like a numbing tide rapidly welling up over them from below, in some confined place from which there was no escape. They were like two small things—two mice—trapped in an inundated cellar, and carried around and around, still alive but helplessly swirling, on the surface of the whirlpool before they finally went under.

Fright was the muted pealing of a bell. A tiny, softened *t-t-t-ting, t-t-t-ting*, over and over. Somewhere unseen around them, hidden, but pertinent to them, having to do with them, having to do with this place they were in.

After the first needle-like shock, they were motionless, only their eyes tracing it in frightened flight, now to this side, now to that, each time too late. It was like a wasp, buzzing elusively around their heads, while they held still, trying to identify it, trying to orient it, to isolate it. It was everywhere, it was nowhere. *T-t-t-ting, t-t-t-tling*, soft, velvety, but unending.

"What is it, a burglar-alarm?" she breathed. "Have we touched something we shouldn't—?"

"It's from over here—the bedroom. There must be an alarm-clock in there—"

They shot for the entrance, mice coursing on the tide of fright. There was a small folding-clock on the dresser. He picked it up, pummelled the top of it, held it to his ear.

T-t-t-ting, t-t-t-ting— It was no nearer than before, it was everywhere at once, a ghost-trilling.

He put it down, ran back again the other way. She after him. "The doorbell, maybe. Oh God, what'll we do?" She shuddered. He ran down a few steps, stopped on the stairs, listening.

"No. It's coming from two places at once. It's coming from down there, but it's also coming from up here behind us—"

She stopped him. "It's no good, it's dark down there, you'd never find it. Come back, we'll try up here again—"

They ran back into the bedroom again, the drowning mice.

"Let's try closing the door," she said. "That may tell us which room—"

She swung the door to. They listened. It went on undiminished, unaltered, unaffected by the closing-off.

"It's right here in this bedroom with us, we know that much now— Oh, if it would only *stop* a minute, give us a chance to collect our faculties—"

He'd dropped to the floor on hands and knees, was padding lumberingly this way and that, animal-like.

"Wait a minute, there's a box under there! Against the wall, under the bed, painted white—I can see it. Telephone-extension. But where's the arm itself—?"

He jumped up, ran over to the head of the bed, shunted it slightly out away from the wall. Then his arm reached around and behind it, at about mattress-level, and brought out the instrument.

"It was hooked on behind there, so he could reach it from his pillow without getting up."

It was still unrecognizable.

"One of these muted bells, so it wouldn't ring too hard in his ears. Must be another one downstairs, and this is an extension here, that's what sent the sound all over the place, got us so rattled."

It was still keeping up, right in his hands while he spoke. Plaintively, untiringly. *T-t-t-ting, t-t-t-ting—*

He looked at her helplessly. "What'll I do?"

T-t-t-ting, t-t-t-tling— It was like a goad, it would never stop.

"Somebody that doesn't know, trying to get him. Trying hard, too. I'm going to take a chance and answer."

Her hand flashed out to his wrist, tightened around it, ice-cold. "Look out! You're liable to bring the police down on us! They'll know it's not his voice."

"Maybe I can get away with it. Maybe if I talk low, indistinct, they won't know the difference; I can pretend I'm he. It's our only chance. We may find out something—even if it's only a stray word or two more than we already know, we'll be that much to the good. Stand close by me. Pray for all you're worth. Here I go."

He lifted the finger which had been holding the denuded hook down, and the thing was open.

He brought it up to his ear as gingerly as if it were charged with high-voltage electricity.

"Hello," he said with purring indistinctness. She could barely hear it herself, he swallowed so much of it.

Her heart was pounding. Their heads were close together, blended ear to ear, listening, listening to this call in the night.

"Darling," a voice said, "this is Barbara."

She glanced over at the photograph on the dresser. Barbara, the girl in the silver frame. My God, she thought strickenly. You can fool anyone but a man's best girl. She knows him too well. We'll never—

His face was white with strain, and she could almost feel a pulse in his temple throbbing against hers.

"Steve, darling, did I leave my gold compact with you? I couldn't find it when I got back, and I'm worried about it. Look and see if you've got it. You may have slipped it in your pocket for me."

"Your compact?" he said blurredly. "Wait a minute." He covered up the receiver momentarily.

"What'll I do? What'll I say?"

Bricky wrenched herself away from him suddenly. She ran into the other room. Then she came back again. She was holding something up in her hand to show him, something that caught the light burnishedly and flashed.

"Tell her yes, and go ahead. Keep your voice low. Keep it low. It's going good so far. She didn't really want that, that isn't why she called him up. If you watch your step, you may be able to find out something."

She crouched against him again, ear to the receiver. He took his muffling hand off the mouthpiece.

"Yes," he whispered. "I have it here."

"I couldn't sleep. That was why I really called you. It wasn't the compact." He shot Bricky a look, meaning "You were right."

That voice was waiting; it was his turn to say something. Bricky's elbow kicked into his side urgently.

"I couldn't either."

"If we were married, that would make it so much simpler, wouldn't it? Then you would have just dumped it out of your pocket onto our own dressing-table in our own bedroom."

Bricky dropped her eyes for a moment and winced. Proposing to a corpse, she thought.

"We've never parted angry like this before."

"I'm sorry," he said half under his breath.

"Maybe if we hadn't gone there, to that Perroquet place, it wouldn't have happened."

"No," he agreed submissively.

"Who was she?"

This time he didn't say anything.

The voice was forbearing with what it took to be his stubbornness. "Who was she, Steve? The tall redhead in the light-green dress."

"I don't know." He gave it because it was the only answer he could give; it turned out to be the appropriate one.

"You told me that before. That was what started it the first time. If you don't know who she was, then why did she force herself in between us like that on the conga-line?"

He didn't answer, couldn't.

"Then why did she slip a note into your hand?" The voice took his silence for continued denial. "I saw her do it. I saw her with my own eyes."

They were both listening intently.

"And after we went back to our table, why did you nod to her, all the way across the room? Yes, I saw that too. I saw it in my compact-mirror, when I didn't seem to be looking. As if to say, 'I've read your message; I'll do what you say.'"

There was a pause to give him a chance to say something; he couldn't use it. "Steve, I've dropped my pride to call you up like this; won't you meet me halfway?"

She waited for him to say something. He didn't.

"Why, your whole mood changed from that point on. It was as though you couldn't wait to see me to my door and get me off your hands. I cried, Steve. I cried when you left. I've been crying from then until now, through half the night. Steve. Steve, are you listening to me? Are you there?"

"Yes."

"You sound so far-away, so— Is it the telephone or is it you?"

"Poor connection, I guess," he said, close-mouthed.

"But Steve, you sound so—so cagey, as though you were

afraid to talk to me. I know it's silly, but I have the most curious impression that you're not alone. There's the oddest wait before everything you say, almost as though someone were there right beside you giving you stage-directions."

"No," he whispered deprecatingly.

"Stephen, can't you talk louder? You're whispering, almost as though you were afraid of waking someone. And if you're awake yourself, who else is there in the house to be afraid of waking?"

The dead, thought Bricky, with an inward grimace.

He clapped his hand to it. "She's beginning to tumble. What am I going to do?"

She sensed that he was about to hang up in sheer desperation, as the quickest way out. "Don't. Don't do that, whatever you do. Then you *will* give yourself away."

He went back to it again. "Stephen, I don't like the way you're acting. Just what is going on up there? This *is* Stephen, isn't it?"

He muffled it again. "She's catching on. I'm sunk."

"Wait a minute, don't lose your head. I'll get you out of it. Turn it my way a little."

Suddenly she spoke out, full voice, in a maudlin, drunken singsong aimed straight for the telephone-mouth.

"Sugar, come *awn*. I'm getting tired waiting. I want another drink. How much longer you gonna stand there talking?"

There was a flash of shock at the other end, that was almost like a molecular explosion; without sound or substance to it, yet he could almost feel the concussion of it whirling through the wire toward him, it was so intense. And then the voice withdrew. Not in physical distance but through strata of pain. Withdrew to a remoteness that could never be bridged again.

When it sounded again, there was no indignation. There was nothing. Not even acute coldness, which is an inverse form of heat after all. There was only classic, neutral politeness.

The voice said just two things more. "Oh, I'm sorry, Stephen." And breathed once or twice in agony between. "Forgive me, I didn't know."

There was a click, and silence.

"That was a lady," Bricky apotheosized her ruefully when he'd hung up in turn. "A lady through and through."

He drew the back of his hand across his mouth remorsefully. "Gee, that was cruel. I wish we hadn't had to do that. She was engaged to him after all—whoever she is." Then he looked at her curiously. "How were you so certain that would do the trick?"

"I'm a girl myself, after all," she said wistfully. "We all work on the same strings."

They thought about her for a moment longer, both turning to look at her, over there in her silver frame. "She won't sleep tonight," he murmured. "We've given her a busted heart."

"She had to have one, one way or the other. The funny part of it is, though, she'll suffer more this way than she would if she'd found out he was dead. Don't ask me why."

They left her, then, and returned to their own concerns.

"Well, we know a little more than we did before," he said. "We've filled in another little chunk of missing time. They went to the show at the Winter Garden, *Hellzapoppin*, first, and then they went to this place where they had the trouble. The Piro—what'd she say it was?"

"The Perroquet." She had the night-life of this city that she hated at the tips of her fingers at all times. "I know where that is, on Fifty-fourth Street."

"But that still don't bring it up to the point where he came back here and it happened. There's still a chunk out, between the time he left her at her door and—"

She was thinking about it.

"There's something right there. And something big. The biggest thing we've had so far all night. He *must* have gotten a note, there must have been one." She went over closer to the picture. "This doesn't look like the face of a girl who would make up a thing like that, out of her own jealous mind. Take a look at her. She's too pretty and too sure of herself to think up things to worry about. If she says she saw it, she saw it, you can bet on that. There *was* a note. The thing is, what became of it? If we only knew what he did with it."

"Tore it up into a million little pieces, I guess."

"No, because if he did that while he was still with her, that would have been admitting he *had* gotten one after all, and he didn't want her to know it. And then once he'd left her, there was no longer any reason to tear it up, she wasn't around to claim it any more. He could leave it whole, the way it was. And most likely he did. What I'd like to know is, where did he have it hidden while he was still sitting with her in the club? He had it on him *somewhere.*"

"We've turned out all his pockets and it's not in any of them—"

She tapped the curve of her underlip thoughtfully. "Let's go at it this way. Quinn, you're a man. I imagine you'd all act pretty much the same in a given situation. You're in a night-club entertaining the girl you're engaged to, and you've just been handed a note by a stranger, a note you didn't want her to see. What would you be likely to do with it, where would you be likely to put it? Answer quick now, without taking too long to think it out. If you start thinking about it, that'll make it artificial."

"I'd roll it up in a little pill and pitch it."

"No. You're on a conga-line when it's first slipped to you, there isn't any chance for you to do that. If you take your hand off your partner's waist you're likely to go out of step and disorganize the line."

"Well, I could drop it straight down the floor under me, without hardly moving my hand at all; just let it fall."

"No again. That way it would be carried backward along the floor, under the line, and all your fiancée would have to do when she came up to that point would be to reach down for it herself. The main thing is, she didn't see him do either of those things, and she was watching him from two positions away down the line—which is close enough to be accurate. He got it and then it disappeared, not another sign of it, either being thrown or being pocketed."

"Then he must have kept it folded flat on the inside of his hand."

"Exactly. Now here's what I'm trying to get at by testing you. The line breaks up and he takes her back to their table. That's when he stuffed it away some place, as soon as he had the table between them to cover him. Now try again. You're sitting at the table with her, and she's already starting to throw the incident up to you, so you can't just be passive about it and let it ride. You're covered up to here—" She drew a line across him just above the belt. "It's in your hand yet, from the conga-line, and you've got to get it out of your hand fast. You can't use your upper pockets, nor your wallet, nor your cigarette-case, because she'll see all that, that's above the water-line."

"I'd throw it away *under* the table—"

"Never. One reading isn't enough, especially on a conga-chain while you're kicking out with both feet. You want to look at it again, to study it or decide what to do as soon as you're alone and you safely can. He became uneasy from then on, she said to you just now. Showing that the note gave him a problem, he had to make a decision. That kind of a thing's never thrown away after one quick glimpse. It was unfinished business. He kept it. But *where?*"

"Maybe he slipped it *under* the table-cloth, on his side."

For a minute she stopped, startled. Then she said finally, "No-o. No, I don't think he did that. That would still mean leaving it behind, when they got up to go. It would also mean some stranger would eventually get hold of it. He'd be less likely to do that than even to just throw it away. And I don't think he *could* do that without her noticing the rippling of the cloth his hand would make. Remember, he's trying to quiet down a girl who's mad and has a right to be, a girl sitting squarely opposite to him, and they have six eyes and about a dozen extra senses."

He was trying, but he wasn't shining much. "Gee, I dunno—I've about run out of places. I'd *sit* on it, maybe, while I was still in the chair, but then as soon as I got up I'd be worse off than before."

"Never mind, Quinn." She shook her head dispiritedly. "You'll make some woman an honest husband. You're certainly no good for intrigue."

"Well, I never *had* a note handed to me in a night-club by somebody, right while I was with somebody else," he mumbled apologetically.

"I'm willing to take your word for *that*," she assented drily.

They went inside again. She stood, looked down at *it*. All night long, it seemed to her, that was all they'd been doing, standing by it, looking down at it.

"Try that little watch-pocket or whatever you call it, just under the belt in front. Did we turn that one out before? I can't remember."

He crouched, hooked his thumb to it, drew it out again. "Empty."

"What are they for, anyway?" she asked dully. Then before he could answer, "Never mind. This is no time to be learning the ins and outs of the men's tailoring business."

He stayed down like that, at the crouch, dribbling his fingers undecidedly against his own kneecap.

"Quinn, could I ask you to— Would you mind turning him a minute?" she said hesitantly.

"The other way? Do you think we ought to disturb—?"

"We've done so much already, emptying the pockets and all, that I don't see that it matters."

He turned the form over, face down, as gently as he could. A slight, involuntary twinge of distaste struck through them both, quickly quelled.

"What'd you want that for?" he asked, ridging his forehead at her.

"I don't know myself," she said lamely.

He stood up again. They looked at one another uncertainly; at a loss, not knowing what to do next.

"It's not on him, that's a cinch. He may have put it some-where around the place here, after he got back. The desk—we haven't looked that over yet."

"That's going to be an all-night job," she said, going over to it. "Look at the way it's crammed with stuff. I tell you what; you go inside and take a look through the bureau-drawers, I'll give this a quick going-over."

Tick-tock, tick-tock, tick-tock— In the silence of their preoccu-pation with their separate tasks it sounded twice as loud.

"Quinn!" she called suddenly. He came in on the fly.

"You mean it was in there? You came across it that quick?" She was standing, however, with her back to the desk.

"No. Quinn, he was very well-dressed. I just happened to turn and something caught my eye. He has a hole in the heel of one sock, it's showing just above the shoe. That doesn't go with the way he's turned out. The left one, Quinn." He was already over by it.

The shoe dropped off with a light thud. The "hole" had vanished with it. "The note," he said.

He was already smoothing and starting to read the crum-pled little slip of paper by the time she got over to him. They read it together the rest of the way. It was hastily scrawled in pencil, on some impromptu edge that didn't take pressure very evenly; the sort of a note written where there were no writing facilities readily available.

"Mr. Graves, I understand? I would like to speak to you in private, at your home, after you have taken the young lady home. And I don't mean some other time, I mean right to-night. You don't know me, but I feel like a member of the family already. I wouldn't want to be disappointed and not find you there."

Unsigned.

She was hectically elated. "She did, see? She did! She did come up here. She was the woman of the matches—we were right about it. I forget which one of us it was—"

He was less positive, for some reason. "But the mere fact that he received the note and tucked it in his shoe doesn't prove she actually did show up here."

"She was here, you can count on that."

"How do we know?"

"Listen, anyone that would go this far would go the rest of the way, don't kid yourself. This was no shrinking violet. A girl or woman that would scribble out such a defiant note, and strong-arm her way onto a conga-line, and smuggle it into the hand of a prominent well-to-do man like Stephen Graves, without even knowing him, mind you, and under the very nose of the girl he was engaged to marry, wouldn't let anything stop her from coming around here and calling on him, once she'd made up her mind to it! Get this: 'And I don't mean some other time, I mean right tonight.' That dame was *here*, you can bet your bottom dollar!"

Then she added, "And if the character-reading approach doesn't cinch it for you, give it the blindfold-test. That ought to do it."

"What do you mean?"

"She goes with the kind of perfume that the match-folder gave off, and that I guessed at in the air of the room here when we came in the first time. The kind of a dame who would write a note like this is also the kind of a dame whose handbag would reek like that. She was *here*," she said again.

"It still doesn't follow from that, that she shot him. She might have been here all right, and left, and then this cigar-mangling guy came in after she was already gone."

"I don't know anything about him. I do know there's plenty of shooting-material right here in this note, even before she got to the point of personal contact with him."

"There is kind of a threat in it," he admitted.

"*A* threat? The whole thing is threat, from the first word to the last. 'Mr. Graves, I understand?' 'I wouldn't want to be disappointed and not find you.' What else would you call that?"

He was reading it over again. "It's some kind of a shake, don't you think?"

"Sure it's a shake. A threat almost always spells a money-squeeze, and particularly when it's from a woman to a man."

"'I feel like a member of the family already.' What does she mean by that? He was engaged to this Barbara. It makes it look like it's someone he got tangled up with before then, and when she heard about him becoming engaged— All except for one thing—"

"Yeah, I thought of that too, when I first read it. All except for that one thing, as you say."

"'You don't know me.' So how can a guy get tangled up with someone, and still not know her? Unless maybe she's fronting for some other dame, making the approach. She's the, how would you call it—middleman? Maybe a sister, or someone like that."

She lopped that off short. "Nuh, never. That's one thing, if you knew more about women— You'll never find a woman using another woman for go-between, in a squeeze-play stemming from heart-interest stuff. Don't ask me why, but that's the hard-and-fast of it. A man might, in business or some kind of crookedness. But never a woman, in anything of this kind. She either does the dirty work herself, or it doesn't get done."

"Then he wasn't tangled with her. And yet she had something on him."

"And he knew she had something on him, or at least had a hunch she did.

The way he acted after getting the note shows that. He met the writer of it part of the way, on her own ground. Look, see what I mean? Barbara was jealous of another kind of a note, which she thought this was. Of a friendly, a too-friendly note, from somebody that he knew, that he was flirting with behind her back. All he had to do to calm her down was show her this, show her what kind of a note it really was. But he'd rather keep it to himself, even at the cost of letting her work herself up and of parting from her on bad terms. Why shouldn't he want to show it to her? Or better still, why didn't he get up from the table then and there, go over and accost the woman before she left the place. 'What d'you mean by this? Who are you? What're you driving at?' Force the thing out into the open." She shook her head. "He had more than a slight suspicion that there was something behind it that needed to be handled with kid gloves, and you can't tell me different. That she had at least part of a leg to stand on, if not the whole two; that there was fire *somewhere* behind the smoke. He played it her way, soft-pedalled it. And why should he have to? People don't do that. Would *you*—?" Then she quickly cancelled that out. "Oh, never mind you; you're no good at that stuff, anyway. I forgot that, from before."

He had been prepared to look flattered for a moment; he let the look slip off again.

"In other words," she went ahead, "it rang the bell somewhere or other, deep inside him, when he got it. It wasn't just a bluff, out of thin air."

She was starting to get herself together, as if ready to go out again. "All that's neither here nor there. The main thing is, we've got her now. I'm almost sure we've got her. And I'm going out and find her."

"But we still don't know her name, what she looks like, where she hangs out."

"We can't expect life-sized photographs to be handed us in this. I think we're doing pretty good as it is, starting in from scratch the way we did. At least she's become a live person now, she's real, instead of being just a will-o'-the-wisp like she was until now. Just a whiff of perfume in a room, that's already gone. We know that she was at the Perroquet around midnight; she must have been seen there. His girl told you something about her. What was it, now? A tall redhead, a light-green dress. Number Three on the conga-line. They can't *all* have been tall redheads in light-green dresses down there tonight." She flung her hands encouragingly wide, to impress it on him. "Look at all we've got!"

"The place'll be closing by now."

"The people that count, the people that can really help, they'll still be around. Waiters, checkroom girl, washroom attendant, all like that. I'll trace her from there if I have to go over the hairbrushes in the dressing-room one by one for stray red hairs—"

"I'm going with you." He went over to the bedroom-doorway, put out the light in there. Then he went toward the bath. "Just a minute," he said, "I want to get a drink of water in here, before we go."

She went on out to the stairs without waiting. She thought he'd be right after her. Then because he wasn't, she stopped and waited, two or three steps down from the top. Then because he still didn't come, she turned and went back again the two or three steps, and into the lighted room once more.

She could see him standing there motionless just past the bath-entrance. She knew even before she went in and joined him, that he'd found something, that he'd seen something, by the intent, arrested way he was holding himself.

"What is it?"

"I called you and you didn't hear me. This was lying in the tub. That shower-curtain must have hidden it from us until now. When I was getting a drink, my elbow grazed the curtain and it fell further back than it was. And this was there, on the dry bottom of the tub."

It was light blue and he was holding it taut between both hands. "A check," she said. "Someone's personal check. Let me see—"

It was made out to Stephen Graves, for twelve thousand five hundred dollars and no cents. It was endorsed by Stephen Graves. It was signed by Arthur Holmes. It was stamped, in damning letters diagonally across the face of it: *Returned—No Funds.*

They exchanged a puzzled look across it, she now holding one end, he the other. "How'd a thing like this get into the bottom of a bathtub?" she marvelled.

"That's the least important part of it. That's easy enough to figure out. This check must have been in the cash-box in the first place. The hole I made in the wall is up over the bottom of the tub in a straight line. When I pulled the cash-box out and opened it, the check must have slipped out and volplaned down into the tub without my noticing it. Then the slant of the shower-curtain hid it from me until just now. But that isn't the thing. Don't you see what it could mean?"

"I think I do. There's a pretty good chance of Holmes being our jittery cigar-chewer, don't you think?"

"I'm betting on it. Here's something to kill someone for—twelve-fifty—oh—oh!"

"Then maybe this Holmes came around here tonight to see him, either to make good on it then and there, or to ask him not to prosecute until he'd raised enough money to make good on it in the near future. And because Graves wasn't able to find the check when he went to look for it, Holmes thought he was trying to put something over on him. They got into an argument about it, and Holmes shot him."

"Then, in a way, I'm still responsible for his death—"

"Forget that. Holmes didn't have to kill him, even if he did think he was holding out the check on him. Holmes," she said thoughtfully, backing the crook of one finger to her mouth. "I've heard or seen that name before, somewhere, tonight. Wait a minute, weren't there some cards in his wallet? I think it was on one of them."

She went out into the other room and knelt down there on the floor again. She took up the wallet, shuffled through the two or three cards that had been in it the first time. She looked up at him, nodded. "Sure, I told you. Holmes was his broker. Here it is right here."

He came over and joined her, check still in hand. "That's funny. I don't know much about those things, but don't clients usually give checks to their brokers, and not the other way around? And a bad one at that."

"There could be a reason for that. Maybe Holmes misappropriated some securities that he was holding, or handling for Graves and then Graves demanded an accounting sooner than he'd expected, so he tried to gain time by foisting a worthless check on him. When that bounced back and Graves threatened to have him arrested—"

"Any address on that?"

"No, just the brokerage firm-name, down in one corner."

"Well, I can get to him." He took a hitch in his belt. "I'm *going*," he said determinedly. "Come on, you can go down to the bus terminal awhile, and wait for me there—" Then, as he saw she didn't make any immediate move, "You agree with me that it *was* Holmes now, don't you?"

"No," she said to his surprise. "No, I don't. In fact, if anything, I still think it was that conga-line dame."

He flourished the check at her. "But *why*, when we've just turned this up?"

"Several little things, that you won't take any stock in. First of all, if Holmes *did* kill him, it was to cover up this check. Right? Then he never would have left here without it. Once he'd gone as far as to kill him over it, he would have looked for it until he'd found it. Because he'd know that would point straight at him when it *was* found. Just as it is doing at this minute."

"Suppose he did look for it and wasn't able to find it?"

"You found it," was all she replied to that. "And then another thing that makes me think it was the woman who was here at the end—I know this one you're going to laugh at, but—Graves had his coat on when he died."

"Aw, Bricky—" he started to protest.

"I knew you wouldn't take it seriously, but the impression I get of him, don't know why, is that he was the type man wouldn't have received a woman with his coat off, not even a blackmailer. And it was pretty late by then and he'd been in it all evening. I think if it was Holmes who'd been here at the end, we'd have found him lying just in his vest, or maybe even just in his shirt-sleeves. But that's just the meaning it has to me, I don't ask anyone else to try to get that out of it. It's more of a hunch than anything else. Anyway, to me it still spells the woman."

After a moment he laughed cheerlessly. "First we didn't have anything. Now we've got too much again."

"What I said before still holds good. More so now than then, even because the time has been clipped that much shorter. One of them is still the wrong one, one of them the right one. But we can only afford to pick the right one the first time out. We can't go after either one of them together. Because even those fifty-fifty odds are too high for us to take. If they paid off wrong, that would let the other one go by default. Suppose Holmes is the wrong one after all? Then by the time we've found that out, there's no more slack left to go out after the woman."

"But it's him and no one else. Everything here is trying to tell you that with all its might."

"There's motive enough here for Holmes to have shot him," she agreed. "Plenty, and to spare. But we're not even sure that he was up here tonight. The check and all that, it's just, what do they call that stuff?"

"Circumstantial," he supplied grudgingly.

She nodded. "It's circumstantial with her too. It's circumstantial all the way around. He got a note from a woman in a night-club, saying she was coming up here. And a woman *was* here. But that doesn't mean it was one and the same woman. It might have been two entirely different women. A man named Holmes gave him a check that bounced. And a man was up here tonight arguing with him and chewing on a cigar. But they also might have been two entirely different men."

"Now you've split them in four."

"There's still just two, one for you and one for me. I'll still take her, and you take him. And back here by quarter to six, like we said before."

The lights went out and the dead man disappeared in the dark. They went downstairs.

They parted this time without a kiss. The pledge of constancy had been given once, it didn't have to be renewed.

"I'll be seeing you, Quinn," was all she murmured, standing beside him in the shrouded doorway.

She waited for a few moments, in order not to interfere with his going. When she came out into the open in turn, he was gone from sight. As gone as though she'd never seen him. Or rather, as gone as though she would never see him again.

Only the city was there, lazily licking its chops.

IT SHOULD have been easier this time than the last, but he had his doubts it was going to be. He had a name and an occupation this time—two names, first and last, and an occupation—and all he had to do was match them up with a present location. The time before all he'd had was a broken button and a character-istic—left-handedness—and he hadn't even been sure of that. When he thought of the courage he'd had expecting to get any-where last time—well, no wonder it had ended up in smoke. But then when he thought of how much less time he had this time, it almost seemed to make it equally futile.

There were three of them in the telephone book. He tackled it that way first. But that didn't mean anything. That was only the one borough, Manhattan. That left out Brooklyn, Queens, the Bronx, Staten Island. That left out the hinterland, all the way up to Croton, maybe beyond, God knows where. That left out the depths of Long Island, all the way out to Port Wash-ington. And being a broker—he didn't know much about them, but he thought of them as mostly living outside in the suburban belt, he didn't know why.

One of the three was on Nineteenth, one was on Sixtieth,

one was on a name-street that he'd never heard of before. He took them in their order in the book.

The operator rang and rang, and he wouldn't let her quit. No one answers a phone quickly, at such a Godforsaken hour of the night.

Finally there was a wrench and a woman's voice got on. It sounded all fuzzy from sleep. This was Nineteenth.

"Wa-a-al?" it said crossly.

"I want to talk to Holmes, to Arthur Holmes."

"Oh, ye do?" the voice said with asperity. "Well, you're just a little bit too late. You missed him by about twenty minutes."

She was going to slam up, he could tell by the tenor of her answer. Slam up good and hard.

"Can you tell me where I can reach him?" He almost tripped over his own tongue getting it out fast enough to beat her to it.

"He's over at the station-house. You can get him there. What do you want to be ringing me here for?"

He'd given himself up. He'd gone there of his own accord— Maybe the thing was over already. Maybe all this had been unnecessary; maybe they'd been torturing themselves half the livelong night for noth—

But he had to know. How was he to know? Maybe even this woman didn't know. She didn't sound like— She sounded like some kind of a maid or housekeeper around the premises.

"He's—he's a broker, isn't he? A stockbroker—you know, market—"

"Hohl— *Him?*" Fifteen years of suppressed discontent were in it. A lifetime of smouldering rancor packed into one syllable. The receiver even at his end should have softened with the searing heat of it and slowly melted into a gummy stalactite. "He'd like to be. He's the desk sergeant at the Tenth Precinct-house, around on Twentieth Street, and that's all he'll ever be, that's all he's got sense enough to be, and you can tell him I said so, too! And while you're at it, tell him to quit shooting off his fat lying mouth so, in every beer-joint he puts his foot in, all to mooch a few dirty drinks. One time he's the Governor's private body-guard, another time he's with the secret service, now he's a broker. I'm getting sick of all kinds of drunken bums calling me up at all hours of the night—"

He hung up with a vicious poke at the apparatus.

One of *them*. He didn't want to come any closer to one of *them* than he was already, a couple of miles away on a wire. He didn't even want to come this close to one of *them*. That was what he was doing this whole thing for, to stay away from *them*.

It took him a minute to get over it. But he had to go ahead. He didn't want to any more after that, but he had to.

Sixtieth.

This time there was no wait at all. Even at this hour. The person must have been sitting there beside it, or waiting just a few steps away.

It was a young voice. It sounded about twenty. Maybe that was its guilelessness, giving that impression. Some voices never grow up. It was bursting with pent-up impatience, impatience that had been veering over into fear. It was breathless with it. It couldn't wait, it had to get it out.

The call was his, but it appropriated it. As though there could only be one possible call at this particular time, and this must be it. It drowned out his opening phrase. Just gave it half an ear, enough to assure itself that it was of masculine timbre, and that was all, that was sufficient.

There was absolutely no breath-punctuation in the voice's flow.

"Oh, Bixy, I thought you never were going to call me! Bixy what took you so long? I've been wilting away here for hours. I've been all packed and waiting and *sitting* on my things! I tried to call you two or three times and there was some sort of a mix-up, they didn't seem to know who I meant, isn't that ridiculous? Bixy, I got so worried for a minute or two, I couldn't help it." The voice tried to laugh at itself, lamely. "All my jewelry and everything—what would I do? It only occurred to me afterwards. And I already sent him the wire, as soon as I left you. I know you told me not to, but it seemed the only fair thing to do. So now we *have* to go ahead and carry it out—"

The flow stopped. The voice knew. He couldn't tell how, he hadn't made a sound, but suddenly it knew.

"It isn't—?"

The voice was dying. Not physically maybe, but it was shrivelling up. "I'm sorry to get in the way. I wanted to—I was calling Arthur Holmes."

The voice was dead now. The dead voice said, "He's in Canada, fishing. He left Tuesday a week ago. You can reach him at—"

"Tuesday a week ago? Never mind."

"Please get off the line. I'm expecting a call." He got off the line.

The next was the name-street.

The operator said finally, "They don't answer."

"Keep trying."

She went ahead.

It stopped finally. He thought she'd quit. It took him a minute to catch on. She hadn't quit, it was that it had been picked up; it was open at the other end, and yet there wasn't a sound to show that it was. Otherwise, if she'd quit, his nickel would have come back. Somebody listening without speaking? Somebody a little afraid?

So it had begun auspiciously, if by this indication alone.

Neither end spoke. He waited to see. Somebody had to give in. He gave in first.

"Hello," he said softly.

A throat cleared itself at the other end. "Yes?" a voice said reticently.

It was beginning good, it was beginning like the real thing. He was afraid to hope yet, he'd already been disappointed so many times before this.

The voice was a man's. It was very low, and very wary. Even in its "yes" it was watchful.

"Is this Mr. Arthur Holmes?"

He had to hold him fast first; make sure it was he, and then hold him there.

Then once he'd done that— So he had to go easy himself to start with.

"Who is this?"

He hadn't admitted that he was Holmes; Quinn tried to get around that by taking it for granted that he was.

"Well, Mr. Holmes, you don't know me—"

The voice didn't fall for it. "Who is this that wants to speak to Mr. Holmes?"

He tried it again. "The name is not known to you, Mr. Holmes."

Again the voice side-stepped. "I didn't say that this was Holmes. I asked what your name was. Unless you tell me who you are first, I can't tell you whether you can reach him or not. It's quite likely that you can't, particularly at such an hour. Now don't take up any more of my time unless you tell me who you are and what you want of Mr. Holmes."

That "what you want" was what he'd been waiting for. It gave him an opening-wedge.

"Very well," he said with deceptive submissiveness, "I'll tell you both things. The name is Quinn; that of a stranger. It's not known to Mr. Holmes. What I want is to—I want to return a check that belongs to Mr. Holmes."

"What?" the voice said quickly. "What was that?"

"I say, I have a check that belongs to Mr. Holmes. But I have to know if I have the right Mr. Holmes. Is this the residence of the Arthur Holmes that's connected with the brokerage firm of Weatherby and Dodd?"

"Yes," the voice said quickly, "yes, this is."

"Well, now will you let me talk to him?"

The voice hesitated only briefly. The voice took the plunge. "You are," it said quietly.

He'd won the first round. He had him hooked. He didn't have to worry about losing him from now on. All he had to do, now, was bring him in closer.

He repeated what he'd said twice already. "I have a check that belongs to you." He let that stand by itself, for the other to nibble at.

The voice felt its way carefully. "I don't understand. If you say I don't know you, how could you have?" The voice picked up speed. "I'm afraid you must be mistaken."

"I'm holding it right here in my hand, Mr. Holmes."

The voice faltered, ran down again. "Who's it made out to?"

"Just a second." Quinn took a moment or two off, for artistic effect, as if peering at it closely. "Stephen Graves," he said, with that slightly stilted intonation that accompanies reading aloud, in contradistinction to impromptu speech. He was playing it this way consciously; the effect he wanted to convey, at this stage, was of innocent, haphazard possession, rather than dangerous knowledge. There was still too much distance between them.

There was a catch in the voice; as though it had knotted up suddenly in its owner's throat. It said nothing, but the sounds it made trying to free itself carried over the wire.

Boy is he guilty, Quinn kept thinking. Boy is he guilty. If he gives himself away like this out of sight, can you imagine—?

The knot had been effaced; the voice spoke suddenly. "Nonsense, there's no check of mine made out to any such person. Look, my friend, I don't know what's up your sleeve, but I advise you not to—"

Quinn kept his tone even, colorless. "If you'll compare it with your stub you'll see I'm telling the truth. The number in the righthand corner is 20. It's the twentieth check in that particular book. It's drawn on the Case National Bank. It's dated August the twenty-fourth. It's to the amount of twelve thous—"

He sounded as if he was falling apart there at the other end. Something knocked hollowly, as if the instrument had slipped out of his hand and he'd had to retrieve it.

I've got him, Quinn revelled. Oh, this time I surely have.

He could wait. The thing to do from this point on was to improvise as he went along, fit his responses to the circumstances as they presented themselves.

"And how'd you—how'd you come to get hold of such a check?"

"I found it," Quinn said matter-of-factly.

"Would you—would you mind telling me where?"

It was doing things to him. He'd breathe just once, quickly. And then he'd forget to breathe the next two or three times he should have in-between. Then he'd breathe again just once, quickly. Quinn could hear the whole process as plainly as if he were holding a stethoscope to his ear instead of a telephone.

"I found it on the seat of a taxi. It looked like somebody who was in it before me opened their wallet in the dark and it slipped out." Let him think it was Graves.

"Who was with you when you found it?"

"No one. Just me by myself."

The voice tried to use skepticism as a sort of probe, to draw out the admission it believed to be there, lurking just below the surface. "Now don't tell me that. There are always two heads in anything like this. Come on, who was with you?"

"No one, I tell you. Didn't you ever hear of anyone happening to be by himself sometimes? Well, I was."

The voice had wanted to hear that. The voice liked it that way. He could tell.

"Who'd you show it to afterwards? Who'd you speak to between the time you found it and now?"

"No one."

"Who's with you now?"

"No one."

"What put the idea into your head of calling me up at four-thirty in the morning about it?"

"I thought maybe you'd like to have it back," Quinn said disarmingly.

The voice considered that. Not that it was kidding him any, but it tried to give the impression of deliberating, weighing the matter. As though there could be more than one an-swer to his suggestion. "Let me ask you something first. Sup-pose—this is just theoretical—suppose I say I don't want it back, that it's of no value to me, then what do you do with it? Throw it away?"

"No," Quinn said evenly. "Then I'll probably keep it and look up the payee; Stephen Graves. See if I can locate him."

That got him if nothing else had until now. And plenty else had until now. Quinn could almost hear his heart turn over and do tailspins; all the way up through his throat and across the wire.

There was a break; somebody else got between them. The operator said: "Your five minutes is up. Deposit another nick-el, please." Meaning Quinn.

He glanced down at the one he'd been holding in read-iness in his palm. In case the conversation hadn't taken the successful turn it had.

He held it out a minute, to try out something.

The voice cried out wildly, "Wait a minute! Don't cut us off, whatever you do!"

Quinn dropped in the nickel. There was a click and then they went on as before.

Me afraid of losing him? Quinn thought. He's the one afraid of losing me. The voice had had a bad fright. It decided not to do quite so much feinting.

"Well, all right, I—I would like to see this check you're holding," it capitulated. "It's of no possible value to anyone. There was a mistake, and—"

Quinn gave him the axe on that. "It was returned by the bank," he said flatly.

The voice swallowed that; literally as well as metaphorically. "Let me ask you— You said your name was Flynn?"

"Quinn. But that doesn't really make any difference."

"Tell me something about yourself. Who are you? What do you do?"

"I don't see that that has anything to do with it."

The voice tried again. "Are you a married man? Have you a family to support?"

Quinn shied off a little, while he looked this one over. What's he asking that for? To figure how large a payment it'll take to shut me up? No, there must be some darker purpose behind it. To try and find out if I'll be missed if—if anything happens to me.

He could feel the hairs on the nape of his neck tighten a little. "I'm single," he said. "I live by myself."

"Not even a room-mate?" the voice purred.

"Nobody. Strictly lone-wolf."

The voice mulled that over. It sniffed at the trap. It edged closer. It reached in for the bait. And the primary bait, Quinn sensed, was no longer the check itself. It was his life.

"Well, look, Quinn. I'd like to see the check and—maybe I can do something for you."

"Fair enough."

"Where are you now?"

He wondered if he should tell him the exact truth. He told him. "I'm on Fifty-ninth Street? You know the Baltimore Lunchroom on Fifty-ninth Street? I'm in there, speaking from there."

"I'll tell you what I'll do. You'll have to give me a little time to get dressed—I was in bed, you see, when you rang. I'll get dressed and come out. You go to—let's see now—" The voice was trying to work out something. But something more than just the selection of a meeting-place for the two of them. Quinn gave it its head, waited. "I'll tell you. You go over toward Columbus Circle. You know where Broadway splits off from Central Park West, forming a narrow little triangular block. There's a cafeteria there with two entrances, open all night. You go in there and— You have no money on you, have you?"

"No."

"Well, go in anyway; they won't bother you. Say you're waiting for someone. Sit by the window, close up against the window, on the Broadway side. I'll contact you there in fifteen minutes."

Quinn thought: Why shift me to another place? Why not just meet me at the place I'm in already? He's afraid there's a set-up here, I guess; that I've got someone else planted out of sight. He also took note of the expression he'd used; he hadn't said "I'll meet you," he'd said "I'll contact you." He's going to case me first, case me good, before he comes near me, he told himself. He's playing it smart. But no matter how smart he plays it, that won't save him. I've got that check, and he has to have it back. If we take all night and cover all New York between us.

He played it dumb, for his part. Played it dumb and unsuspecting. "Right," he said.

"Fifteen minutes," the voice said. The conversation ended.

Quinn left the phone. He went into the men's room, planted his foot up against the wall, and stripped off his shoe. Then he took the check out, covered it with an extra piece of paper to protect it, and put it down flat on the bottom of the shoe. Then he put his foot back in again. He was taking a leaf from Graves and the note he'd received at the night-club.

He came outside again, and on his way out to the street stopped for a moment beside the rack where they had the trays and cutlery.

There was no one in the place but himself, and the attendant behind the counter wasn't watching him. He picked up one of the chromeplated knives and surreptitiously fingered the edge of it. They weren't very much good; blunt. But he had to have something; even if only for moral effect rather than actual use. He sheathed it in one of the paper napkins and bedded it slantwise in his inside coat-pocket.

He walked the park-breadth over to Columbus Circle and got to the second place in about twelve minutes out of the fifteen he'd been given. He sat down at a table up against the window on the Broadway side and waited.

You could look straight through the place. For instance, from the Central Park West side, if you were out there in the dark, either on the sidewalk or in a car up against the curb, you could look in through the window, across the entire lighted depth of it, to where he was sitting, obliviously looking out the other way.

Quinn knew that, knew that was why he'd picked this place.

He glanced around that way, to the far side of him, once or twice. One time he thought he saw the dark, blurred form of a car, that had been motionless until his eye caught it, glide slowly onward in the gloom. But it might have been just some legitimately passing car, halting for the lights as it neared the Circle.

The fifteen minutes was up, then eighteen, then twenty.

He began to get uneasy. Maybe I had him figured wrong; maybe he just wanted time to make a getaway. Maybe he's more afraid of coming near me than of not getting the check back.

It's him, all right, it's him, and now maybe I've fumbled the thing, lost him again. His forehead started to get damp, and every time he'd wipe it dry, it would get damp all over again.

The phone suddenly rang, up by the cashier's desk. He looked around, then looked away again.

Somebody began to thump on glass. He looked around again, and the cashier was motioning him.

He went over and the cashier said, "There's somebody on here says he wants to talk to a man sitting by himself up against the window. Now look, people aren't supposed to get calls here at my desk—" He handed it over to him nevertheless.

It was he. "Hello, Quinn?"

"Yeah, what happened to you?"

"I'm waiting for you at a place called Owen's. I'm at the bar there. It's down on Fifty-first."

"What's the idea of doing that? You told me here first. What're you trying to do, give me the run-around?"

"I know, but—you come where I am now. Take a cab, I'll pay for it when you get here."

"Are you sure you're not kidding this time?"

"I'm not kidding. I'm in the place already, waiting for you."

"All right, I'll see whether you are or not."

SHE PACED back and forth in front of the place, grinding her fist into its opposite palm. They wouldn't let her in any more. The sign over the entrance was out. The trashcans full of refuse were out. The last lush was out. It was dead. Dead, but not quite cold yet, still only in the process of giving up the ghost. Every few moments a solitary figure would emerge and walk away, somebody who earned a living inside. This was the five o'clock in the afternoon of the night-club workers, whose clock goes in the opposite direction to that of the rest of the world.

While she paced, picketing the place for information so to speak, she kept thinking it out. Inside there, in this place I'm doing sentry-duty before, a redhead in a light-green dress handed Graves a note earlier tonight. I've got the place and I've got the note. All right, I've got that much. Let's see now. To write that note in the first place she needed a pencil and paper. Those are things that the average chippy of her kind doesn't carry around with her ordinarily; she sends most of her messages with her eyes and hips. Maybe this one did have pencil and paper; if she did, that's my tough luck. Let's say she didn't have, though. Then in that case she must have had to borrow them from somebody in there. She wouldn't be likely to interrupt one of the dancers on the floor and ask "Can you lend me a pencil and paper?" She wouldn't be likely to accost some pair or group at one of the tables and ask it. What's left? The waiter at her table, if she sat at a table. The man behind the bar, if she sat at the bar. The girl behind the hat-check counter. The attendant in the powder room.

That narrows it down to somebody who works in there.

That's what I'm doing out here now.

Even in their street-clothes she could more or less identify them at sight as they came out one by one. This trim, pert little good-looker, emerging now modishly garbed as any of her customers, for instance, couldn't be anyone but the checkroom girl in such a place.

She stopped short as she felt Bricky's hand come to rest on her sleeve, and then a look of genuine surprise overspread her face at the discovery that the arresting hand was feminine for once. She even seemed a trifle frightened or guilty for a moment, as one dreading retribution, until the question had been put.

"No, it works the other way around at my stall," she said in a fluting, baby voice. "They all take out their own pencils and use them, where I'm concerned." She opened her handbag and dug up a fistful of assorted cards and scraps of paper bearing names, addresses, telephone-numbers.

One escaped, and she thrust it away with her foot. "Let it go," she said, "I've got enough without that." She put the rest away. "No women borrowed a pencil from me; in fact I haven't one to lend." She went on up the street, with a little twittering sound of diminutive feet.

This colored damsel coming out, equally modish in her turn, could only be the powder-room attendant.

"Wut kine pencil?" she answered the query aloofly. "An eyebrow pencil?"

"No, the regular lead kind, the kind you write with."

"They doan come in there to write, honey, you got the wrong number."

"No one did ask you for one, though, all evening long?" Bricky persisted.

"No. That's about the one thing they left out. Come to think of it, that's the one thing I ain't got in there to give. You've give me an idea; I think I'll get me one tomorrow night and have it in there, I might get a call for it."

A man came out.

He stopped and shook his head. "Not at my end of the bar. Better ask Frank, he works the other end."

Another man came out right after him. "Are you Frank?"

He stopped and smiled and singed her with his eyes. "No, I'm Jerry, but I'm not doing anything. Don't let the name stand in your way."

This time she was the one who had to go away, ten yards or so away, until he was gone and the coast was clear again.

But by that time somebody else had already come out and was well on his way. She had to run up the street after him to overtake him.

"Yeah, I'm Frank."

"Did a girl borrow a pencil from you tonight, at your end of the bar? She was a tall girl, and she was red-haired, and she was in a light-green dress. Oh, it was a long time ago, earlier in the night, but see if you can remember— Did someone? Did anyone?"

He nodded. She got it.

"Yeah," he said, "someone like that did. I remember. It was way back around twelve o'clock, but someone did."

"You don't know her name, though?"

"No, that I don't. I've got an idea she works in one of the other clubs around here—"

"You don't know which one, though?"

"No. The only reason I say that is because I happened to overhear somebody else say to her, 'Whatcha doing in here? You through at your own place already?'"

"But you don't know—?"

"I don't know who she is or where she works or anything else about her. Only that she borryed a pencil from me and bent over close, scribbling something behind her arm for a minute, then looked up and gave it back to me."

He stopped by her a moment longer. There wasn't anything else for either one of them to say.

"Wish I could help you."

"I do too," she said wanly.

He turned and went away. She stood there looking down at the sidewalk at a loss.

That was as close as she could probably hope to get. So near and yet so far. She raised her head. He'd turned a second time and come back to her again. "It seems to have you worried."

"Plenty," she admitted forlornly.

"Here's a tip for you. I don't know if you're in club work yourself or not, but they've got funny habits. There's a theatrical drugstore they all hang out in after the clubs've closed up. People that aren't in the know, they think they step out with these stage-door johnnies, go on champagne parties. Well, some of them do some of the time, but most of them don't most of the time. Don't you believe it. Nine times out of ten they head for this place like a bunch of kids when school's been let out. They like it better. They gang up there and drink malted milks and let their hair down. Go over there and take a shot at it. It's worth trying, anyway."

Was it! She broke away so fast she left him standing there staring after her.

She ran all the way. It was only down a couple of blocks from there.

They weren't exactly lined up at the fountain, as he'd led her to expect. Maybe that was because it was too late and the majority of them had already disbanded. But there were a group of three still lingering down at the far end. One of them had a Russian wolfhound with her. She must have brought it out for an airing before going to bed for the morning. They were all ganged up around it, feeding it crumbs from their plates and making a fuss over it. Its owner was in what might be called a state of street-wear deshabille. She had a polo coat thrown over her shoulders, and under it peered the bottoms of a pair of boudoir pajamas, stockingless ankles, and house slippers. None of the three was a redhead.

Their heads came up. Their attention left the borzoi and settled fleetingly on Bricky instead.

"She means Joanie, I guess," one of them said. She addressed her directly, and rather fatuously. "That who you mean?"

How could she tell, if she didn't know herself? They didn't know her last name, it appeared. "I just know her from in here," one said.

"Me too," a second one added.

"She didn't show up tonight," the third one supplied. "Why don't you go around to her hotel, look her up there? It's just down the line a ways. I think it's called the Concord or the Compton or something like that." Then she qualified it: "I don't know if she's *still* there, but she was a couple nights ago. I walked her over as far as the door, to give Stalin some exercise."

They shrugged her off. Their gnat-like attention went back to the borzoi again, as being the more interesting of the two rival bids for attention.

The hotel had every earmark of one of those shady places catering to card sharps, confidence men, and other fly-by-nights. It held no terrors for her, though. She had met its type of denizen on the dance floor every night of her life, for years past. She went up to the desk with the assurance of one who doesn't expect to be turned away. An evil-looking night-clerk with a cast in his eye, a collar that hadn't been changed in a week, and a whiff of stale alcohol on his breath, shifted over a little to match her position.

She leaned comfortably over the desk on the point of one elbow. "Hello, there," she said breezily.

He widened his mouth and showed her a space between two of his teeth. It was probably supposed to be some kind of a grin.

She swung her handbag around on the end of its strap with her free hand.

First around one way, then back around the other. "What room's my girlfriend got?" she said unconcernedly, staring off across the mildewed lobby. "I wanna run up a minute and tell her something I forgot. You know, Joanie. The one in the light-green dress. I only just now left her this minute in the drugstore, but—" She gave him a snicker; "this can't wait, it's too good." She bent over and slapped hilariously at her own thigh. "Is she gonna *die*!" she brayed.

"Who's that, Joan Bristol?" he asked, with a fatuous look that was an invitation to her to share the joke with him, whatever.

"Yeah, yeah, yeah," she rattled off, as if that were to be taken for granted. Giggling, she poked him in the side. "Listen, you wanna hear something funny?" She bent her head over in the direction of his ear, as if about to whisper something to him confidentially. He inclined his head accommodatingly.

Suddenly, with the typical volatility of the gamin-part she was playing, she changed her mind. "Wait a minute, I want to tell her first. I'll tell you when I come down." She took a step away from the desk, but not without chucking him under the chin first. "Stay there now, Pops; don't go 'way." Then quite by way of parenthesis, still all a-chortle over this other, more important matter: "What room'd you say it was, again?"

He fell for it. She'd worked hard at the little act, and it had gone over. "Four-oh-nine, sugar," he said amiably. He even straightened his weather-beaten tie, caught up in the momentary mood she had managed to create. Of intimacy that took no account of visiting-hours, it was so close. Of harmless, giddy frivolity.

He took a step in the direction of the decrepit switchboard, which it was also evidently part of his duties to attend to.

"Oh, skip that," she called out ribaldly, flinging her hand at him. "She don't have to put on airs with me. Who's she kidding? I know she's two weeks behind in her rent."

He guffawed with mealy-mouthed laughter, and the intended announcement over the house-phone went by the board.

She stepped into the Cleveland-Administration elevator with an exaggerated swing of her hips, and the venerable contraption started to creak slowly upward under her. The stationary doors were not solid, but grilled ironwork. As the descending ceiling of the street-floor came down and cut her off from his sight, it seemed to scrape the raffish smirk from her face in time with its own passage, like a slowly-falling curtain of sobriety passing over her features, and dimming them again to taut gravity.

She and the colored man toiled upward for four endless, snail-like floors together, and then he stopped the mechanism and let her off. He seemed to intend to wait for her return there, at floor-level, so she got rid of him with a pert: "That's all right, I'll be in there quite some time."

He closed the rickety shaft-door, and a line of light ebbed reluctantly down the glass, like something being slowly siphoned off; left it shadowed and blank.

She turned and walked down the musty, dimly-lighted corridor, along a strip of carpeting that still clung together only out of sheer stubbornness of skeletal weave. Doors, dark, oblivious, inscrutable, sidling by; enough to give you the creeps just to look at them. All hope gone from them, and from those who passed in and out through them. Just one more row of stopped-up orifices in this giant honeycomb that was the city. Human beings shouldn't have to enter such doors, shouldn't have to stay behind them. No moon ever entered there, no stars, no anything at all. They were worse than the grave, for in the grave is absence of consciousness. And God, she reflected, ordered the grave, for all of us; but God didn't order such burrows in a third-class New York City hotel.

It seemed like a long corridor, but maybe that was because her thoughts were quick. They were churning wildly, while her feet carried her toward the imminent showdown that lay just ahead, around the turn.

"How am I going to get in? And if I do, how am I going to

know, how am I going to find out if she killed him? They don't tell you these things. Not the whole majestic State of New York can make such words pass their lips, as a rule, so how can I, alone, unaided? And even if I do, how am I going to get her back there, all the way up to East Seventieth Street, without causing a big commotion, calling on the police for aid, involving Quinn in it far worse than he is already, getting the two of us held on suspicion for days and weeks on end?"

She didn't know. She didn't know any of those things. She only knew she was going ahead, there was no backing out for her. She could only pray, to the one friendly auspice there was in all this town for her, as she drew closer, closer.

"Oh, Clock on the Paramount, that I can't see from here, the night is nearly over and the bus has nearly gone. Let me go home tonight."

The door-numbers were stepping up on her. Six on this side, seven on that, eight back on this side again. And then a dead end, the corridor ended in a door, the last of them all, at right angles to it: 409, there it was. It looked so neutral, so impersonal—and yet behind it lurked her whole future destiny, in shape unseen.

On this single slab, she thought, on this great square of old, dark, scabrous wood, depends whether I become a human being again or remain a rat in a dance-hall for the rest of my life. Why should one door have so much power over me?

She looked down at the back of her own hand, as if to say: Was that *you?* Gee, you had guts just then! It had knocked just then on the wood, without waiting for the rest of her.

The door swept open before she had time to plan anything, to think what to do when it should open, and they stood looking at each other eye to eye, this unknown woman and she. Hard, enamelled face very close to hers, so close she could see the caked pores in it, like fine mesh. Hostile, wary eyes, so close she could see the red-streaked vessels in their corners.

The upper hall at Graves' house came back to her again, the memory of creeping through there in the dark with Quinn, and she knew, without being conscious of it, that she must be smelling the same perfume again; that was what was doing it, linking the two experiences.

The eyes had already changed. This thing was going to go fast. Hostile wariness had already become overt challenge. A husky voice came up from somewhere below to join them. A voice that didn't let you kid around with it.

"Well, what's the angle? Didje come around to borrow a cup of sugar or didje hit the wrong door? Anything in p'tic'lar in here y'want?"

"Yes," said Bricky softly, "there is."

She must have taken a draw on a cigarette just before she opened the door, the other, and been holding it until now and speaking through it. Smoke suddenly speared from her nostrils in two malevolent columns. She looked like Satan. She looked like someone it was good to stay away from. She was still willing to have it that way herself—so far. Her arm flexed, to slap the door closed in Bricky's face.

Bricky wanted to turn around and go away, turn around and go away fast. Boy, how she wanted to turn around and get away from there. But she wouldn't let herself. She knew she was going to get in there, even if it was to her own destruction. That door had to stay open.

She did it with her foot and with her elbow.

The woman's muzzle became a white cicatrice of menace.

"Take that out of the way," she warned in a sort of slow-rolling growl.

"We don't know each other personally," Bricky said, borrowing her huskiest dance-hall tones, "but we've got a friend in common, so that makes it even."

The Bristol woman gave her head an upward flip. "Wait a minute, who are *you*? I never saw you before in my life. What d'ya mean a friend?"

"I'm talking about Mr. Stephen Graves."

A white flash of consternation came over the Bristol woman's face. But she might have reacted that same way, Bricky realized, even if she'd only been up there trying to blackmail him and then had walked out again, without anything else.

Until now, on a strip of background-wall visible just behind her, there had been a vague outline-shadow discernible. Not a very sharply etched one, just a faint tracing cast by some impediment in the way of the light coming from the room off to one side. It now moved very subtly, slipped off sidewards, disappeared—as though whatever was causing it had altered position, withdrawn, was secreting itself.

The caraway-seed centers of the woman's eyes flicked briefly in that same offside direction, then immediately straightened back again, as though she had just received some imperceptible signal attuned to herself alone. She said tautly, and with an undertone of menace: "Suppose you come in a minute, and let's hear what's on your mind." She widened the door. It wasn't done hospitably, but with a sort of commanding jerk, as if to say: Either come in of your own accord, or I'll reach out and haul you in.

For one moment more Bricky was a free agent; the hallway stretched unimpeded behind her. She thought: Here I go. I hope I get out of here alive. She went in.

She moved slowly past the other woman, turned aside into a tawdry, smoke-stenched room. Behind her the door champed back into its frame with a sound of ominous finality, as though it were meant to stay that way for good. A key ticked twice; once against the lock in turning, the second time against the keyhole in withdrawal.

She's locked me in here with her. I have to stay and win now, I can't get out again.

The battle was joined. A battle in which her only weapons were her wits, her sheer nerve, and the feminine intuition that even a little chain-dancer is never without. She knew that from this point on every veiled glance she cast around her, every slightest move she made, must be made to count, because there would be no quarter given, no second chances.

The room was empty, apparently. A door, presumably to a bath, was already firmly closed when her eyes first found it, but the knob had just stopped turning, hadn't quite fallen still yet. If it appeared that she didn't know too much, the door would stay that way, wouldn't open again. But if it developed she knew too much— Therein lay her cue; how to find out just what there was to know here, and what too much of it was. That door would tell her. She already had a yardstick to measure her own progress.

For the rest, drawers in the shabby bureau were out at narrow, uneven lengths, as though they had recently been emptied. A Gladstone bag stood on the floor at the foot of the bed. The bag was full, ready for removal. A number of objects were strewn about on top of the bureau, as though the room's occupant had returned in some turmoil, flung them down on entering. There was a woman's handbag, a pair of gloves, a crumpled handkerchief. The handbag had been left yawning open, as if the agitated hand that had plunged into it in search of something had been too hurried to close it again.

The Bristol woman sidled in after her, surreptitiously ground something out under her toe, but then a moment later, as she turned to face Bricky, was holding a half-consumed cigarette between her fingers again. Bricky pretended she hadn't noticed it smoking away on the edge of the table, ownerless, until now. A man will often leave a cigarette balanced on the edge of a table or some other bare surface, a woman hardly ever.

It really was superfluous. That flexing of the doorknob just now, that shifting of light-tones on the wall before, had been enough to tell her all she needed to know. *There are three of us here in this place.*

Joan Bristol drew out a chair, adjusted it, swerved it, so that its back was to the closed door. Then she invited: "Help yourself to a seat." Even if Bricky had wanted to sit somewhere else, she made it the only one available by taking the only other one herself. She lowered herself into it as though she were on coiled springs ready to be released at any moment.

She moistened her rouge-matted lips. "What'd you say your name was again?"

"I didn't say, but you can put me down as Caroline Miller."

The other gave her a smile of disbelief, but took it in her stride. "So you know some guy named Graves, do you? Tell me, what makes you think I know him? Did he mention me to you?"

"No," Bricky said, "he wasn't doing any mentioning of anybody."

"Then what makes you think I—?"

This would have been sheer repetition, and she wanted to get past this point. "You do, don't you?"

Joan Bristol tasted her own rouge some more, reflective. "Tell me, you been over to see him lately?"

"Pretty lately."

"How lately?"

Bricky said with crafty negligence: "I just came from there now."

The Bristol woman was tautening up inwardly. You could tell it quite easily on the outside, though. Her eyes strayed to some indeterminate point over and beyond Bricky's shoulder, as if in desperate quest of further guidance. Bricky carefully avoided turning her head to follow the look with her own eyes. There was nothing but a door there, anyway.

"How'd you find him?"

"Dead," said Bricky quietly.

The Bristol woman didn't show the right type of surprise. It was surprise, all right, but it was a vindictive, malevolent surprise, not a startled one. In other words, it wasn't the news that was surprising, it was the source of it.

She didn't answer right away. She evidently wanted to "confer" with the recent shadow on the wall. Or it did with her. A brief spurt of water from a faucet somewhere behind the closed door, turned on, then quickly off again, was the signal to this effect.

"Excuse me a sec," she said, getting up. "I must have forgotten to tighten the tap in there."

She sidled around Bricky's strategically-planted chair and slipped inside to the bath without opening the door widely enough to show anything beyond it. She closed it behind her for a moment, so the visitor couldn't turn her head and look in.

She had given Bricky the chance herself. The chance to

find whatever there was to find, if there was anything. It was only good for thirty seconds. For the space of time it would take to receive a whispered instruction in there on how to proceed. And it wouldn't occur again. Almost before the knob had fallen still in the door behind her, she was up out of the chair. She only had time to go for one thing. She made it the open handbag atop the dresser. It was the obvious place. More than that, it was the only accessible one, within the limitations of time and space granted her. The bureau-drawers were presumably empty, their position implied that. The Gladstone bag was presumably locked already, its fullness indicated that.

She darted across the intervening room-space, aimed her hand at the gaping bag, plunged it in. Outright evidence she knew she couldn't expect. That would have been asking too much. But something, anything at all. And there was nothing. Lipstick, powder-compact, the usual junk. Paper crackled against her viciously probing fingers from one of the side pockets. She drew it hastily out, flung it open, raced her eyes over it. Still nothing. An unpaid hotel-bill for $17.89, from this place they were in. A man would have left it there. Of what value was it? It had no connection with what she was here after.

And yet some inexplicable instinct cried out to her: "Hang onto it. It might come in handy." She flung herself back into her original seat again, did something to one of her stockings, and it was gone.

An instant later the door reopened and the Bristol woman came out again, her instructions set. She sat down, fixed Bricky with her eyes, evidently to keep her attention from wandering.

"What'd you do, go up there to Graves' place alone? Or'd you have somebody with you?"

Bricky gave her the knowing look of someone who is over seventeen. "Sure. You don't suppose I take my grandmother along at times like that, do you?"

Her interlocutor got what she'd wanted her to out of it. "Oh, times like that, that's it."

"That's it."

"Well, uh—" She nibbled some more at her lip-rouge. "Somebody stop you at the door and tell you, that how you found out? Were there cops outside, people hanging around, lots of excitement, that how you knew he was dead?"

Bricky was answering these questions on instinct alone. Until they came out, she didn't know herself how they were going to come. It was like walking a tight-rope—without a balancing pole and with no net under you.

"No, no one was around. No one knew it yet. Think I'd have walked in? I was the first one found him, I guess. See, I had a key to the house; he'd given it to me. I went in and all the lights were out. I thought maybe he hadn't got home yet, so I'd wait for him. I went up, and there he was, plugged."

Joan Bristol kneaded her hands together with feverish interest in the recital. "So then what'd you do? I suppose right away you beat it out and hollered blue murder, brought them all down on the place."

The demi-mondaine sitting in Bricky's chair gave her another of those worldly-wise looks. "What d'you think I am, sappy? I beat it out all right, and fast, but I kept the soft-pedal on. I put out the lights and locked up the door after me, and left the place just the way I found it. Sister, I didn't breathe a word. Think I wanted to get mixed up in it? That's all I need, yet."

"And how long ago was it you were up there?"

"Just now."

"Then I guess nobody knows yet but you—"

"You and me."

She had a slight sense of motion taking place behind her. The air may have stirred a little. Or something may have creaked.

"Did you come down here alone?"

"Sure. Everything I do, I do alone. Who've I got?"

The mirror on the dresser, aslant toward her, showed her the hinged end of the door behind her slowly bending outward. The surface of the glass wasn't wide enough to encompass the other end, the actively-turning end, show her that.

She didn't have time to turn her head. She only had time to think: The door has opened behind me. There's somebody about to— That shows they did it. I've hit the jackpot. My trail was the hot one, Quinn's the cold.

That knowledge wasn't going to do her any good now. She'd asked for it, and she was about to get it.

Bristol asked her one more question; more to hold her off-guard a split moment longer, than because she needed to have it answered any more. "And how'd you come to tie me up in it? Where does your coming around here figure in?"

There was no need for her to worry about the answer; none was expected. Two and two had already been put together quite successfully without her further aid.

Something thick and pimply, full of tiny little knots, suddenly blanketed itself around her face from behind. A Turkish bath-towel wound into a bandage-arrangement, most likely, although she had no leisure to identify exactly what it was. She reared up galvanically, and lost one hand behind her, secured at the wrist by some powerful grip. The Bristol woman had jolted to her own feet in time with her, and she secured the other. The two were brought together at her back, crossed over, and tied crushingly with long thin strips of something, perhaps a dismembered pillow-case or linen face-towel.

She couldn't draw free breath for a moment, the rough-spun towelling muffled her whole face. The horrible thought that she was about to be smothered to death then and there occurred to her—but she realized dimly that they wouldn't have gone to all the trouble of tying up her hands if that had been their purpose. That alone kept her from going into an unmanageable paroxysm of struggle that might have brought about the very result it was trying to evade, as has happened in so many countless cases before.

Then a rough hand, heavier and larger than the other woman's, fumbled a little with the towel, brought it down half-face, freeing her eyes and nostrils. The remainder was tied far more tightly than the whole had been, with such constriction at the back of her head that she had a feeling as though her entire skull was going to be crushed with the pressure. But at least she could get air into her lungs and relieve the bursting coughing that had already started in.

Bristol was still in front of her eyes, as they came clear, addressing someone unseen behind her back. "Watch her mouth now, Griff. You can hear everything through these walls."

A man's voice growled: "Get her feet—them high heels are barking my shins."

The woman crouched down out of sight—the snowy mantle of the towel prevented acutely downcast vision—and Bricky felt her ankles knock together and some more thin strips whip dexterously in and out around them, lashing them together. She became a helpless sheaf, tied at both ends.

Joan Bristol came up into sight again. "What's the play now?" she asked. The man's voice said: "Don't you figure we ought to—?" He didn't finish it.

Bricky got the uncompleted meaning by indirection, via the suddenly-taut look on the woman's face. Her blood ran cold. He'd said it as calmly as though they were talking about lowering a shade or putting out a light.

The woman was scared. Not for Bricky's sake, just for their own. She must have known him better than anyone, whoever he was; known just how capable he was of doing it.

"Not here in the room with us, Griff," she said bleakly. "They know we were *in* this room. That's begging for it!"

"Naw, you don't get me," he argued matter-of-factly. "I don't mean chop-chop, that kind of stuff." He went over to the window, drew the sash up carefully, like one of those men who are handy to have around the house, suggesting an improvement. A patch of electric-lighted mold was revealed, on blank brickwork opposite. He edged his head forward a little and looked speculatively downward. Then he turned and spoke to the woman quietly. "Four floors ought to be enough." He motioned expressively with one hand. "The three of us get drinking up here, she goes over to the window to try and open it, get a little air in, it jams and— How many times does that happen?"

Bricky's heart was burning its way out through her chest like a blow-torch. "Yeah, but there's always a follow-up. That's no good for us this time, Griff. We'd get hooked here for hours, answering all kinds of police questions, and they're liable to work their way back a little too far—and before you know it, *other things*'ll come into it."

She shot him a look that was only meant for the two of them, but there were three of them there that understood it.

"What're we gonna do, leave her behind us here?" he snarled.

The Bristol woman raked distracted fingers through her hair. "Look at the mess y' got us into now," she bleated querulously. "What the hell did y'have to—"

"Shut up," the man answered flintily.

"She knows already. What d'you suppose brought her down here?"

"Then why the hell didn't you handle it right in the first place, like you were supposed to?"

"I couldn't manage him, he got out of hand. I only went down to the door and let you in thinking you could throw a scare into him, get him to come across. That didn't mean you had to sign off on him!"

"What'd you expect me to do, when he made a grab at it like he did, let him take it away from me? You saw what happened. I had to cork him up in self-defense. Anyway, what's the good of talking about it now? You loused it up and the damage is done. It's this twist we've got to think about now. I still think the smart thing would be to—"

"No, I'm telling you, Griff; no! That would be the dumb thing to do, not the smart thing. Let her chirp after we're gone. It's still only her word against ours. She went up there too, didn't she? She coulda done it just as well as us. Just let's get out of here—"

He flung open a closet-door on the other side of the room, looked in. "How about this? Let's stuff her in here, ditch the key. It backs up against a dead wall, so she'll never be heard. That ought to be good for plenty of head-start. It'll be days before they get around to busting this door open—"

They lugged her across to it between them, her legs trailing after her. They thrust her inside like some sort of a mothproof garment-bag.

"Better hitch her to something," he said, "otherwise she might try thumping against the door with her whole chassis." He rigged up a sort of halter-arrangement of sheeting-strips, passed it under her arms, wound it around one of the clothes-hooks behind her. She was left upright, with her feet to the floor, but unable to shift out from the rear wall of the closet.

The woman said: "Can she breathe in here, in case they take some time to—?"

"I don't know," he answered callously. "She should find that out and tell us about it afterwards."

They closed the door on her. A sudden pall of darkness obliterated everything. The key was withdrawn, the key that they were going to throw away somewhere outside. She could still hear them through the door, for a brief moment or two longer, making their last-minute preparations for departure.

"Got the bag?"

"What about that stew down at the desk? He must've seen her come up here."

"I can handle that easy. Where's that pint of rye I bought this afternoon? I'll offer him a goodbye-slug across the desk. He always goes around behind the letterboxes to down a shot. You duck out while he's back there, and make like she's with you, talk to yourself or something."

"What about the jig on the elevator?"

"We'll take the stairs. We've done that plenty of times before when we got tired waiting for him to come up, didn't we? The pushbutton don't work, that's all; he didn't hear us ringing it. Come on, you ready?"

"Hey, I'm missing that hotel-bill. We've got to settle up before we can get out of here. It must have fallen on the floor somewhere around the room here—"

"Never mind looking for it now; let it go. He can make out a new one for me down at the desk—"

The outer door closed and they were gone.

Going over to the third and final place in a cab, Quinn thought he understood what was behind all this complicated maneuvering. Holmes didn't want to walk into a trap. Therefore, to avoid one, he'd first of all moved Quinn out of the place he'd originally been in to a second place. He'd scrutinized him there unseen. But there still being no absolute surety that Quinn was alone, even though he seemed to be, he'd shifted the rendezvous to still a third place. This gave him the opportunity of being the first one on the grounds, and thereby being sure that the surroundings were sterile. To plant accomplices Quinn would have had to do it in full sight of the prospective prey.

He made it in about seven or eight minutes, no more. This Owen's had a good deal of the look of one of the old-time speak-easies of two decades before. It was the ground-floor of a brownstone house, and you went in by the basement. It had a neon sign to blazon it, but it was past the legal closing time by now, and that was out. Most of the people were out of it too. But he jumped down and went in anyway.

There was a man sitting there in a booth by himself, facing the front. His hair was frosting around the edges, but still dark on the crown of his head. He had on rimless spectacles, and they gave him rather a sedate look. Much too sedate to be sitting by himself at a bistro around five in the morning. He looked more the type to be at home nodding over a paper under a lamp, and with the deadline set for eleven. He had on a light-gray suit, and a light-gray hat hung from a wall-hook over his table. His hand was curved around a highball, and a second one, ownerless, stood on the opposite side of the table.

As Quinn came in he unobtrusively pointed one finger upward, then dropped his hand back to the table again.

Quinn went over and stood looking down at him. He sat looking up.

There was a curious moment of abeyance, of staring without speech, rendered grotesque by their nearness to one another.

The man at the table spoke first. "You're Quinn, I guess."

"I'm Quinn, and you're Holmes."

"How much is your taxi bill?"

"Sixty cents."

"Here's the money." He let the coins flow out of a hole at the end of his hand, as thought the change were something fluid.

Quinn came back in again in a moment. He hadn't moved, still sat there like that. Quinn stopped again where he'd been before, by the edge of the table.

Holmes gestured sketchily toward the plank-seat across from him. "Sit down."

Quinn sat tentatively, considerably to the outside of it, away from the wall.

Again they looked at one another, the young fellow in his early twenties, the man in his late forties or perhaps even fifties. Holmes was older, more experienced. It showed itself almost at once. He was more in command of the situation; even this situation, which should have been to his disadvantage. Not even virtue, being on the right side, can make up for lack of experience.

"There's a drink for you," he said. "I had to order ahead, so I'd be allowed to stay in here. It's past closing time."

Quinn thought, but without putting much stock into it: Be funny if he'd slipped something into this. That was 1910 stuff, though. He didn't take it seriously.

Holmes almost seemed to have read his thoughts. "Take mine instead, then," he said. "I haven't put it to my mouth yet." He drew the other glass away from in front of Quinn, tilted it to his lips, drank deeply.

"Whenever you say," he said ironically.

Quinn looked around him surreptitiously, thinking; This is no place to browbeat it out of him. I can't do much with him here. I shouldn't have let him pick the background.

Again Holmes seemed to read his mind. "Do you want to come out to the car instead?"

"I didn't know you had one. Why didn't you pick me up with it in the first place, instead of letting me do all this chasing back and forth?"

"I wanted to get a line on you first. I didn't know what I was up against." You still don't, thought Quinn bitterly.

Holmes drained his drink to the bottom, stood up, took down the light-gray hat and fitted it on his head with as much painstaking care and precision of adjustment as though he were leaving a business luncheon at high noon instead of an extorted rendezvous around crack of dawn. He looked a degree less sedate with his hat on, but only a degree; he was still every inch the dignified, austere, pontifical business-man. He started for the entrance, the invisible reins of the situation tight in his hand.

Quinn rose and took a step or two in his wake, leaving his drink untouched. Then he glanced back at it. I might need that for what's coming, he thought, I feel sort of saggy inside. He dropped back to the table a moment, drank it down in two or three long gulps, and then went out after Holmes. In no time he already felt better, more able to handle the situation that he was about to plunge into.

The car was a few doors down. Holmes was already standing waiting beside it, to show him.

"I didn't mean to rush you," he said urbanely, and motioned him in.

Quinn let him sidle it into motion. Then he said tersely, "Where y'heading?"

"Just coast around a little, I thought. We can't sit talking in it at the curb at this hour, we'll get a cop down on us, sticking his nose into the car."

"What's wrong with that?" Quinn chopped out.

Holmes said suavely, "I don't know. Do you?"

"I was asking you," Quinn said.

Holmes smiled at the asphalt surfacing out ahead of their oncoming bumper, as though he had discovered something amusing about it. There wasn't anything; it was like all other asphalt surfacing.

The car dawdled westward; it had to, Fifty-first was a westbound street. Neither of them said anything. Quinn thought: I'll let him begin; why should I make it any easier for him? He has to begin sooner or later. The play is with him; I'm carrying around his ticket of imprisonment and execution on me—supposedly. Whatever Holmes thought he kept locked up inside his head; it didn't come through to his face.

He wheeled them around northward into Sixth. They went

up that, then at random they turned east again through one of the even-numbered streets. It was impromptu, Quinn could tell that by the abrupt swing he gave the wheel at the last moment. They went straight through over to about First Avenue, and then went north some more. Finally he seemed to come to a decision. He turned off at a street that became a ramp, dipping under the East River Drive, and ended up against the water's edge with no bulkhead of any sort to protect it, in a sort of landing stage or apron just above the heaving gemmed blackness of the river.

He stopped only after their front tires were already tight against the low stone curbing that rimmed it.

Quinn held his peace. He thought, Two can play at your game. Holmes shut off the engine and killed the front lights.

All the filigree coruscation went out of the water, but it was still there. They could smell it at every breath, and sometimes hear it. It made a little chuckling sound every now and then, like a very small infant.

"You're pretty close to the edge, aren't you?" Quinn remarked.

"The wheels're blocked. You're not nervous, are you?"

"I'm not nervous," Quinn said flatly. "Should I be?"

Holmes turned his head slightly aside.

"What're you looking at your watch for?"

"I was trying to figure how long ago you met me at Owen's."

"Twenty minutes," Quinn said, "and this should have been all over with by now."

"It's going to be. Have you got the check? How much do you want for it?"

Something's wrong, thought Quinn. I'm not handling myself right. I'm in the wrong situation. I wonder how he came to get the upper hand, at what point along the way?

He pinched the bridge of his nose tight for a minute.

Holmes was hunched forward, making a papery noise with his hands down close against the dashboard lights. "Here's two hundred dollars," he said, "now give me the check."

Quinn didn't answer.

Holmes turned around and looked at him. "Two hundred and fifty." Quinn didn't answer.

"How much do you want?"

Quinn spoke slow and quiet. This was his inning now. "What makes you think I want money for it?"

Holmes just looked at him.

"Here's what I want for it: I want a written confession that you killed Stephen Graves tonight. If you don't give me that, then I'm going to take you and the check, both, to the police."

Holmes' lower jaw kept trying to adhere to his upper, and falling away loose again. "No, wait—" he said two or three times over. "No, wait—"

"You weren't up there tonight, Mr. Holmes?"

The lower jaw suddenly clamped tight and didn't fall away any more; so tight that not a word came through.

"He's dead up there. And you're the man that did it. You don't really think I found that check skating around town loose in a taxi, do you? Where d'you suppose I found it? Where I found Stephen Graves' body lying sprawled out!"

"You're lying. You're trying to take me for something that you couldn't possibly know."

"I was up there."

"You were up there? You're lying."

"You and he were sitting face to face in those two leather-covered chairs, in that second-floor room, that study, at the back. He had a drink, but he didn't offer you one. He had a cigar, but he didn't offer you one. You chewed one of your own to pieces. I'll even tell you what kind it was. Corona. I'll even tell you what you had on. You had on a brown suit. You put on a gray one to come out and meet me now, the second time, but you had on a brown one then. You're missing a half-button from the left sleeve. Never mind jerking your hand back; let it ride, let it grab at the cuff of this one. I know anyway, without that. Now am I lying? Now do you believe I was up there? Now do you believe I saw him dead—and know that you killed him?"

Holmes didn't answer. Again his head turned aside.

"Never mind looking at your watch. Your watch can't save you."

Holmes put it away. He spoke at last. "Yes, my watch can. You're just a kid, aren't you? Gee, I almost feel sorry for you, son. I didn't know you were as young as you are, over the phone."

Quinn blinked.

"You're having a lot of trouble with your eyes, aren't you? Lights on the dashboard've got rings around them, haven't they? Like big soap-bubbles. That's it."

"That's what?"

"See, you talked too much. You've talked yourself into the grave. If you had just kept your mouth closed, I really would have believed you found that check in a taxi. You would have gone to sleep here in the car. And you would have awakened in a couple of hours beside the river here, *without* the check. But otherwise unharmed. Maybe with a ten-dollar bill in your pocket to sugarcoat the experience. Head weighs too much, doesn't it? Too heavy for your neck. Keeps toppling over, as if it were made of solid rock."

Quinn suddenly pushed at it and held it back.

Holmes smiled a little, patronizingly. "If you'd stuck to your own highball-glass, this wouldn't have happened to you, you would have been all right. You were suspicious, but not suspicious enough. You took the wrong glass. Mine. I'm a chess-player. You're evidently not. Chess is figuring out your opponent's move before he makes it."

He stopped and watched him some more. "Tie too tight? That's right, pull the knot down. Bust open the neck of your shirt too. That's right. Doesn't help much, though, does it? Can't keep it from happening. You're going to sleep. Here in the car. You're going into the river. Without a mark on you. I'll take the check off you before you do, don't worry. I'll find it, it's on you. You wouldn't have come to the pay-off without having it on you somewhere. It's stuck in your shoe, probably. That's about where your type of youngster would think was a clever hiding-place for it."

Quinn ripped himself off the seat as though he were pulling out stitches binding him to it, clawed for the door-catch in a sort of toppling, forward fall. Holmes kept him up off the floor by slipping an arm around under his stomach and drew him back onto the seat again, like a topheavy sack.

"What's the good trying to get down? Even if you did get out, you probably couldn't stand up any more anyway. You'd only fall down on the ground outside."

One of Quinn's legs flexed a couple of times, trying to gain altitude.

Holmes rotated the little lever, brought the window down on that side. "Trying to kick out the glass? You haven't the strength of a kick left in you—" He turned suddenly and caught at Quinn's flailing hand. "What's that you've got? A table-knife?

What can you do with that? Look how easy I can twist it away from you. You're all rotten with sleep."

He flung it out forward through the side-opening. "Did you hear it splash? That's water in front of us, that even black line you see. Right over the hub-cap."

He held one arm propped against the side of the car, with an attitude of patient waiting, holding Quinn passively walled-in behind it. Something like a futile sob sounded blurredly deep down in the latter's throat.

"Now you can't move at all, can you? That's right, make a lazy pass with your hand, like you were brushing away gnats. That's about all you're still able to do. In a minute you won't be able to do that, even. There go your eyes. Down—down—down—"

I found out one thing, anyway, Quinn thought foggily. I was on the right track. But I found out too late—

"You won't get away with it, mister," he mumbled drowsily, as his head went down for the last time. "Bricky knows. There are two of us, not just one—"

SHE LEANED there bound and helpless in the dark. They'd never make that bus now. Poor Quinn would wait there for her at the Graves house with the dead man to keep him company, until broad daylight; until someone happened on him there, and gave the alarm, and they arrested him for it. And that would be the end of it; he'd never be able to clear himself. After all, this Bristol woman and her partner hadn't left anything half as incriminating behind them over there as that broken-into wall safe that he was responsible for. She could accuse them all she wanted to afterwards—that is, *if* she survived this walling-up alive—but it wouldn't do any good. She hadn't been an eye-witness to his first entry; she hadn't even set eyes on him until afterwards. Her word would be worthless.

Precious minutes ticking by. Minutes that were drops of her heart's blood. It must be all of five-thirty by now. In another ten minutes at the latest she and Quinn should have been starting for the bus terminal. What a fat chance now. She might have known the city would outsmart them. It always did. Just a small-town boy and a small-town girl—what chance did they have against such an antagonist? He'd go up the river to the electric chair. And she'd turn into a tough-gutted chain-dancer in a treadmill, without a heart, without a hope, without even a dream any more.

Precious minutes trickling by, that couldn't be stopped, that couldn't be called back again.

Suddenly that other door outside had reopened and someone was in the room again. For a minute wild hope flashed through her mind. Ah, the happy ending, the camera-finish, like in the storybooks, like in the pictures! Someone to rescue her in the nick of time. The besotted hotel-clerk come up to investigate, his suspicions aroused by her non-reappearance when they left? Or maybe even Quinn himself, drawn here by some miraculous sixth sense—

Then a voice spoke, cottony with subdued rage, and the bottom dropped out of her hopes again. It was Griff, Bristol's accomplice. The two of them had come back again. Maybe to finish her off, here and now, on the spot.

"Why'dn't you think of that sooner, you half-witted dope? What's the matter, your brain missing a cylinder?"

"I'm going to ask her now," Bristol's voice answered him grimly. "I would've the first time, only you came out of there too fast for me. There must have been *something* there that tipped her off to me. It's a cinch she didn't pull my name and address out of a trick hat—"

The closet-door swung out and blinding light spilled over her, shutting off her eyes for a moment. She was aware of herself being loosened from the hook that had held her fast. She was hauled out into the open once more, between the two of them. The towel-gag was lowered sufficiently to enable her to speak.

Joan Bristol held the back of her hand poised threateningly

toward her lips, ready to swing it and flatten them. "Now you try to scream and I'll dent you in!"

She couldn't have, even if she'd wanted to. All she could do was pant and sag exhaustedly against the man who was holding her up.

Bristol raised a hand to her hair, took a half-turn in it, and drew her head back at a taut inclination. "Now, no stalling. What I want to know is this: just what was it over at the Graves place that hooked you onto me? How'd you know I knew him, and how'd you know where to find me? I'm going to let you have it, and I'm going to keep on letting you have it, until you give me the straight goods on it!"

Bricky answered in a muffled but unhesitant voice. "You dropped your hotel-bill over there. I found it lying in the room with him."

The blow, when it came, was rabid and with a sound like a paper bag full of water dropping from a third-floor window, but it wasn't from Bristol to Bricky, it was from her own team-mate to Bristol. She staggered five or six steps back away from the commingled little group they made.

"Why, you—!" he grated. "I mighta known you'd do something like that! It's as good as leaving your calling-card sticking out of his vest-pocket! I oughta slap you down to the soles of your feet!"

"She's lying!" Joan Bristol shrilled, one side of her face slowly reddening as with an eczema. "I could swear I still saw it in my handbag after I got back here—!"

"Did you take it out to show it to him? Answer me! Did you? Yes or no?"

"Yes, I did—I—you know, as part of the build-up, to show him how bad I needed money. That was at the start, before he got tough about it. But I *know* I put it back again, Griff! I know I brought it back here with me!"

Bricky shook her head, within his boa-constrictor-like grasp. "It fell out. It was for seventeen dollars and eighty-nine cents. It had 'Past Due' stamped on it, in sort of purple ink. It even had your room-number on it."

He gave her a merciless shake. "Did you bring it here with you? What'd you do with it? Where is it?"

"I left it there where it was. I was afraid to touch anything. I left everything just the way I found it."

Bristol closed in again, the sting of the punitive blow evidently lessened by now. "Don't take her word for it, she may have brought it with her. Frisk her and see if it's on her."

"You do it, you're a dame. You ought to know where—I'll hold her."

Her hands went quickly and thoroughly about their business. She missed it by inches. Bricky's legs were tightly bound together at the feet, anyway. She held them that way, compact. It was within the top of one of her stockings, to the inside. The Bristol woman poked a finger down into each, at the outside of the leg.

"She hasn't got it on her."

"Then we'll have to go back there and get it! We can't leave it lying there, it's a dead give-away. You chump, I ought to bust your neck lopsided for you!"

The threat glanced off his partner's pelt unheeded. She was thinking. "Wait a minute, I've got the play, Griff," she said in a rapid, bated voice. "We'll take *her* back there with us, and we'll leave her there with him. Fix it to look like she did it to him. You know—" She hitched her head toward Bricky with unmistakable meaning; "do what you wanted to do in the first place, only do it over there. Give them a double-header to figure out. That way we're in the clear. It don't have anything to do with us."

He thought about it for a minute, brittle-eyed.

"It's the only out for us, Griff. Rub out this detour by finishing her off where she started out from."

He was starting to nod, faster and faster. He got through nodding—fast too—and sprang into action. "All right, fix her up to get her past that desk downstairs. She's pie-eyed, see, and you've got to hold her up. I'll still get him out of the way like I told you. We're helping her home, that's all. Leave her hands the way they are, just loosen her feet so she can move on them."

They were numb from constriction, she couldn't use them at first, even after they'd been freed.

Bristol took her own coat, slung it around Bricky's shoulders, concealing the defection of her arms. That wasn't particularly grotesque, there was a new style that had come over from London lately for women to wear their coats just that way, leaving their arms out of the sleeves.

"Take the towel off her chin," the man said. "You'll have to. Here, use this on her."

He brought something out from behind, handed it over to Bristol. Something that glinted and was black. Probably the one that had been used on Graves.

It disappeared under the enshrouding coat, and Bristol's hand ground it hard into Bricky's spine, deep as a spinal anesthetic being administered with a snub-nosed, triggered needle.

"Now wait here with her. I'm going down ahead and get the car out of bed, and get rid of that stew down at the desk. Gimme about ten minutes, the garage is a couple blocks over. Better take the stairs."

The door closed after him and the two women were left alone.

They didn't speak; not a word passed between them. They stood there curiously rigid, one directly behind the other, the coat hooded between them, raised in the middle like a small tent with the passage of Bristol's hand.

Bricky thought: I wonder if she'd shoot, if I made a sudden step to the side, tried to break contact with the bore of the gun? Somehow she didn't make the attempt, and not altogether through fear either. They were taking her back to the very place she had wanted to take them all along: to the scene of the murder. A feat that she probably would never have been able to accomplish single-handed, particularly in the case of the man. Why not wait? That was the better place for it. True, this opportunity might not recur up there—but why not wait and see? There was always Quinn.

Bristol shifted a little, spoke at last. "That's long enough. Start walking over to the door now. Now let me warn you for the last time. If you let a peep out of you, on the stairs or on the way through the lobby, or outside while we're walking over to the car, this goes off into you head-first. And don't think I'm kidding. I've never kidded about anything in my life. I was born without a sense of humor."

Bricky didn't answer. She probably had been, at that, she reflected. It must be hell to be like that *all* the time; dead sore at the world and dangerous.

They went out of the room, and along the musty corridor of before. Behind one of those doors the loose, tinny jangling of an alarm-clock went off just after they'd gone a few steps past, and a curious transmitted shock passed from one to the other, that was almost like electric current passing through the gun for a conductor.

She heard Bristol let out a deep breath behind her. She knew without having to be told how close that accidental, extraneous thing had come to exploding the weapon.

They turned aside where there was a dark-red exit-bulb burning, passed through a fireproofed hinged door, and started down an emergency staircase. Its lower reaches brightened imperceptibly with light from the lobby. They could already hear Griff's voice, somewhat hollow and resonant in the open down there, before they were quite clear of it.

"Take another one. Go on, don't be afraid, that's what it's for."

"Wait a minute," Bristol whispered tensely behind her, and held her motionless at the foot of the stairs. The desk was out of sight from there, around an el-shaped turn. They had to go straight past the front of it, however, to reach the street.

Somebody gave a strangled cough, and Griff's voice sounded again. "Easy, easy. Don't swallow the whole bottle."

"Now," Bristol hissed, and urged her forward via the gun, as though it were some sort of a handle which controlled her movements.

He was there by himself, leaning engagingly forward over the desk on both arms. In front of him there were just the tiers of pigeonholes, cutting off the view from the rear.

The two-headed, four-legged, curiously-humpbacked creature that was the two women, the two women and a gun, slithered rapidly by. He didn't turn his head or seem to be aware of them at all, but he fanned one hand loosely behind his back, sweeping it repeatedly in the direction of the entrance. As though he had a funny sort of waggy tail there, cropped short.

They were in the car already when he joined them. It was down further, away from the hotel entrance, and Bristol had her in the back with her, waiting. He got in in front, and they still didn't say anything between the three of them. Bristol had shifted the gun around to her side now, because of the impediment of the back of the car-seat. Bricky sat there docilely, made no move to resist. She wanted them to reach there unhindered fully as much as they wanted to themselves.

The night was falling to pieces all around them, cracks and slivers of light showing through all over more and more.

They made the run up swiftly and remorselessly. Just before they took the final turn around into Seventieth, Bristol warned him in a slurred undertone, as though just the two of them were alone in the car: "Watch it, now. Don't pull up unless you're sure."

They turned in and he ran straight past the house first of all, as though it had nothing to do with them, as though they had some destination miles from here.

It held its secret well. Well and long. There was no sign of life, inside or out. It was just as it had been yesterday morning at this same early hour; the morning before.

Their three faces had turned to it as one, as they went by.

Was he back yet? Was he in there? Oh, God—now and only now was she beginning at last to get frightened.

Griff swerved in abruptly only after they were well past it; reversed and backed up a house-length or two; braked finally, but still a good three or four doors down from it. Then they watched again briefly, from their stationary position now.

Nothing.

"Still good for another quick trip in and out again," he murmured tight-lipped. "Come on, let's go."

Her heart was racketing wildly as they hauled her out to the sidewalk, sandwiched her in between them, and advanced rapidly toward it in the gun-metal pall that overhung the street. They hustled her up the stoop and into the concealment of the vestibule with quick looks this way and that to make sure that no one was observing. No one was.

"Made it," Joan Bristol exhaled relievedly. "Where's that key she had on her? Hurry up."

They thrust her inside between them, closed it again after them. She'd played the game through to the end. And this was the end now. Now that they'd closed this door on her, every second was going to count. If he came back even five minutes from now, he'd be five minutes too late; he'd find her here—like Graves was. And even if he came back right now, that mightn't help much; it might only mean the two of them, instead of just one. These people were armed and he wasn't.

Maybe—maybe he wouldn't come back at all. Maybe *he'd* had something like this happen to him too, only somewhere else.

The darkness inside the house was as impenetrable as ever. Bristol cautioned Griff the same way Bricky had Quinn the first time they came in here—it seemed like years ago. "Don't touch the lights, now, until we get up there." But they hadn't been two murderers stealing in in the dark, they had only been a couple of kids trying to straighten themselves out, get a new start.

Griff lit a match; dwarfed it in the bowl of his two hands to an orange-red pinpoint. He led the way with it. Bricky trudged at his heels, still armless under the coat, the gun still fused to her living back. The Bristol woman came last. The silence around them was overpowering and, to Bricky at any rate, charged with such high-voltage tension that it was as though the air were filled with static electricity, creating little tingling shocks at every step.

Suppose he was waiting up there in the room ahead, with the lights out? Suppose he heard them, came forward now, saying "Bricky, is that you?" She would be bringing death upon him. And if he wasn't up there, then she had brought death upon herself. But of the two choices, she preferred the latter.

Then again, what was the difference either way? It was too late now; they'd missed the bus. The city was the real victor. Just as it always was.

The opening to the death room loomed black and empty before them in the stunted rays of his match. He whipped it out and for a moment there was nothing. Then he lit the room lights, and they shoved her in there with the dead man. Into the emptiness where there was no Quinn waiting to help her.

Griff said : "All right, now, hurry up and get it. Let's do what we have to, and get out of here fast!"

Bristol scanned the floor, turned on Bricky menacingly. "Well, where is it? I don't— Where'd you say you saw it?" She was still holding the gun in her hand, although she'd shifted out from behind Bricky's back.

"Over there by him, is where I said," Bricky answered in a listless voice.

Then she added: "And you believed me."

"Then you didn't—!" the other woman yelped. She swung toward her confederate. "See, I told you!"

His open hand burst into Bricky's face. "Where've you got it?"

She staggered lopsidedly, then came up again, smiling bleakly. "That's your problem."

His voice calmed suddenly. The calm voice of murder. He

always seemed calmest when contemplating that. "Let me have that," he said to Bristol. "I'll do it."

The gun passed back to him again. "Get away from her. Move over."

She was suddenly alone there, by herself.

He was coming toward her; he must have wanted to make it a contact wound. So the possibility of self-destruction could enter into it, afterwards.

It only took him a second or two to move forward, but her thoughts took hours. She was going to die now. Maybe that was better. It was too late now to take that bus—the bus for home. The clock said—

THAT WAS the last thing she saw. She closed her eyes on it and waited, like a prisoner facing a firing squad.

The roar of the gun jarred them open again. She thought it was the loudest thing she'd ever heard. Louder than the loudest backfire, louder than a tire blowing out right in front of your face. She wondered why it didn't hurt her more. She wondered if that was what death was always like, just that stunned, deafened feeling—

Griff was lumbering erratically around just in front of her, two or three feet in front of her. Was it he doing that, or was it she? He had too many arms, he had too many legs, there was too much of him—

The gun, still streaking its sputum of smoke after it, was vibrating jaggedly, tilted upward in his hand. Another hand had his collared by the wrist, made a bulge there. The crook of an arm was wrapped around his neck, elbow pointed toward her. Above it, his face was contorted, suffused with dammed-up blood. And behind it, another face peered, equally contorted, equally blood-heavy. But not too much so to be unrecognizable.

The boy next door, fighting for her. Fighting for her—the way the boy next door should.

Suddenly there was a floor-shaking collapse. No more Griff, no more double arms and legs and heads in front of her, no more anything else. Two bodies threshing around on the floor.

Joan Bristol flashed past her, coming from the recesses of the room, an andiron snatched up from before the fireplace raised high above her head.

Bricky's hands were tied; she couldn't reach for her and grab her. But if the boy next door could launch himself against a gun with his bare hands, then she could launch herself against an andiron with no hands at all.

She slithered one leg out until it was almost calf-low to the floor, deftly spoked it between Bristol's two scampering feet.

Joan Bristol went down face-first in a rocking-horse fall, and the andiron went looping futilely through the air, clanged against a wall somewhere.

Bricky flung herself down on her before she could get up again, knelt on her bodily with both knees at once, pinning her flat. Every time Bristol tried to squirm free and unsaddle her, she raised one knee slightly, slammed it down into her again with redoubled force.

She didn't have time to glance at the men. An arm was swinging over there, pounding into the side of a head like a mallet. Twice, three times. Suddenly they broke into two, one of them staggered upright, one of them stayed flat. The one coming up was bringing the gun up with him.

"I'll be right with you, Bricky," a winded voice gasped from over there.

She looked then. Griff was face-down to the floor. He

twitched a little, raised a dazed hand to the side of his head, but he stayed flat the way he was. Quinn was standing watchfully over him for a second. He was the one had the gun.

"I can't hold her down—" she panted.

He went over to Graves' desk, picked something up, came around in back of her, and sawed her hands apart. Both of them were still breathing too fast to be able to talk much.

He took the same bonds he had just removed from her, re-knitted them, and fastened them around Joan Bristol's hands, behind her back.

"Do that, uh, to him too," she heaved.

"You bet." He went into the bedroom, came out with linen stripped from Graves' bed, ripped it and went to work.

"I saw them coming in with you, outside on the street. I was watching from one of the front windows on this floor. Something about the way you were walking between them, sort of stiff, told me they had a gun on you. I backed up into the bathroom and laid low—"

"They did it, Quinn. We got the right ones at last."

"I know it wasn't Holmes. Gee, I had a narrow escape, though—" He stood up, surveyed his own handiwork. "That'll hold them for a few minutes anyway, if not for long. No need to gag them; let them attract all the attention they can. In fact, we want them to, we'll do it for them."

"Quinn, what good is it to us now? There they are, but what's the difference? Look." She pointed. "Two past six."

"Let's try for it anyway. Let's go down there. If it isn't that one, there may be another later in the day—"

"It's no use, Quinn. We talked that over. We won't be strong enough to take the later one. You'll see. The city's awake now."

"The cops're awake too. We *will* be stuck if we just stand here— Come on, Bricky, try, try!" He caught her by the hand, pulled her out of the room after him, down the stairs.

"Pick up your valise. Open the door and stand there by it. I'll use the phone down here, it'll only take a minute."

He picked up the phone. "Ready?" She was standing there out in the vestibule, valise in hand, poised for instant flight. "Get on your mark, get set, here goes."

He said into the phone: "Give me the police." Then he said to her, "Hold that door out of the way for me." She pushed it back with her arm and held it wide.

"Hello, is this the police? I want to report a murder. At—" He gave the house-number. "—East Seventieth Street. You'll find Stephen Graves lying dead on the second floor of his house there. In the same room with him you'll find the two people who did it. You'll find them tied up and waiting for you, if you don't take too long getting there. In the desk, also in that same room, you'll find a special delivery letter. That'll give you the reason. Oh, and one other thing—you'll find the gun that they did it with, downstairs in the vestibule, under the doormat, waiting for you. Hunh? No, this isn't a rib. I only wish it was. Me? Oh, just a—just a fellow who happened to be passing by."

He flung the instrument down without even bothering to re-hook it. "Go!" he shouted to her, and came scurrying after her.

He dipped down for a minute, shoved the gun under the doormat, and then went floundering outside and down the stoop-steps after her.

"Their car!" she called back, pointing as she led the way. "He left his keys in it."

He slammed into it after her, swerved it out away from the curb. They'd hardly rounded the corner than they could already hear the keen of some approaching radio patrol-car, still invisible, racing up from the opposite direction.

"Gee, they're fast," he said. "If we'd had to stay on foot, they would have already grabbed us by now."

They went tearing down Madison, almost empty of traffic at that hour. Twice Quinn took a chance, drove through a red light slackening speed but not stopping.

"We'll never make it, Quinn," she shouted above the hiss of wind.

"We can try, at least."

The sky kept getting lighter over in the east. Another day, another New York day was on the way. Look at it. Even dawn in this town was no good.

You've won, she kept thinking bitterly. Are you happy? Does it do you good to know you've got us, you've wrecked us, a little fellow and a little girl like us? The odds were fair and square, weren't they? Like they always are when you're involved, you top-heavy, bone-crushing bully. Some odds. Some fight. You rotten place, trying to look pretty in the early morning; you—you New York.

A tear whipped straight across her temple, from the corner of her eye toward her ear, carried that way by the backthrow of the wind they were making.

His hand stole a moment from the wheel, squeezed hers tight, so tight the skin wrinkled, then beat it back again fast to the throbbing rim to keep the life from being crushed out of them. "Don't cry, Bricky," he said looking down the avenue ahead, and swallowed hard.

"I'm not," she said smoulderingly. "I wouldn't give it that much satisfaction. Let it dish it out all it wants to, I can take it."

The buildings kept shooting up taller ahead of them all the

time. With every block they seemed to put on additional inches, though it was just the over-all aspect of the skyline and not individual rooftops that altered. From eight and ten stories to fifteen, from fifteen to twenty, from twenty to thirty and more. Higher, higher all the time, encroaching on the sky, leaving less and less of it, until sometimes it was just like a jagged irregular manhole-opening over them, with the cover left off. Bright blue up there. And below dimness, perpetual dimness and labyrinths of concrete from which there was no egress.

They'd shifted over now, they were going down Seventh on their way toward the Thirties. Broadway, on their right, kept edging closer through each successive side-street opening. Then suddenly, just as the Forties were ending, it sheared straight across their path, forming the X, the double triangle, that everyone calls Times Square but that's really two other squares, Duffy above the waist, Longacre below.

The most famous patch of asphalt on the face of the earth, this is, and yet so commonplace, so like nothing at all, when you're on it. The Palace and the State Building on the left, the wedge-shaped Times skyscraper straight ahead, and on the right, as the building-line suddenly veered way out and left a gap, that odd-shaped tower-cube abruptly struck up into the paling-blue morning light—

She grabbed at his arm so unexpectedly, so fiercely, the whole wheel came around with it, and they were nearly flung up against the statue of Father Duffy. Their front wheel on that side took a bite out of the sidewalk, then came down off it again as he swerved crazily the opposite way. It took him another half-block to straighten them out, get the machine under control again.

She was up on her knees, facing backward on the seat, her

hand still riveted to his shoulder, pummelling it with joy and babbling into the wind racing backward.

"Quinn, look! Oh, Quinn, look! The clock on the Paramount says five-to! It's only five to six now! That one back there in the room must have been fast—"

"Maybe this one's slow— Don't, you'll fall out."

She was blowing kisses to it, she was almost beside herself with ecstatic gratitude. "No, it's right, it's right! It's the only friend I ever had in this whole town. I knew it wouldn't let me down. That means we can still make it, we still have a chance—"

The Times monolith clipped it, and it was gone now. She'd never see it again. If her heart had its way, she'd never be here where it was. But with her chin resting low on the top of the seat, she peered backward to where it had been, in grateful, misty-eyed goodbye.

"Get down on the seat, I'm going to make a turn."

The razor-edged sharpness of it lifted two wheels clear, and they were in Thirty-fourth. And there, on the second block over, between Eighth and Ninth—there it was ahead of them, under way already, the big cross-country bus. . . .

It had just finished clearing the terminal ramp as they got there, turned and straightened itself out, and now it was beginning to pick up speed, point westward, headed for the river tunnel, the Jersey side—and home.

So close, and yet so out of reach. A minute sooner and they would have been on it. She made a little whimpering noise in her throat, then choked it down. She didn't ask him what they were to do, nor he her; instead he went ahead and did it.

He wouldn't give up. He sent the lighter, more maneuverable thing that they were in winging after it. They gained, they closed, they caught up. It slowed ponderously as it neared Tenth to make its turn for the tunnel approaches, and they coasted deftly up alongside of it. A friendly red light did the rest, stopping the big and the little alike with overawing impartiality.

It came to a shuddering elephantine stop, and they to a skittish grasshopper-like one.

They were already out and on the ground before it had quite finished, and pounding pleadingly on the glass inset of its pneumatically-controlled door. And she, at any rate, bobbing up and down in frenzied supplication.

"Open up, let us in! Take us with you! We're going your way! Ah, let us in! Don't leave us here, don't make us stay behind— Show him the money, Quinn; quick, take it out—"

The driver shook his head and scowled and swore at them in pantomime through the glass. And the red light lasted and lasted, and he couldn't shove off, had to sit there looking at their agonized faces. Anyone with a heart would have had to give in. And he evidently had some such thing inside him that he used to pump his blood with. He gave them a final black look, and he glanced around to see if anyone was noticing, and then he grudgingly pulled the control lever and the door swung hissingly open.

"Why don'tchuz get on where you're supposed to?" he bellowed. "Whad-dya think this is, a crosstown trolley stopping at every corner?" And things like that that drivers say when they're afraid of being thought soft-hearted.

She went reeling down the aisle, found a vacant double near the back. A moment later Quinn had dropped down beside her, their borrowed car jockeyed over to the curb and left behind, their tickets jealously clutched in his hand. Tickets for all the way, tickets for home.

The bus got started again.

They were well out in the Jersey meadows, the tunnel behind them, New York behind them, before she'd gotten enough breath back to talk at all.

"Quinn," she said in an undertone, so she wouldn't be overheard by those around them, "I wonder if we'll be able to make it stick? What we did back there just now. Do you think those two will be able to talk their way out of it? After all, we won't be there to give our side of it."

"We won't have to. There'll be others who can put the finger on them so effectively they'll never be able to wriggle out of it."

"Others? You mean there are witnesses?"

"Not witnesses to the murder. No one saw that. But there's one member of his own family, in particular, whose testimony will be enough to convict them."

"How do you know?"

"There's a letter from the younger brother, Roger, back there in Graves' desk, where I told them to look for it. The one I told you was away at college somewhere. It was sent special delivery, he must have gotten it sometime yesterday. I came across it while I was waiting for you to show up. In it the kid tried to tip off the elder Graves, so he wouldn't come across if the Bristol woman tried to put her hooks into him."

"How'd he know?"

"He was married to her."

She held her lips parted for a moment. "Then that explains what had us so stumped in that note from her to Graves. 'You don't know me, but I feel like a member of the family.'"

"That's it. One of these undergraduate gin-marriages. Only it wasn't even a real one at that; it was spiked, phony. She still has a husband at large somewhere, so in order to steer clear of a bigamy rap, she went through a mock ceremony with him. It's the dirtiest thing I've heard of in years."

"How'd he come to get tangled up with such a bum?"

"She was entertaining at a roadhouse near his college, and he used to go there Saturday nights with his pals, that's how he first met her. He's just a kid, what do you expect? The kid fell for her, the kid got high, and the kid proposed marriage. She and this former vaudeville partner of hers looked him up, and they found out he came from a prominent family and meant dough. That made it different. So they rigged this thing up and they took him."

"But that's pure corn, that goes back to about 1900."

"They got away with it. Sometimes the oldest things work the best. Just listen to this. The partner used to do a vaudeville act in which he impersonated a rube justice of the peace. So all he did was do the act over again, for the kid's benefit, and the kid believed he was really married to her. He planted himself somewhere nearby, she and the kid drove out with their witnesses one Saturday night, and a counterfeit ceremony was performed. I suppose the gin helped a lot."

"And you mean he didn't tumble—?"

"Not for two months after, according to his own letter. It was kept secret by mutual consent. The kid went ahead with his courses and she went ahead with her entertaining. The partner came back to town here and laid low, naturally. Those were a couple of very profitable months for the two of them."

"What lice there are in this world."

"They were on a part-time man-and-wife basis, the kid and her, and week-ends, which was the only time he could see her, was when the touch used to go on him. They bled the kid white, took him for all they could."

"And then, I suppose, the pitcher went to the well once too often."

"That's about it. All the dough was coming from Stephen Graves in the first place, not the kid, naturally. So when the take started to climb up a little too high, he cut off the kid's funds."

"That blew the lid off."

"They didn't trust each other, she and the partner. When the easy money stopped short, he must've thought she was trying to double-cross him, hold out on him or something. Anyway, he did the last thing he should have done; rushes back up there and shows himself around, trying to find out what's what. The rest you can piece out for yourself."

"Just about."

"The kid caught sight of him hanging around her dressing-room, recognized him, and at long last tumbled to the frame that they'd worked on him. I guess he would have killed the two of them if he could have got his hands on them, but they lit out just one jump ahead of him."

"I bet they did."

"Only they weren't satisfied even yet. Success must have gone to their heads or something. They figured the stunt might be good for one more lump payment at this end, before Roger could get to his older brother and warn him what was what. After all, there was a debutante-age sister to be considered, and all that stuff doesn't do anyone any good, even when they're innocent parties. And that's where the shooting came in. The special delivery from the kid beat them to Stephen by just a couple of hours' time; he was ready for them by the time they showed up."

"I can fill in the rest of it myself; I overheard that part of it from them. Instead of bluffing easy and getting frightened, he turned the tables on them. The woman went in first to cinch the deal, leaving the man waiting for her outside the house. Graves told her to go to hell, and told her he was going to bring police action against her. She lost her head, ran down to the door, and let her accomplice in. He pulled a gun on Graves. Graves grabbed for it, and Graves lost his life."

"And I nearly lost mine. And you nearly lost yours."

"You mean when you jumped them back there?"

"No. Holmes. Before then."

"Why? What happened?"

"Holmes. He wasn't the right one. But he was so scared stiff about that check, that when he found out Graves was dead and he might be accused of having done it, he lost his head and nearly turned himself into the very thing that he was trying so hard not to be suspected of. Murder, with me the object."

"He tried to——?"

"He did more than try. He practically had the thing finished. He put something into my whiskey, and he was going to roll me over into the river. I think he already had me out of the car; I don't know, I was only half-conscious by then. Your name saved me. I happened to mumble that you'd know he did it anyway, that it wouldn't save him to get rid of me. That threw him into reverse. It doubled his fright, but at least it snapped him out of it. Instead of shoving me in, he spent the next quarter of an hour dashing cold water into my face and walking me around and around the car, so the sedative would wear off. Then he rushed me back to his place and filled me full of pitch-black coffee.

"By the time that was over—I dunno—we sort of believed each other. Don't ask me why. I guess we were both too worn out to be suspicious any more. I believed he hadn't done it, and he believed I wasn't just trying to shake him down on the strength of the check.

"He told me he hadn't meant to do it. For that matter, I guess they never do. He'd simply been caught short, and to cover himself up he'd palmed the check off on Graves. But then he'd already raised the money to make it good even by the time he went over to see Graves last night. Then he found he couldn't square it because Graves couldn't find the blamed thing any more when he went to look for it. It had fluttered out of the cash-box when I broke into the safe the first time, you remember.

"He was uneasy, of course, in fact highly agitated about it; but he realized that Graves was a gentleman, would be above holding it out on him purposely for the sake of forcing him to pay ransom for it or anything like that. Graves was cold to him, after such a thing having happened, but they had no outright row or anything. He left with the understanding that Graves wouldn't prosecute, and that he was to call back again today, when Graves had had more time to look for it. He was expecting the Bristol woman at the time; Holmes' unannounced visit had taken place just before hers.

"Anyway, I let him have the check back. It would only have enmeshed him in the murder if it popped up afterwards—and I was dead sure by that time he hadn't been guilty of that. He made out a new one right under my eyes, predated it to match the old and mailed it back to Graves in an envelope; the estate can cash it."

He took something out of his pocket and showed it to her.

Her face paled a little at the sight of so much money; for a minute she thought—

"No, don't be frightened," he reassured her. "It's honest this time. Holmes gave it to me. He insisted on my taking it, after he'd heard our story, yours and mine. I'd told him about us, how badly we wanted to get back home. He said he had a fellow-feeling for me; we'd both been guilty of mistakes, on one and the same night, that might have led to serious consequences—me by breaking into that safe and he with his bad check—but that we'd both been given another chance, and we'd both probably learned our lessons. And he was so grateful and relieved at getting out of the mess, he made me a present of this. This two hundred cash. He said it would come in handy for a nest-egg, for us to start off with back home. He said later on, if I feel I'd like to, I can send it back to him a little at a time.

"It's enough for us to get a new start on. You can do a lot with two hundred dollars in our town. We could make a first payment on a little place of our own and—"

She didn't hear him. She wasn't listening any more. Her head had dropped to his shoulder, was rocking there gently in time with the motion of the bus. Her eyes drooped blissfully closed. "We're going home," she thought drowsily. "Me and the boy next door, we're going home at last."

THE END

DISCUSSION QUESTIONS

- Were you able to predict any part of the solution to the case?

- Aside from the solution, did anything about the book surprise you? If so, what?

- What role did the New York City setting play in the narrative?

- Did any aspects of the plot date the story? If so, which ones?

- Would the story be different if it were set in the present day? If so, how?

- If you've read other books by Cornell Woolrich, how does this one compare?

- Are there any present-day writers whose work reminds you of Woolrich's?

- If you've seen the film based on this book, discuss the adaptation. What stayed the same? What changed?

H.F. Heard, *A Taste for Honey*

Dolores Hitchens, *The Cat Saw Murder*
Introduced by Joyce Carol Oates

Dorothy B. Hughes, *Dread Journey*
Introduced by Sarah Weinman
Dorothy B. Hughes, *Ride the Pink Horse*
Introduced by Sara Paretsky
Dorothy B. Hughes, *The So Blue Marble*

W. Bolingbroke Johnson, *The Widening Stain*
Introduced by Nicholas A. Basbanes

Baynard Kendrick, *The Odor of Violets*

Jonathan Latimer, *Headed for a Hearse*
Introduced by Max Allan Collins

Frances and Richard Lockridge, *Death on the Aisle*

John P. Marquand, *Your Turn, Mr. Moto*
Introduced by Lawrence Block

Stuart Palmer, *The Puzzle of the Happy Hooligan*

Otto Penzler, ed., *Golden Age Detective Stories*

Ellery Queen, *The American Gun Mystery*
Ellery Queen, *The Chinese Orange Mystery*
Ellery Queen, *The Dutch Shoe Mystery*
Ellery Queen, *The Egyptian Cross Mystery*
Ellery Queen, *The Siamese Twin Mystery*

Patrick Quentin, *A Puzzle for Fools*

Clayton Rawson, *Death from a Top Hat*

Craig Rice, *Eight Faces at Three*
Introduced by Lisa Lutz
Craig Rice, *Home Sweet Homicide*

Mary Roberts Rinehart, *The Haunted Lady*
Mary Roberts Rinehart, *Miss Pinkerton*
Introduced by Carolyn Hart
Mary Roberts Rinehart, *The Red Lamp*
Mary Roberts Rinehart, *The Wall*

Joel Townsley Rogers, *The Red Right Hand*
Introduced by Joe R. Lansdale

Roger Scarlett, *Cat's Paw*
Introduced by Curtis Evans

Vincent Starrett, *The Great Hotel Murder*
Introduced by Lyndsay Faye
Vincent Starrett, *Murder on "B" Deck*
Introduced by Ray Betzner

Phoebe Atwood Taylor, *The Cape Cod Mystery*

Cornell Woolrich, *The Bride Wore Black*
Introduced by Eddie Muller
Cornell Woolrich, *Waltz into Darkness*
Introduced by Wallace Stroby